C.G.BLAINE

This is for every therapist whose couch I've graced. What up.

Part 1
Bennett

-1-

Snakes

A STACK OF VIDEO GAME cases crashes to the floor when I bump into the dresser. I cringe and glance over my shoulder. Despite my utter lack of stealth, the guy named Guy remains unconscious in his bed. Exactly how I want him to stay until I successfully sneak out of his apartment. I finish slipping on my shoes and back out of his room, pulling the door shut like I'm defusing a bomb. It latches without a sound.

Claiming victory, I turn to escape down the hall, only to slam straight into a hard body. A gasp slips out of me, a grunt from him. I would topple backward if not for him grabbing my arms to keep me upright. I tilt my chin up, and startled gray eyes meet mine.

Whoever he is brings a finger to his lips. "Shh."

He checks through the open doorway behind him. A naked girl rolls across the bed in her sleep, the sheets tangled around her legs, and he lets go to ease the door closed with the same caution I used. A kindred spirit also making a break for it. When he turns back to me, a flash of amusement crosses his face before he drags me behind him to the living room.

Apparently, we're in this together now.

"I'm missing my belt," he says, scanning the floor.

While he searches around, I pick up my bag off an end table. In the process, I knock over a frame. *Smooth, Bennett.*

I set it back up and take in the photo of Guy and his sister—the naked roller. They're posing in front of a tacky backdrop covered in trees, their smiles almost as disturbing as their color-coordinated outfits. We took similar photos at a department store I worked at in high school. But never of twenty-something twins who'd won a hundred thousand dollars off a lottery ticket and quit their jobs, thinking they were set for life. More like a few months since they live together in a two-bedroom, one-bathroom. As always, my drunken ability to choose a quality man amazes me.

He's tearing apart the couch when I start inching toward the entryway.

"Is it worth it?"

Cushion in hand, he looks up and notes me slinking away. "You're right. She can keep it as a souvenir."

But on our way past the kitchen, I spot the belt by the refrigerator. I detour for it, pulling off my heels to avoid them clicking across the linoleum. He waits by the open door when I return.

I slap the leather against his palm. "She'll have to remember your time together some other way."

"You're a fucking angel," he says, following me out of the apartment.

I stop in the hallway to put my shoes back on, not sure anyone's ever referred to me as such before. When my foot lifts, he extends a hand, so I can steady myself. "And you're a fucking gentleman."

His lips twitch, fighting off a smile. "The people on the other side of the door might not share these opinions of us."

"Trust me, I'm doing him a favor by skipping out on him." I teeter, switching legs, and he steps closer, not trusting my balance. It's automatic, and it makes me think he really is a gentleman deep down.

With both my feet back on the ground, he tugs me in the direction of the elevators before letting go. The harsh overhead lighting intensifies the pounding in my skull. I made it through my entire college career without a debilitating hangover, so it makes nothing but sense that I wake up the day after graduation with one. I squint and drag my hands down my face. My escape partner flips a light switch on the wall, darkening the corridor.

He's a hero as well.

A little old lady with blue hair walks her dog off the elevator before he and I lean against opposite walls. He tips his head back and closes his eyes, slapping at the buttons. A few light up but not the right one.

"Want to try that again?" I ask.

An eye opens, and he pokes the lobby button with one finger. His other eye slits. "You owe me a condom, by the way."

"Excuse me?"

One side of his mouth turns up. "Your dude came in, asking his sister for a condom. I provided."

"Such a waste," I mumble.

He raises his eyebrows and fully opens both eyes as we stop on the fourth floor. "Go on."

I shake my head. "I'm not telling a complete stranger about the sex I had less than five hours ago."

He pushes the third-floor button as the doors close. "You know who I went home with last night, where I woke up this morning, and that I'm a fucking gentleman. I know you practice safe sex, rock the shit out of a pair of heels, and believe you're more trouble than you're worth." He presses the next floor's button when we stop on three. "We're practically best friends."

I purse my lips as I think it over. It really doesn't matter, since after this, we will never see each other again. "Fine," I say, making him perk up even more. "Did you know a snake's saliva contains digestive enzymes powerful enough to break down bone?"

He makes a face. "I do now."

"They can digest everything, except for the claws and hair of live prey."

"Why are you doing this to me?"

I let my head rest on the wall behind me and stare up at the mirrored ceiling. "I wondered the same thing when he insisted I watch him feed his snake and explained the entire process."

"No…" The reflection shows him sticking his foot out of the elevator to keep us on the second floor a little longer.

"All I could think about the entire time was that, less than five feet away from my head, a mouse was being digested."

His eyes meet mine in the mirror. "On behalf of men everywhere, I am so sorry. You deserve better from us."

I smile, and he lets the doors shut.

It's early on a Saturday, leaving the lobby deserted, except for a mailman shoving letters into tenants' boxes. I stop and dig through my bag for my phone. "Shit, I forgot to charge it."

"Thank God you have backup this morning." He pushes one of the glass doors open, holding it for me. "After you."

I put on sunglasses on my way past. "I'm not getting in a car with you."

"I'd be worried if you did." He snags my elbow, redirecting me the other way, and points to a coffee shop across the street. "We're going to get a coffee, order you an Uber, and you're going to give me the name of a business within walking distance of wherever you live. That way, when I turn out to be a psycho stalker, you and your loved ones are safe."

"You won't just follow me?" I ask.

He shrugs as we step into the street. "I didn't even think about it until now. But thanks for the idea."

The floor-to-ceiling windows in the coffee shop provide no relief for my headache, so I leave my sunglasses on as we stand in line.

"You look like a lurker with those on," he says.

"I'm cool with it." I give him a once-over. "They make more sense than a stocking cap."

He drags the ugly olive beanie off his head. The dark hair is longer on top than I would have guessed from what was sticking out underneath. Even after combing his fingers through it, he still looks like he rolled out of someone else's bed. "Your turn."

I take off my sunglasses and move forward with the line. "Do you want to stare into my eyes now?"

"Maybe later."

At the counter, he orders a large black coffee. The barista asks for his name.

"Snake," he says, watching me out of the corner of his eye. I pretend not to care.

She writes on the cup and turns her attention to me. I order something complicated to make up for his lack of imagination. Eyebrows raised, he waits for my name.

"Angel."

He covers his mouth with his hand, but his eyes smile. When he reaches for his wallet, I wave him off and toss down cash. "You're paying for me to get home. At least let me buy your coffee."

"I'd argue, but that wouldn't be very gentlemanly, and I have a reputation to uphold with you."

As we wait, he checks his phone. All the while, he chews on his lip, not even seeming aware of it. I wonder if he's serious about trying to keep up a persona or if this is the real him. I decide it is, and in three years, when I randomly think about this moment, he will be the exact same person out there in the world as he is right now, standing in front of me.

"Snake," the barista calls. "And Angel."

He thanks her and picks up our drinks. Walking out, I take mine from him and slide back on my shades. The Phoenix sun has graduated to blinding and murderous. One of many things I won't miss. I sip my coffee that ended up mostly sugar and milk as a black SUV pulls up to the curb.

He steps ahead to open the door. "Your carriage."

"Thank you," I say, climbing in. "I really appreciate it."

"I couldn't have you sneaking back in and marrying snake boy." He purses his lips like he wants to add something, but then he says, "Take it easy," and shuts the door.

The driver asks if I'm ready. I face forward and start to answer until the door swings open.

"I need you to give me your number." The guy sticks his head in, phone in hand.

"You *need?*"

He nods, eyebrows drawn together like it's the most obvious thing in the world. "Need." He pulls off my sunglasses and tosses them on the seat beside me. He's staring into my eyes. "There's something I need to tell you, but I can't right now."

"What could you possibly need to say later that you can't say now?"

"Something that doesn't feel right saying until we've both taken a shower. Please. One text, and I'll delete your number."

I laugh because it makes no sense, and he smiles, holding out his phone. After a second, I sigh and take it. "One message," I say, adding my number to his contacts under the name Angel. "If you send more, I'm blocking you."

"All I need is one."

THE PINK STICKY NOTE SHOWS UP from halfway down our hallway. It hangs eye-level on our apartment door. Keaton calls them mini-mems, short for miniature memos, and uses them whenever I let my phone die. To be fair, it happens with me more often than most people. She writes down what she wants to text me and posts it to whatever surface is closest. It's one of those quirks that's endearing as hell. I unlock the dead bolt as I read it.

Your phone's dead again.

I find another on the other side of the door.

I can't believe you bailed so early.

The way she and her boyfriend were all over one another, it surprises me she noticed me leaving the bar at all.

One on the table where we keep our keys.

Liam's hot cousin showed up just after you left. Some skanky bitch was all over him.

I grab the water bottle from the fridge with one stuck on the label.

Dammit Bennett. That skanky bitch should have been you!

The cousin moved back from LA a few days ago. She convinced herself if we met, the four of us would have a joint wedding, raise our kids in a cul-de-sac, and all be buried under an apple tree together. A sweet thought but far from how I envision my life going.

The pile of pink on a couch pillow surrounded by used tissues hints she squeezed in a movie before passing out.

> *Julia Roberts should star opposite Kate Hudson in a love story.*
>
> *They'd make a beautiful couple.*
>
> *So would we.*
>
> *Marry me?*

On her bedroom door.

> *Don't die before me.*
>
> *Swear!*

She's lying facedown on top of her comforter. I pull off her shoes, cover her up, and pull the note off her cheek.

> *I love you.*

"You too, crazy woman." I leave the door open a crack, so she knows I'm home, and I space out in the shower before crashing onto my bed.

WHEN THE BOUNCING STARTS, I know the only way to make it stop is to open my eyes. They fight me, but I prevail.

Keaton hovers over me, her blonde curls in my face. "I brought you food."

I grunt, rolling over. "You also brought an audience."

Liam waves from the doorway. "You look like shit, Bennett."

"Oh, stop. You'll make me blush."

"Red is a better look than gray." He dodges the pillow I launched and adjusts his glasses. "Your aim sucks too."

"Why do we keep him around?" I ask her.

"Eye candy." Keaton throws the pillow back at me. "Don't go back to sleep." She drags Liam out and shuts the door behind them.

I blink away the sandpaper lining my eyelids and haul myself out of bed. The bathroom mirror confirms Liam's evaluation of gray not being an attractive color on me. Sleeping on wet hair hasn't helped either, but between the shower and nap, my headache has become tolerable. I own the mess and throw my hair up without bothering to run a brush through it.

Liam meets me at the kitchen counter with the greasiest burger in existence. "We weren't sure how hungover you'd be, so we went with very." He slides over a shot and my phone and walks away. "Eat. Shoot. Make sure you didn't declare your love for anyone." The advice of a recently retired frat boy.

Being a rebel, I check my phone first. My belly flips when I see the text from an unknown number. Only one. The smart choice is to delete it, never read it. But curiosity overpowers sense more often than not. I abandon my food, ignoring Keaton's questionable look on the way to my room, and crawl back under the covers. When I open it, I laugh.

He sent an audio message. I don't even hesitate to hit play.

"You're so fucking beautiful."

That's it. Four words and less than five seconds, and I want to know him—what he wants out of life, his favorite song, how he says my name, what his laugh sounds like. I listen again. To how he accentuates each word like it's the most important thing he'll ever say. And again, with my eyes closed. I commit it to memory—him, his words, all of it. Then, I delete the message.

In a week, I'll be gone. The last thing I need is a reason to stay.

-2-
Packing Tape

KEATON STOPS IN MY DOORWAY with her judgmental face on as she examines my camo pants and paint-splattered, ripped-to-shit black tank top. "I thought I put those clothes in the throwaway pile."

"You did," I say, carrying a box over to her. "I dug them out and put them on just for you, baby."

She rolls her eyes, taking the box. As she walks away, she mumbles, "At least change the damn pants."

"But they're comfortable." I pick up another box and follow her to the living room. We stack them next to the others.

"Is it too late to beg you not to go?" she asks, pouting out a lip.

I sigh. The fact that we won't see each other every day is finally setting in for both of us. We've lived together since we were fourteen, when my mother ran off to Europe to find herself. Most shrinks' lives are as miserable and fucked up, if not more so, than their clients. They just know how to hide it better. Mr. and Mrs. Reynolds learned this firsthand when Dr. Ross dropped me off at three a.m. and begged them to take care of me for a few weeks. That turned into months and eventually a full guardianship when she made her move permanent. All my life, she was in search of something. A calling, the right man, inner peace. Nothing ever seemed to make her feel whole, feel alive. Certainly not me.

"Look under the sink," I tell Keaton.

She gives me a dubious look, skipping to the kitchen and opening the cabinet. "No way, Bennie." She squeals, hugging the legless, eyeless body of what was, at one time, a stuffed pig. "You found Snort?"

I shrug. "More like stopped hiding him in the back of my closet."

Her mouth falls open. "I knew you stole him junior year." She smiles and barrels toward me, knocking us both over the back of the couch. "Thank you, thank you, thank you."

"Stop it." I laugh as she rubs it on my face. "He always smells so weird."

"And they say dreams don't come true." Liam drags her off me. She holds Snort up for him to kiss the snout, which he does because he is whipped and proud of it.

"Where's all this help you were bringing?" I grab an empty box. "We were promised big, strong men to carry our belongings down the stairs."

"It's a hundred degrees outside. Unless I can advertise beer and pussy, no sane man's giving up his Saturday."

I shake my head. "The mouth on this one."

"So, what are we moving next?" he asks, rubbing his hands together.

"The beds." Keaton tucks Snort away in a box clearly marked as hers. "They both need to go to the storage unit."

He watches her walk away before he turns to me. "You're good to entertain yourself for twenty to thirty minutes, yes?"

"Sure, I'll even have a beer waiting for you."

"Now you're getting it," he says, already following her.

I start packing up the kitchen cupboards. Most of our stuff will go into storage. Keaton's moving in with Liam, and he has all the basics, as does my new roommate in Portland. I like the idea of only taking the essentials with me and leaving the rest behind. My mother and I are definitely related.

I push on my tiptoes to retrieve the butter dish we've never used off the top shelf and wrap it in newspaper. I set it in the bottom of the box on the kitchen island. When I look up, my heart stops. He's standing in the living room, wearing his ugly beanie and a smile.

"Still fucking beautiful," he says, and it sounds just like I remember.

They say you never know how you'll react to something until it happens to you. But in my case, I respond to seeing a psycho stalker appearing in my living room very much how I anticipated I would—screaming bloody fucking murder.

He starts toward me, shaking his head. "No, no, no."

I back into the counter, looking for anything to use as a weapon. I grab a roll of packing tape with the blade attached, intending to slice any part of him that comes close enough. "Get away from me!"

"It's okay." He holds up his hands as if it will subdue me. *Oh God,* he's going to subdue me. "I'm not—"

Liam charges out of the bedroom, pulling up his jeans. "What the fuck?" He stops a few feet away from the stalker but barely acknowledges him. "Why the fuck are you screaming?"

I open my mouth, but nothing comes out, so I point with the tape dispenser.

Liam looks between us, shaking his head. "Dane? My cousin?"
No.

"She might think I'm a psycho stalker," says the not-psycho stalker.

"And what were you planning to do with that, Bennett?" Liam gestures toward the tape in my hand. "Pack him?"

I toss it down, absolutely mortified.

He walks back to Keaton's room. "Thanks for coming to help, man," he says over his shoulder. "Welcome to the crazy."

The most awkward silence of my entire life follows the slamming of the bedroom door. We stare at each other with a kitchen island and most of the living room between us as he chews on his lip. We aren't Snake and Angel anymore but Dane and

Bennett, meeting for the first time with what feels like other people's memories of each other.

He breaks the standoff first by taking off his beanie. "I think the lesson we've learned today is not to sneak up, unannounced, on someone after joking about being a psycho stalker."

"Or you could avoid both as a general rule."

"True." He sits on a barstool across from me. "While we're exchanging helpful tips, can I give you one?"

"Sure," I say. "Why not?"

"There's a knife block behind you. One of those might have been a little more intimidating than a roll of tape."

If he shares traits with Liam, a reaction will only prolong my torture, so I go back to emptying cupboards and change the topic. "So, you're the hot cousin I was supposed to meet at the bar last weekend."

He steps beside me and reaches the top shelf. "And you're the bangable roommate I was supposed to wash my junk for." He catches the ceramic serving bowl I dropped and adds, "Liam's words."

The red finally hits my cheeks. "Of course."

We set into a rhythm. He hands me dishes, and I wrap them in newspaper. Once a box fills, I mark it for him to carry over to the others.

"I saw you that night," he says as we move on to the drawers. "At the bar."

Rather than sorting silverware, I dump it all in a box. I'll make sure it goes with Keaton.

"When?" I ask.

"You were leaving with that dude. I held the door for you when he didn't." He points at himself and mouths, *Gentleman.*

I laugh, and he smiles, sliding the drawer back in for me.

"You said, 'Thank you,' but never looked up."

I lean a hip on the counter, remembering the gesture, just not him. "I looked back after you said, 'You're welcome,' but you were already walking in."

"Well, that's bad timing." He flips over another drawer full of utensils. The metal clangs as it pours out.

14

We finish packing up the kitchen, and he sets the final box among all the others. I look around at the last four years of my life. Sorted into stacks of brown cardboard that will sit in darkness indefinitely.

"Portland, huh?" Dane's back on his stool.

I hand him a beer from the fridge and take out two more, keeping my word to Liam. "For now. I'm not really sure where I'll end up yet. My sublease is for three months, so maybe San Francisco after that. Or somewhere on the East Coast."

"You graduate college and become a drifter?" He opens his bottle and another for me, eyeing the third but not asking.

He isn't far off, but drifter makes me think of moving without direction or purpose. I know what I want. I just don't know where to find it.

"More like an explorer."

"Drifter."

"Adventurer."

He props himself on his elbows, narrowing his eyes at me. "I've seen two boxes marked for you. Everything else is Keaton, donations, or storage unit. You're going to be a drifter."

I sip my beer and shrug. "I'm cool with it."

I retreat to my room for the last few boxes.

Dane follows, eyes scanning the bare walls and empty closet. "What did it look like in here before?" Before I can answer, he flips open a flap on a box and pulls out a candleholder. "Where was this?"

"On the dresser."

He sets it down, so the blue and purple glass tiles catch the light. "And this?" It's a picture of Keaton and me at her sixteenth birthday party. "Wait, let me guess." He walks toward the dresser and then veers to the nightstand beside the bed. "Here."

I nod, and he heads back for more. This time, he doesn't even ask, placing things around the room.

"Are you planning on unpacking everything?"

He crosses in front of me with a jewelry box. "I'm curious what you kept closest. We surround ourselves with reminders of what matters most to us. The more important something is, the closer we want it. Keaton's obvious." He puts the jewelry box next to her picture and steps back, examining the empty space in front of it. "What goes there?"

I play with the label on my beer, pretending not to hear him. He doesn't know me.

"You have it on right now, don't you?"

"No." But my eyes betray me and flit to my bracelet.

"Can I see?" He walks over, holding out his hand, and I give him my arm.

He turns it over as he traces the black braided cable until his fingers stop at the silver rectangle covering my inner wrist. "*Seek*," he reads the word inscribed and looks up, eyes on mine. "What are you looking for, Bennett?" He says my name like it's the answer to his question, and I pull my hand back.

Guys in my bedroom are supposed to try to get me naked, not ask me to expose myself. But his stare stays steadfast, wanting just that.

Keaton giggles in the living room. In the time it takes to look at the door and back, he's returning everything to the box. She swings around the corner through the doorway. "We're ready to carry stuff to the truck." Her attention lands on Dane. "I see you found that big, strong man you were looking for."

"Hey, Keaton." He glances up. "You have sex hair."

She gasps and dashes away in search of a mirror.

"That was mean," I say, picking up the box he repacked.

"Honesty can't be mean. It can hurt, but it's better than the alternative." He pulls the box from my hands and walks out, leaving me in a room that no longer belongs to me.

-3-
Beanbags

It's bittersweet, setting our keys on the kitchen island. I wrap my arms around Keaton and rest my chin on her shoulder while we say a silent goodbye to the walls and carpet. It feels like the end of something much larger. It is in a way.

She cries on the drive over to Liam's. Between sobs, she asks if I think the apartment will miss us. I tell her it won't have to. Everything around us absorbs some of our energy. Apartments, used shoes, a family heirloom. They all carry a piece of us and everyone else that comes into contact with them. It's why we need to be careful not only of what we let into our lives, but also of what we send out into the world.

She sniffs and asks, "How many beers have you had?"

I scrunch up my nose at her, and she laughs.

We claim emotional overload to get out of unloading boxes. I'm not proud of it, but neither Liam nor Dane objects, so we relax on the tailgate of Liam's truck, sipping our iced lattes and bossing them around.

Once they finish, Liam carries the last and arguably most important thing in. Keaton laughs as they disappear up the stairs. On the surface, they're two people you wouldn't expect to work. She's wanted to be a grown-up since we were kids, and despite what his finance degree would lead you to believe, he isn't interested in becoming an adult anytime soon. But they bend in the other's direction, bringing out qualities in one another that were previously undiscovered. Most people lose a part of themselves to a relationship, but they found themselves when they found each other.

"You staying here tonight?" Dane shuts the tailgate.

"Couch surfer tonight, drifter tomorrow."

He taps away on his phone and heads toward the parking lot. "I'll be back later then."

"You're coming to dinner with us?"

"I am now," he says, not looking back.

I stay on the sidewalk, curious who he is when no one watches. People walk like they live, and he takes each step as if he might change course at any second but never does. Sure of himself while being ready to adapt. I can't even step up onto a curb without rolling my ankle or sidestepping to keep my balance.

I make a mental note to sign up for a yoga class.

The rest of the afternoon, we work to de-man the apartment to Keaton's satisfaction. From Liam's face when Snort goes front and center on the bed, the little guy will find himself in the back of a closet sooner rather than later.

We take a short intermission to shower and change before dinner.

True to his word, Dane meets us at the restaurant. He slides into the seat next to mine at the table without acknowledging me.

An older man in a suit approaches almost immediately. He holds his arms out in greeting. "The Masters boys."

Liam stands halfway to shake his hand and conducts introductions. Mr. Willis, the owner of a chain of clothing stores and one of their grandfather's oldest clients. From what I understand, Masters Financial Group specializes in financial planning and wealth management. Money shuffles from here to there and back again. If the amount grows, they are doing their jobs. I tend to glaze over whenever Liam uses numbers, but that's the gist of it. Now that Liam's graduated, the grooming for them to take over the company can commence. It's the entire reason Dane moved back.

Mr. Willis sets his hand on Dane's shoulder. "Your grandfather told me he'd twisted your arm into coming back."

"More like threatened to disown me, sir." Dane's light tone mismatches the tight smile.

"Well, I know Miles is grateful you two are coming on board." He points a finger at Liam and shakes it around. "He's been talking about handing the reins over since this one declared a major freshman year."

Dane leans over, no longer interested in the conversation. "Coffee, dinner—if we'd met under different circumstances, I'd think you were trying to date me."

"You invited yourself to dinner," I say, playing with the stem of my water glass.

A ghost of a smile appears. "And I'm inviting myself back to the apartment after."

I lick my lips and look away at nothing across the dining room. This is how it starts—flirtatious conversation, his leg brushing mine under the table, then *boom!*—we're six months deep, and I can't remember why it ever happened in the first place.

Our waiter appears, and Mr. Willis claps Dane on the back. "We'll talk shop soon. See what the young blood can offer us."

"Advice on your backswing," Dane mutters as he returns to his table.

Liam rests his head in his hands. "Imagine how many rounds we'll wind up throwing for that man."

They exchange a grunt for a groan, and we order.

ON OUR WAY BACK, Liam deems my departure cause for celebration. He springs for the most expensive champagne at the gas station. Deep down, he'll miss me. Eventually.

Keaton downs three glasses and resumes crying because it's the last time for everything. Last popped cork, last toast, last time

I roll my eyes at her for crying over everything being our last time together. Liam starts to counter each one with a first they'll share, and within a few minutes, she returns to her giggling self.

He's good for her. She'll be fine without me.

Eager to check off a few items from the list they just created, they disappear to the bedroom. As soon as Dane and I are alone again, the vibe changes. A pretense falls away. Neither of us mentioned our initial encounter to Liam or Keaton. It seems like an unspoken agreement that neither of us will.

We finish off the champagne while sitting in beanbag chairs— the only option other than the couch. He's stalking me on social media. Openly since he liked an Instagram post from over a year ago.

"I like you a hell of a lot better in heels than bowling shoes."

I don't say anything, not in the mood to relive my two-month tenure on a bowling league. An ex insisted I try. I despised every second but pretended to love hurling a ball as much as the guy, who I found out was banging the girl at the shoe counter for the entirety of our relationship. He chased me into the parking lot, still buckling his belt. I flung my bowling bag and nailed him in the balls.

Dane tosses his phone on the floor, his attention shifting to the physical me rather than the virtual one. He put his beanie back on a little bit ago. It grows on you. "How far is Portland?"

"One thousand two hundred and sixty-eight miles. At least, that's the number Keaton keeps throwing around."

He picks up his phone and taps away before dropping it again. "It's a sixteen-day walk."

"I should probably drive then." I carry the empty bottle to the kitchen and rinse out the plastic flutes.

When I come back, Dane has switched directions in his beanbag, so we'll face opposite ways. I sit down, and our thighs almost touch, the gap between us gone.

"Did you move my bag closer?"

He shushes me. "What are the odds they're down for the night?"

A hand creeps over to my leg, his skin warm enough that the rest of me feels cold. I remind myself to breathe as his fingers trail up. "She'll be out here by three to ask me to stay."

He looks up in thought and nods. "I can work with that."

He leans in and brushes his lips over my collarbone, sweeping up to my neck. I drag off his beanie, tossing it behind him somewhere. My fingers thread in his too-long-on-top hair. His hand travels higher. I wish it would go back but keep going, wanting to feel him everywhere.

"Can I ask you something?"

"Ask me all the questions," he says against my skin. "Just let me keep doing this." His thumb grazes back and forth under the hem of my dress, sending chills every which way.

"Did you delete my number after sending the text?"

He pulls back until his gray eyes meet mine. I've already decided the answer really doesn't matter. It's trust issues asking, not me. But he nods and gives me one anyway. "It was one of the hardest things I'd ever fucking done."

"Then why did you?"

His focus falls to my mouth as his hand continues its path, the touch lighter ascending my inner thigh. "I said I would."

"I deleted your message," I tell him. "Right after I listened to it."

"I know. I always knew you would."

His hand skims over lace. My heart pounds, and not even sure what I'm saying anymore, I breathe out, "How?"

"I just did." His gaze lifts back to mine. "Any more questions?"

And then we're kissing, hard and desperate. He drags me over, and I straddle his lap, yanking his shirt over his head.

The beanbag gives way under his elbow when he leans back. I laugh as he growls with my lip between his teeth. He stands up like I'm not clinging to him and, in a few steps, lowers us onto the couch. He shoves the fabric between my legs out of the way and slides his fingers into me. My back arches with his mouth on me through the thin material of my dress, and I moan his name, undoing the button on his jeans.

And then he's gone.

21

"Fuck," he says, walking toward the kitchen while I pant where he left me on the couch. He rubs the back of his neck, shaking his head.

"Dane?"

"Sorry," he says, already crossing the room again.

I can't even ask what happened before he's back between my legs, his lips crushing mine. He moves my hand between us, so I'll finish what I started, and he glides his up my side to my breast. But when I reach his zipper, he pulls back.

"I can't do this." His forehead drops to my shoulder, and he groans. "Goddamn it."

Despite his claim, within a few seconds, he presses his lips into my skin. As they move up my neck, I have to take a deep breath.

"If we're not doing this, I really need you not to do that right now."

Dane props himself on an elbow and stares down at me. For the first time, I notice the chain hanging from his neck and the silver bar dangling. His thumb brushes over my cheek. "I really need you not to look and feel so incredible then."

"Why are we stopping?" I trace over the outline of his lips until he bites the pad of my finger.

"Because I already know how that scenario ends. Either I wake up and you're gone with no plans on ever seeing me again or…"

"You leave with the same," I finish for him.

He kisses my palm, then the medallion covering my inner wrist. "And I'm not ready to be done with you yet." His head dips barely enough to touch his lips to mine before he flops over onto one of the beanbags. "So, I need you to keep it in your pants or skirt or whatever."

I roll onto my side to face him. "What do you suggest we do then?"

"This." But other than his teeth sinking into his bottom lip, nothing happens.

"We're going to sit here and do absolutely nothing?"

"Close." He slumps further into the cushy chair and stacks his hands behind his head. "We're going to sit here, and I'm going to stare into your eyes."

The dude who wears the beanie grows on you too.

BY THE TIME THE DOOR creaks open, I'm half-asleep on the couch. Dane's sprawled across both beanbags, covered up with a scratchy blanket his aunt Clara knitted. Rather than stumble around, Keaton climbs over the back of the couch. I scoot as close to the edge as I can without falling off, so she can wedge herself between me and the back cushions.

She drapes her arm over me. "Stay," she whispers.

I close my eyes, not answering her. The only reason I stuck around after I turned eighteen was for her. Now, I need to go for me.

A psychiatrist once told me, my restless desire to get away from what has always been and find what could be stems from my mother's abandonment. I want to discover something, anything out there in the world to justify her leaving me behind. Dr. Rita was probably right, but she also recommended I cut all sugar and caffeine from my diet, so fuck her.

"I can't," I finally say.

Her cheek presses against my back, and she squeezes me tighter. "I know. Just come back."

It only takes a few minutes for her to pass out again. Once her grip loosens, I crawl off the couch, careful not to wake her and re-engage it. Part of me wants to bolt right now in the middle of the night. Avoid the goodbyes altogether. But if anyone in my life deserves a proper, tear-filled goodbye, it is Keaton James Reynolds.

Dane's arm stays draped over his eyes. I'm not even sure he's awake until he flips the blanket up. He shifts over, and the arm slides around me when I cuddle up beside him. He readjusts the blanket over us and grazes his nose down my jawline. Thinking he'll kiss me, I turn into him, but he only drags his lips over mine—slow and light enough that it drives me crazy within a few seconds.

"I'm an idiot for not fucking you."

When I nod, his lips part, so his breath touches the seam of mine.

"Deleting your number was a mistake," he says.

More nodding—not because I agree, but because I want more contact between us. And he gives it to me, bringing his mouth closer, his hand to the side of my face.

"I shouldn't have let you leave the bar."

I don't nod that time, and he stops moving. He studies me with a serious look on his face. Then he sighs and presses his lips to mine.

"Goodbye, Bennett," he whispers.

"Goodbye, Dane."

-4-
Blue-Eyed Badass

My FLIGHT INSTINCTS WIN OUT before the sun comes up. I detangle myself from Dane and quite possibly the roughest blanket known to man. At some point, he pulled his beanie down over his eyes. I hate that it makes me smile.

I shove my dress and shower supplies in my bag and drop it by the door. Keaton has already unpacked her neon-pink sticky notes, and I scribble out three mini-mems.

One goes on her arm.

> *Meet you at your parents' for breakfast. I'll bring the tissues.*

Another on Liam's bedroom door.

> *Try not to be a total douche all the time.*

Dane's note sticks somewhere in the vicinity of his forehead.

> *Two messages.*

On the back, I leave my phone number. I will probably regret it before I reach city limits, but I'll be gone, so it won't matter.

A realization hits me on my way to the Reynolds' house. Phoenix isn't my home anymore. Nowhere is. An odd sense of freedom accompanies the thought. I roll the windows down and decide not to care when my hair whips me in the face.

The place you grow up always smells the same. Even through wall plug-ins and candles, the scent of memories lingers. Prior to my parental discarding, I spent more time in Keaton's bedroom than my own. More time on their couch, in their backyard, at their dinner table. So, the transition to living there full-time took as much effort as not walking home at dark.

When I arrive at the house, Joyce's nose is already red from crying and stays that way all morning. Patrick pats me on the back a lot and prints off driving directions I won't use because, smartphones. They're the parents everyone needs—supportive, nurturing, present. And the closest thing I have or could ever want.

We all hug in a big group on the front porch when I insist on getting on the road. Keaton holds on long after Joyce and Patrick go inside. I promise to charge my phone every day, and she threatens to snail-mail me mini-mems if I don't.

Then I'm in the car, a weight lifting with every mile. I drive straight through, only stopping for gas and coffee and the inevitable pee breaks that occur when fueled by copious amounts of caffeine.

The darkness brings calm. Headlights, different radio stations coming in and out of range, and me on my own for the first time.

The last ten miles, I practice introducing myself to the stranger named Marco, who I'll be sharing walls with for the next three months until his roommate returns from Iowa. At the high-rise apartment building, I haul my bag up three flights of stairs because the elevator is broken. Then I drag it back down one because my apartment is on the second floor.

After the door opens, I receive an up-down from a thick-framed set of glasses. He finishes his inspection and disappears back into the apartment.

"She's here," he says, out of sight.

"What does she look like?" someone asks.

"Cute but blonde. Great eyes, but they're blue."

Me in ten words or less.

I let myself in, and passing a small kitchen, I walk into the living room. Glasses lounges on one side of a worn leather couch. At the other end, a guy looks up from his magazine long enough for a quick pass over me.

"I'm Marco. Room's on the left." He goes back to reading, neither impressed nor un. "We share wine here."

"Thank God," I say, heading down the hall. "I find myself unbearable after drinking an entire bottle alone."

"I like you," he calls after me.

We all want validation, even if it only sounds half-sincere.

I glance around the spacious bedroom. On the nightstand sits a family picture between a lamp and a pair of headphones.

Without the road and music for stimulation, my brain quickly turns to mush. Since my sheets are buried in a box somewhere, I grab a decorative pillow off the mushroom chair and stretch out on the fluffy white rug. My phone vibrates as I settle in. I texted Keaton to tell her I made it and expect it to be her, but an unknown number sends my belly into a familiar flip.

Sources say you're officially adrift in Oregon.

It vibrates again.

Twenty hours straight through? Such a badass!

And again.

So am I. Hence, a third message.

I smile, too exhausted to laugh, and reply, *Rulebreaker! Too bad I have to block you now.*

Go for it, baby. I already have your number, and burner phones are cheap. I'm not going anywhere this time.

27

It surprises me that I'm okay with that. Maybe even more than okay.

The door almost hits me in the head when Marco walks in. "Declan is driving me crazy. I need a mental health break." He tosses down the matching pillow from the chair and spreads out next to me. "Why are we on the floor?"

"I haven't slept in thirty hours and need to crash."

"Perfect," he says. "I could use an angry nap."

We wake up six hours later, order Chinese, and watch trashy reality shows. One day in Portland, and I've found my spirit animal.

-5-
Darkest Desires

MARCO WALKS LIKE HE'S ON a runway. Chin up, shoulders back. He glides down the street, through a store, across the living room. It gives beauty to the most mundane of situations.

"You're my favorite person," he tells me after my first week here. "It used to be the owner of the thrift store who layers three perfumes, only wears ruby-red lipstick, and has a different wig for each day of the week."

A few days later, the lady adopts a blind potbellied pig named Gilda, which she dresses in feather boas, and reclaims the title. Understandable.

The small gallery I managed to weasel a job out of stays closed on Sundays, so we go on excursions. The Japanese Garden, Holocaust Museum, Washington Park. One day, we spend just riding the streetcar and watching people. Most weeknights, I abuse his employee discount at the restaurant where he bartends. Alongside me usually sits whatever guy he's given his heart to. They rotate out on almost a weekly basis, sometimes more often, but for that short time, their worlds revolve around one another.

I've been in Oregon a month when Keaton's name lights up my phone at four in the morning. She proves unable to stop crying and shrieking, leaving me panicked and disoriented from being ripped out of REM sleep. Liam eventually takes over the conversation. He woke her up with an air horn, and on the ceiling in glow-in-the-dark paint was *Marriage Time*. It's the perfect Liam proposal.

"Sorry you'll have to grow old alone, Bennett."

I yawn, not fully functional until five a.m. on a Sunday. "I'm not worried. This is only her first marriage. She has Pinterest boards for three different weddings, and she hates to let things go to waste."

They spend twenty minutes discussing possible dates and venues before I fall back asleep.

I tell Marco about the proposal later while we wander around a used bookstore we stumbled upon. He claims we aren't hiding from his as-of-last-night ex. Although the oversize shades and newsboy hat tell a different story.

He pulls the sunglasses down his nose. "So, after leaving Phoenix and never wanting to return, you'll be making frequent trips back for the next year and a half at least."

"Best-friend duty trumps all," I say, pulling a book off the shelf.

Marco leans over to inhale the air kicked up as I fan through the pages. Old books soothe the soul. The way the pages feel, the scent of the binding and dust and oils from people's skin. They hold a warmth new books can't provide, a sense of a life lived between the covers.

I set it back and follow him to the romance section.

"Give me a number." He twirls a few times for no reason.

"Three."

He gestures to the third shelf down. "Another."

"Seventeen."

His finger skims over the spines as he counts seventeen in from the end. "*Darkest Desires*." He pulls it out and drops onto a dusty couch. "Sit. We'll alternate reading chapters."

I settle on the other end and extend my legs, overlapping them with his in the middle. "It has to be a romance? True love, happily-ever-afters aren't exactly my jam."

He finally slides off the shades to better glare at me. "Not everyone's destined for soul-crushing love. The kind that creeps in and takes over from the inside out. For some of us, this is as close to happily ever after as we'll ever be. Mine or someone else's, real or fiction—I want to experience it." He turns to the first page and glances up again. "Unless it's that sweet, no-steam, only-holding-hands shit. I want, at minimum, one person to whip their dick out."

"I say the same thing at the start of each day."

He makes a face and digs his phone out of his pocket. "But first, we show the world how much fun we're having."

Once he's updated every channel of social media available, we read about Daphne and Denton and their epic love threatened by her jealous stepfather and an unplanned pregnancy. A few chapters in, Marco becomes so enamored with the story, he takes over as permanent narrator.

"Denton still couldn't quite place his finger on what about the dainty woman fascinated him; nevertheless, he knew precisely where he'd like to place his finger on her."

As I settle back to listen, Dane texts. He sends an update every few days on what I'm missing. Pictures of Liam's latest cooking attempt, videos of Keaton passed out in strange places, audio clips that share his most random thoughts. They are the reminders I never imagined I would want, but I wait for them.

> *Fuck, those heels do it for me. And the dress.*
> *And the body underneath. Thank Marco for*
> *thoroughly derailing my afternoon.*

I check Marco's feed, and sure enough, there I am, standing by the book bin, perusing discounted titles.

The two of them have been a part of each other's online lives since Marco saw one of Dane's messages on my phone. It was a review for a new toothpaste he'd started using, which he awarded four out of five Dane stars. To prove he was a verified purchaser, he included a picture of himself brushing his teeth. Shirtless, of course, and flexing, as one does while brushing their teeth. All smooth skin and hard muscles and foaming from the mouth.

Marco dubbed him The Great Dane and followed him on Instagram, hoping for more topless bathroom selfies. I'm sure he's been disappointed with the half-eaten sandwiches and new-sock-Saturday posts.

The caption under Marco's picture of me reads: *Ewww, am I rite?* I kick him, but he barely notices, too entranced with the words on the page in front of him. "*He maneuvered gracefully through the crowd toward her, every inch of her body aware of every move of his.*"

So much for being a gentleman, I reply. *Illusion shattered.*

Oh, baby, those were the respectable thoughts.

"*He caressed her cheek, the touch jolting awake Daphne's most sensitive flesh from hibernation. His words stoked the womanly desires already set ablaze, and she ached for this man deeply.*" Marco fans himself with his hand. "Whoa."

I fold my feet up underneath me before I send, *What were the others?*

Dress hiked up. Legs wrapped around me. That mouth moaning my name again.

"*Denton's fingers trailed down her bodice. Her body shivered in anticipation of where his exploration would lead him next as he pushed her legs apart.*"

Dane: *Want more?*

I hate how fast I answer, *Yes.*

Wear those shoes to the engagement party. I'll show you every single one.

"*Daphne grasped Denton's throbbing girth, desperate for his seed to—* hey!"

I rip the book away and toss it on the floor. My phone too. Gently and onto a rug, but far enough away that I can't reach it.

Daphne is a bad influence. Or Marco. Or Portland in general because I can't be trusted anymore when it comes to Dane Masters. Not even from a thousand miles away.

− 6 −
Musical Chairs

I LAND IN PHOENIX LESS than ten weeks after I left. Keaton squeals before I even see her and bounds toward me. She hits hard, her arms locking around me.

Waiting where she left him, Liam holds a sign: *GO BACK!* He tries to get the people around us to join him in chanting the same.

God, I missed them.

We drive to the wedding venue Keaton insists on me approving before they book. The garden, ornate archways, balcony surrounding the ballroom all fit her dream wedding perfectly. I give my blessing, and Liam winks at me. He texted me over a week ago when he found out they'd had a cancellation for next June. Knowing how much she wanted it, he already put the deposit down. Which means it's official. My best friend is getting married.

The engagement party is at the Reynolds' house. We arrive just in time for Liam to help Patrick move flowerpots from one side of the backyard to the other. It improves the aesthetic or something.

Parents mourn their children when they leave home, keeping their rooms untouched as a memorial of sorts. Either that or they turn the space into a home gym they never use. My substitute parents are remember-when types, everything exactly where I left it when I moved out four years ago.

I drop my bag and fall back on the bed.

No one ever technically told me my mother wasn't coming back. I came to the conclusion on my own when we redecorated the guest room and everyone started calling it Bennett's room. A few boxes showed up a week later with stuff from my old bedroom to confirm. They went in the trash, unopened, before either Joyce or Patrick came home. Everything in them was tainted by *her*, and it was easier to go on like she never existed.

Like mother, like daughter.

I shower off the smell of passenger 7C and change. By the time I emerge, the backyard has transformed into something off Keaton's Pinterest board. Mason jar candles everywhere; strings of soft, glowing bulbs around the fence line; tables with white cloths; and gorgeous flowers in wine-bottle vases as centerpieces. We play music through the speakers Liam hooked up while we fill water glasses and finish arranging the place settings.

The second Keaton disappears into the house, I swap Dane's name card over to my table. I set him straight across from me. No offense to Aunt Peg, but he's nicer to look at.

Since the bookstore, his texts have returned to random updates until a few days ago. He sent a stern reminder of his footwear request, telling me not to bother showing up without the heels. They are under my bed in Portland.

Guests start arriving as the caterers and bartender set up. Introductions are made, families mingle, and I answer the same questions for different groups of Keaton's relatives.

The Reynolds clan is massive—six siblings on Patrick's side and five on Joyce's. All but them continued on until they hit a minimum of four offspring. After every single family gathering, Keaton thanks them for stopping with her.

I say, "I'm great. How are you?" thirteen times before escaping to the kitchen where I want to stay for the remainder of the night.

Liam meets me by the fridge and massages my cheeks. "Remember, it's a marathon. Smile breaks are important."

I stretch out my jaw. "I met your parents. They love Keaton."

"Duh. It's Keaton. The first time she went to their house, she took Mom some specialty tea and Dad an assortment of meat sticks."

"We scoured the city for those damn tea bags."

He smiles the smile of a man ridiculously in love, and I remember why I like him so much.

"All right," he says. "I'm going in. Wish me luck."

"Luck," I call after him.

Two steps onto the deck, and someone shouts his name. He looks back, pretending to cry. I laugh as he trots down the steps, arms spread wide to embrace them.

"Bennett?"

I cringe, recognizing the voice, but slap on a smile mid-spin. "Ford?"

"I knew it was you the second I stepped in the front door." Keaton's cousin wraps me in a hug. "I'd recognize that laugh anywhere."

"Well, I tried changing it, but it ended up being this whole thing."

He shakes his head, pulling back. "They drag you here, kicking and screaming?"

"No. But they bribed me with a plane ticket and open bar."

"You're not the one making the drinks, are you? I swear, sometimes, I still wake up in the middle of the night and taste that shit you used to mix." His smile softens, his eyes melt, and the puppy-dog look returns full force.

Ford's crush has been going strong since the first summer Keaton and I were inseparable. He always found a reason to come to the house—mowing the yard, cleaning the pool. But it was over for him the second I met his older brother, Bentley. The first guy with a six-pack to pay attention to me. Add in the way he acted like a complete dick to everyone but me and his golden tongue, and the gangly, younger Reynolds never stood a chance.

I step back far enough that Ford's hands fall away.

"How's the rest of the garage?" I ask. Their parents named them all after cars with the twins, Chevy and Lincoln, rounding out the all-boy group.

"Busy." He sticks his hands in his pockets. "They voted me family rep for the night, but we're all hoping to make it to the wedding."

I'm hoping they all won't.

Joyce's voice carries in from outside. He glances over his shoulder. "I should probably go sacrifice myself to the mob. Come with me?" He reaches his hand out. We both stare at it hanging in the air between us—him wanting me to take it, me willing him to take it back.

He lowers it to his side when I shake my head.

"I plan on hiding until dinner. I have a limited number of facts to dole out about Portland and need to ration." I turn around to face the counter.

"See ya out there then," he says.

I wave over my shoulder and pour a near-overflowing glass of wine. Ford can make a situation awkward but dealing with him is easy enough. It's Bentley at the wedding I dread. The last time we saw each other didn't end well.

I take a few gulps to distract myself and smell a lotion that's on the counter. It reminds me of an old lady, so I hide it in a drawer. "No, Joyce."

More people trickle in but none I know. I check my phone. If Dane wants to dictate what I wear, he could at least show up on time to see I haven't listened. A few seconds after my phone clatters to the counter, the screen lights up. I reach for it, but hands run up my arms, the kitchen window reflecting Dane behind me.

"Waiting for someone?" He leans down and kisses my bare shoulder. "Or do you always scowl at your phone when you check it?"

His arms wrap around me, pulling me back against his chest. I sink into him. He smells clean and reminds me of being on the water.

"I thought you weren't sneaking up on people, unannounced, anymore."

"I sent you a text. I just wasn't patient enough for you to read it." He picks up my phone and shows me.

You're so fucking hideous.

I laugh, and he nuzzles against my neck.

"That's the sound I wanted to hear."

He backs up, his hands lingering as I spin around. A reflection can't do him justice. His hair, shorter than last time, is still wet; he left an extra button undone at the top of his shirt; and his eyes are fixed with a sexy stare.

"You look pretty awful yourself," I say.

"You accidentally used five words in a sentence that only needed three." He counts off each word on his fingers as he mouths, *You. Look. Pretty.*

I laugh again, and he grins.

Clinks from outside precede Patrick's ten-minute warning to dinner. "In other words, get your drinks and sit down," he says.

Dane hands me my wineglass off the counter. "Shall we?"

I follow him out, wishing I'd booted Uncle Jimmy from beside me instead of poor Aunt Peg.

We go in opposite directions at the bottom of the deck. Keaton looks like she needs saving from a group of family members. A cousin reaches out, tugging at one of her loose curls. Her fists clench at her sides, fighting the urge to slap the hand away.

"Here you are," I interrupt her cousin Steph. "I need some clarification on how you want the servers to carry the trays."

Keaton feigns an exhausted hostess face. "There's always something." Her arm hooks through mine, and we walk away. "I fucking love you. She's already trying to find out when I'm popping out a kid, so we can coordinate births."

"Picture it, Keats … you can share a birthing tub." I yelp when she pinches me.

Everyone is taking their seats, and I weave through the tables. Joyce squeezes my arm on the way past, the way a mother does to remind her children that she's proud of them for doing absolutely nothing. I smile at her, even gladder I buried the lotion.

I'm drinking my wine down to an acceptable level when the chair next to me pulls out. Dane sits down.

"What are you doing?" I ask.

He flicks the place card in front of him. "I might have spiced up the seating arrangement a little. Looking at you from across the table all night was not an option."

"Now who's Jimmy going to talk to about his divorce?"

Dane makes a face, setting down his beer. "Who's Jimmy?"

"Keaton's uncle. The one you switched chairs with."

He shakes his head, about to say something until Ford walks up behind us. His eyes dart between Dane and me before stopping on the table between us.

"Hey, Ford." I tack on a smile because he seems flustered. "This is Dane, Liam's cousin."

"Hey," he says, making one more sweep between the two of us. "They said I was over here ... somewhere."

Dane points across from me. "I think I saw your name over there." He winks at me.

I start to get an idea of what happened and spot Uncle Jimmy a few tables over where I saw Ford's name earlier. Dane and I aren't the only ones wreaking havoc on Keaton's carefully constructed seating chart. Unfortunately for Ford, the game of musical chairs hasn't quite worked out as he'd planned. He reluctantly goes to the other side of the table, his right hand rubbing up and down the left side of his jaw. All of his brothers do the same thing when annoyed. Same hand. Same side.

"Great memory," he says. "Dane, was it?"

Dane nods. "You and Bennett must know each other through Keaton. Everyone here under thirty seems to be another one of her cousins."

"Yeah, Bennett and I have known each other a long time."

"She's never mentioned you though." Dane rests his arm on the back of my chair, prompting another pass of Ford's hand over his jaw. "So, I'm guessing you don't know her very well."

It's the last thing he says through dinner.

OTHER THAN PAUSING FOR BITES, the only times Ford stops talking is after asking, "Did you know Bennett (fill in the blank with a fact about me, such as I played the trumpet in band or slept through most of prom)?"

Dane shakes his head and sometimes glances at me out of the corner of his eye, but most of the time, he just appears bored. He even starts texting under the table. And the more uninterested Dane, the smugger Ford. I can't decide whether he's trying to chase him off by proving how well he knows me or by making me sound like the dullest person alive. Either way, it seems to work.

We're finishing our entrees when a higher power intervenes. Ford's phone lights up on the table. He hesitates, hand hovering, but eventually excuses himself to answer. I relax in my seat, hoping he gets lost on his way back.

As soon as he walks away, Dane's entire demeanor changes. His body shifts toward me, a smile spreading over his face, and he pulls his phone out from under the table.

"First off"—he checks his screen—"AP classes all through high school? You're a nerd. With such a huge brain, there is no excuse for failing your driving test twice. And as for prom, tell me the truth—was your date just so terrible that you pretended to oversleep?" His expression goes serious again as he leans in and points at his face. "Trumpet. Four years. Marching band. Tell me that doesn't turn you on."

My mouth falls open. "I didn't think you were even listening to him."

"Not only was I listening, but I was also taking notes." He sets his phone in my hand. "The guy was telling me everything I needed to know about Bennett Alexus Ross. I couldn't risk him realizing it and have him stop."

I read through his thoughts on everything Ford said, and he has plenty. "You played him?"

"Like my fucking trumpet," he says. "I feel kind of bad though. It sounds like he's dedicated a lot of time, and I kind of lucked my way in."

"And what exactly have you lucked your way into?" I ask, handing his phone back.

"I'm not entirely sure, but I'll let you know when I figure it out."

He pushes my hair behind my ear. I press my lips together and glance away, but his fingertips trail along my jaw, bringing my face back. We're closer than necessary for a conversation we stop having. Surrounded by people yet completely alone while he once again stares into my eyes.

"Heels or not," he says, his voice low, "I want you right now."

A blush creeps up my neck, and his gaze dips and slowly rakes over me, staying in certain places longer than others. I can practically feel him touching me, my chest rising faster. He locks in on my thighs, on the extra half-inch of skin on display when I shift and the hem of my dress slips up.

Someone reaches between us, and we both sit back. I look up as Ford sets a glass of wine in front of me.

"Sounds like it'll be a while until dessert, so I grabbed you one of these."

"Thank you," I say, forcing a smile, but my eyes go straight back to Dane.

A corner of his mouth perks up. He tilts his head toward the house, and I can't stand up fast enough.

"I'd better check inside to see if Joyce needs help with anything." Before anyone points out she's over on the grass, playing croquet, I walk away.

Dane's already following when I reach the steps to the deck. Other than Ford, no one pays attention to the way he stalks me across the yard, his eyes burning through me. A group of servers gathered inside slows me down, so by the time I reach the living room, he isn't far behind. I turn around in the hallway outside my room, and he runs straight into me, pinning me against the door.

"I'm calling for a do-over on the first time this happened."

He drops his forehead onto mine and grips my hip. I force a breath, my body responding like a fucking Daphne.

"Will there still be a naked girl rolling across the bed?"

"I'll need to get you undressed first."

The door gives behind me. My back hits the other side by the time it shuts again. He grasps the backs of my thighs, lifting me.

Dress hiked up, legs wrapped around him. I feel him through his slacks, long and hard, and when he thrusts forward, I moan, his name attached.

"I've been dreaming of that," he says in my ear. "One more time, baby."

He rocks against me, and I can't help it.

"Oh my God, Dane."

I pull his face to mine, not sure how I've lasted this long without his lips on me. I unbutton his shirt while he carries me to the bed, and I push the fabric off his shoulders. It hits the ground after he lays me down. He lowers on top of me and takes the same leisurely path his eyes strolled earlier, kissing his way down my body. His breath is warm through my dress and then hot on my thighs.

But everything turns cold when someone knocks.

Fuck.

Dane's head pops up from between my legs, and I push onto my elbows, my pulse racing. I can't remember if either of us locked the door.

"Hey, Bennett," Liam says.

I consider not responding, but then he might try to come in. "Yeah?"

"Keaton's looking for you. She needs help with some sparkly baggie things."

"The gift bags. Okay. I'll be out."

Dane bites my inner thigh, and my teeth sink into my bottom lip in a poor attempt to suppress a moan. I fall back on the bed and add, "In a bit."

He grins and runs his tongue over the same spot.

My hands push through his hair, and his thumbs are hooked in my panties when Liam says, "Oh, and Dane? Your dad's here."

"Thanks, man," he calls over his shoulder.

"Dane," I whisper-yell and shove him with my foot. He catches my ankle and secures my leg to stop me from trying with the other foot. I wiggle in a futile effort to break his hold, and he chuckles.

"Stop it." He crawls up to hover over me. "You're getting me all worked up again, and talking to my dad with a visible hard-on will be incredibly awkward for everyone involved."

The silver bar swinging between us has a dotted line etched in the metal on both sides. I wrap its chain around my fingers, glaring at him.

"It's just Liam," he says. He kisses my knuckles when I continue to pout. "He won't say anything unless Keaton outright asks him."

"He's right," Liam confirms from the hallway.

"Liam," I shout. "Go away!"

Dane laughs, and I can't help but smile at the way he chews on his bottom lip.

Once he pulls me off the bed, he picks his shirt off the floor. I check the mirror and fix my hair, so I won't give Keaton a reason to be suspicious of my disappearance. We share almost everything, but I'll avoid anything Dane-related as long as possible. Whatever this is won't change my mind about leaving Phoenix. I don't need her thinking otherwise.

He steps behind me and folds his arms around me. "We're spending time together before you leave," he says, looking at me through our reflection. "No nosy couple or another guy vying for your attention. Just you and me."

I turn around in his arms. "Are you asking or telling?"

"Does it matter?" He kisses the tip of my nose and walks away without my answer.

But, no, it really doesn't.

I HELP KEATON SET UP a table by the front door for guests to grab a thank-you bag on their way out. After eating all the candy out of a few, we set them aside. We move a few more over to eat later. A break before dessert was a terrible idea.

When I step back out on the deck, Patrick waves me over to him and Joyce. At first, I think they're talking to Liam's dad and probably a cousin—a young blonde dressed more for a nightclub than a backyard. Then I see Dane with them, his back to me. By the time I figure out what is about to happen, it's too late.

Patrick puts an arm out for me, and Dane glances back. He wipes a hand over his mouth, hiding a smile. At least one of us finds meeting the parents without warning entertaining. I step under Patrick's arm, and he pulls me against his side.

"This is our other girl, Bennett."

They always introduce Keaton and me the same way—"our girls"—never differentiating between us. It throws people off when they later learn I go by a different last name or our birthdays are a few months apart. We all secretly enjoy it, Patrick the most.

"Greg here is Liam's uncle, and this is his wife, Aubrey. I believe you've already met his son, Dane."

Greg takes my hand in both of his, squeezing it. They carry themselves the same, straight backs and strong shoulders. But Dane's eyes hold a softness missing from his father's.

"A pleasure, my dear. I hope Dane's represented the Masters name well."

Dane rolls his eyes, and I smile.

"If anything, he's saved it from the damage done by Liam."

Patrick chuckles as Joyce covers her face, embarrassed over nothing. "She's kidding," she says.

"Of course she is." Greg steps back beside Aubrey. Her hand goes straight to his chest to claim him.

She can't be more than a few years older than me, but anyone younger must pose a threat, judging by the way she clings to him. It makes me sad for her.

Patrick and Greg transition into a conversation about classic cars, and I excuse myself. I continue the tour of family and friends for the rest of the night, flitting in and out before anyone traps me for long. Ford stays away, only swooping in for a hug before he leaves. He reminds me we'll see each other at the wedding, then heavily hints we should meet up sooner. I answer with a noncommittal shrug.

Every so often, Dane catches my eye and smiles or trails his fingers across my back as he walks behind me. It turns into a game—how close we can get without talking to the same people.

By the time most of the guests have cleared out, I haven't seen Keaton for a while. I find her in the family room, spreading blankets out on the floor, and tackle her in the middle of them. We sprawl out on our backs to stare at the ceiling like we've done an uncountable number of times over the years. At one time, we did this in the backyard, but after a few coyote sightings in the area, Patrick insisted we camp in a safer location.

"Which of us is getting up to shut off the light?" I ask.

"I got this." She pulls out her phone, and a minute later, Liam walks in with Dane right behind him.

"What do you want, woman?"

"Can you shut off the light, please?"

He narrows his eyes but flips the switch next to the doorway. The ceiling lights up in glowing stars—not the cheap yellow shapes in an eight-year-old's bedroom, but bright dots of different sizes, creating a night sky above us. Constellations, a shooting star. All the beauty of the universe without the intimidating vastness. You can disappear into it without being lost.

"Is this what you're doing for the rest of the night?" Liam asks.

"Yes," we answer in unison.

"I warned you about them," he says to Dane. But a second later, he drops onto the floor between us and elbows until I scoot over to give him room. "Lucky for you two, I dig me some crazy."

With the three of us spread from the fireplace to the coffee table, it leaves less than enough room for the next body that comes crashing down. Dane crams into the space beside me. "Must be genetic."

When I turn my head, he smirks and slides his arm under mine between us. With his fingers brushing over mine, I look up at the ceiling and pretend fake-stargazing together isn't a straight re-creation of one of Keaton's visions of the four of us.

I FALL ASLEEP WITH MY cheek resting on a bicep but wake up with it pressed against the wooden leg of the table. I roll onto my back, sure I'll have an indent. Next to me, Keaton's sprawled out, half on top of Liam. As I get up, I take his glasses from his hand and set them on the coffee table. The last time I saw my phone, it

This was on the counter in the kitchen. Now it's here, next to the TV remote.

I check for the text I know will be waiting.

> Dane: *Tomorrow. Tell me when and where. I'll be there.*

— 7 —
Not a Date

THE NEXT NIGHT, MY PHONE lights up at precisely nine. I can't check it because I'm standing in front of the fireplace in the family room, trying to act out *frog in your throat* for Liam. It isn't going well. Keaton curls up in a ball in hysterics as I once again stick my tongue out while hopping around.

He resorts to threats while I grab at my neck. "I swear to God, Bennett…"

The timer beeps, and he rips the paper off the coffee table to unfold it. "THAT was a frog?" He throws the paper and then swats at it when it floats back toward him.

"Careful," I say. "We have a bad history of throwing things during game night."

It's the reason we stopped a few years ago. Joyce hurled a wineglass while screeching out an answer and nailed Patrick in the head. New carpet and a few stitches later, it was clear we had taken it too seriously and needed a break.

I pick up my phone, seeing the text from Dane. "I'll be back later."

"Going for a walk?" Keaton asks, eyebrow raised.

It takes a second to remember our code for meeting a boy. I shrug, not wanting to lie to her. "I might have a craving for ice cream." *Yes.*

"Bring me something back." *Tell me about it later.*

"Bring me something too," Liam shouts after me.

He's going to be so disappointed.

I don't notice Dane on the front porch until he catches my wrist. He pulls me over to him, his mouth colliding with mine. I grasp at the back of his neck, wanting him closer, and his hands slide down my backside. His tongue parts my lips, and a low sound rumbles from the back of his throat. All want and no patience. It's how a night ends, not how you start one.

When he forces his lips away, his thumb skims over my cheek. "Is it too soon for me to miss you? Because I'm pretty sure I fucking missed you."

A therapist once told me it's not our choice. He was trying to convince me I missed my mother even if I wouldn't admit it. According to him, missing someone deals with an influx of hormones and chemicals in our brains, created by family, friends, someone who makes your pulse race. You get high on them, your brain addicted, then when they're gone, the levels plummet to normal. You withdrawal, feeling the absence of the hormones they provided and therefore them. But even if Dr. Preston was on to something, he expected me to scream at a plant and call it Mommy, so goodbye credibility.

I lead Dane off the porch, and his fingers interlace with mine.

"I thought you were going to wait in your truck."

"If I had kissed you like that in the truck, we wouldn't have stopped. I doubted you would let me fuck you on the porch."

I want to believe that's true. Just like I want to believe I haven't fucking missed him too.

His truck is exactly like Liam's, except red instead of blue. Company vehicles given to anyone bearing the company name as their own.

"Do you even like finance?" I ask as he drives. Where to I have no idea. I haven't bothered asking, and he hasn't offered to tell.

"No. It's boring, and the clients are rich assholes who've completely lost touch with reality." He glances over and smiles. "You're going to ask me why I do it then."

Since he keeps crawling into my head, I decide to return the favor. "And you're going to say because it's family and nothing is more important than that."

He thinks about it for a few seconds. "Tell me something that is more important."

"You," I say. "You should never give up your own happiness or peace of mind or sense of self for someone else. Anyone who asks you to isn't worth the sacrifice, and anyone who is never would."

A streetlight hits his face, highlighting the sharp line of his jaw. "I guess it's a good thing I'm in it for the money then."

He looks over, his grin spreading. I laugh. He's messing with me.

"We're here, by the way." He pulls into the parking lot of a big-box store and parks next to a faded blue minivan with a dent in the side door.

"Are we going grocery shopping?" I ask, climbing out.

We meet at the back of the truck. "Why? Were you hoping for something more along the lines of dinner and a movie for our date? Because we've both already eaten, and I fall asleep during movies."

"When did this become a date?"

He tucks me under his arm, shielding me from the wind on our way inside. "You're right," he says. "It's not a date. If it were, I would tell you."

"Considerate of you, but most guys would ask."

"Too risky. You might say no, and I'd need to respect your decision."

I roll my eyes and lean into him as he kisses the top of my head. Through the automatic doors, he stops for two shopping carts and pushes one toward me.

"I'll meet you at the registers in fifteen minutes."

"You haven't told me what we're buying," I call after him.

He shrugs, still walking away. "Follow your heart."

My heart leads me to garden gnomes dressed as gangsters, a sparkly phone case shaped like a unicorn, and the liquor aisle.

When we meet back at the front of the store, Dane crashes his cart into mine. He examines my items and fishes out the tequila bottle. "I like how your mind works, Bennett Ross, but this might not go with what I picked up."

In the bottom of his cart is a bottle of wine, a blanket, throw pillows, and candles.

I narrow my eyes at him. "Not a date, huh?"

He tilts his head back and forth, thinking it over, and then he smiles. "No. Now, it's a date."

— 8 —
Date

I BLINK AT HIM. "YOU can't just declare us on a date."

"I just did though." He pushes his cart into a checkout lane, and mine goes abandoned.

The man in front of us balances a kid in each arm and a phone between his ear and shoulder as he points out what brand of cigarettes he wants. Incredible talents develop when the need arises.

Dane picks up a container of mints from the display and shakes them at me. "Do you like these?"

"No." Not entirely sure how annoyed I am with him yet, I cross my arms. "Buy the cinnamon ones."

His lips twitch, and he switches them. They go on the conveyer belt along with everything else. While we wait on the cashier, he tugs me over to him by the arm. "Pout all you want, baby. This is happening."

I sigh and let myself lose the battle. "Fine, but I don't sleep with guys on the first date."

"Respectable," he says, securing his arms around my waist. "That's why I'm calling coffee and dinner dates one and two. We can say me grinding on you in your bedroom is three if you want. I'll leave it up to you."

"Four dates in three months? No wonder we're not getting anywhere."

He lets go of me to pay. "When you fall for a drifter, you take what you can get."

If I hadn't already decided to give in, I would when he looks back and smiles.

The hot wind blows on our skin as we walk back to the truck. His hand finds my lower back when he opens the passenger door for me, and I brush against him, climbing in. Then he's crawling in after me. I laugh, falling back on the bench seat with him following me down.

"What about the candles?"

"There's a lighter in here somewhere," he mumbles into my neck. "And we can drink the wine out of the bottle. The pillows can go under your sweet little head."

"And the blanket can shield us from the kid watching from the car a few spaces over?"

He kisses his way to my lips before he checks to confirm. "Think of it as an added challenge."

I push on his shoulder, and he sighs, crawling backward out of the truck.

DANE LIVES IN A QUIET neighborhood with tree-lined streets and older houses. Ones built with actual character that look different from those on each side. Fences and manicured lawns and more than one car in most driveways. It's where you expect to find already-established families, not someone who graduated college two years ago.

The inside of his red-brick bungalow almost mismatches the outside. Exposed brick borders the tops of the slate-colored walls, and wood beams run the length of the high ceilings that vault in the living room. In the kitchen, all the pots and pans hang from a rack suspended over a large island with a concrete countertop, and the cabinets are white and open.

"This was my mother's house," he says.

I don't need to ask. The word *was* always sounds different when referring to someone who died. It carries a heaviness or absence or both.

He hands me a glass of wine as I look at the pictures of him and her on the mantel over the fireplace. Her red hair caught the light, no matter the angle, and she had one of those smiles you couldn't help but stare at, sincere and telling. The photos progress from Dane as a toddler to a teenager, not following his life past a certain point.

"You were still in high school," I say.

"Just before graduation. She'd been in remission for over a year but only lasted a few months after the cancer came back." He shakes his head, taking in the room like he's seeing it for the first time. "She called this her *Maison de la vengeance*—Revenge House. Every time my father pissed her off, she would renovate a room and send him the bill. She made me promise to never sell it."

"My kind of woman." I eye him and sip.

"Oh? You like that idea?" He steps closer when I nod and sets my glass on the mantel. "Too bad you'll never get one of your own."

"And why's that?" I start to back up, but he catches me and pulls me flush against him.

"Because I'm impossible to stay mad at."

With a quick grin, he picks me up over his shoulder. I let out an embarrassing giggle as his arm tightens around the backs of my thighs. He carries me through the living room, swiping the plastic bags off the couch on the way. I land on my back on a bed, and he shakes the bags out next to me. The glass candles crack together, rolling toward me, but my attention stays on him dragging his shirt over his head. He lowers himself onto the bed and nudges the hem of my top up. It lands on the floor beside his shirt. I shove the candles off in the same direction.

"You won't stop this time?" I ask.

We're both on our knees, chest-to-chest, my arms around his neck while he unclasps my bra. He tosses it over the edge of the bed, and his eyes wash over me.

"The whole damn house can burn down for all I care."

His mouth covers mine, and we fall back on the mattress. I push his jeans down until he kicks them the rest of the way off. One pillow flies over his shoulder, followed by the other. Item by item, our date goes in a pile along with our clothes. The mints go last, the container rattling when it bounces.

A hand slides between my legs, but his fingers barely graze over me. Even when my hips move to meet them, the contact remains minimal.

"Tell me you'll stay for breakfast in the morning."

The tips of his fingers conduct another pass before retreating, and I almost whimper.

"No sneaking out," he says, "or leaving without a goodbye."

My eyes close when his palm presses against me, but it disappears after a second. *Torture.*

"Say it, Bennett. Say you'll wake up in my arms and eat shitty pancakes across the table from me."

His eyes wait for mine when they open. He starts skimming his thumb in a circle, and I'm so done.

I blow out a frustrated breath. "Fuck me right now, and I'll stay until lunch."

One corner of his mouth lifts into a sexy smirk. "Deal."

His fingers finally dip inside me, and I'd cancel my flight if he asked. I grab the back of his head, yanking his lips to mine. My body's already humming when he reaches in the drawer of the nightstand. I notice the chain missing from his neck lying on top. A book sits next to it with a piece of paper sticking out for a bookmark.

What he keeps closest to him.

Dane holds the condom wrapper in his teeth, tearing it open. His hips settle between my thighs, and the way he stares down at me makes it hard for me to breathe. It only lasts a few seconds— me not breathing, him looking at me like we're something important. Then he thrusts into me.

Hard.

I suck in air, and his eyes shut until he retreats. I lock my legs around him, and he bites my jaw, burying himself in me deeper. We aren't sharing a moment anymore, but rough and needy, finishing what we started on a couch a few months ago. His grip digs into my skin as my nails scrape over the muscles of his back. I moan, and his tongue shoves into my mouth like he needs to taste the sound. It sends a shiver through me. Everything builds fast from there. A tingle in my toes and a tension in my core battle for control neither can win.

"Dane…" I lose the rest as my thighs tighten on his hips, wanting more of him.

He presses his nose against my neck. "Fuck, baby."

The sound of his voice sends the world spiraling, taking me with it until it all drops out. His short breaths work their way through my skin while my body quivers around him. I come apart, crying out his name and not knowing my own. He pumps into me harder, and then he groans, his muscles rigid with one last thrust.

I melt into the mattress as he stills, and our eyes meet. His fade back to the ones from before, looking at me like I deserve a special place on his nightstand. I breathe through it this time. Force myself to live in it. His focus lowers to my mouth, and he drops his lips onto mine. A slow kiss. Soft and lazy and the type that takes up residence in your chest. After he pulls back, his thumb runs along my bottom lip.

"Get dressed." He gives my lip a tug and rolls off me.

Usually, I'd have already calculated how long until I could get out at this point, but as I watch him gather his clothes off the floor, an unfamiliar sense of rejection grabs hold. I wrap my arms around my chest and sit up, suddenly very cold. "I thought I was staying the night."

I cringe at the slight shake in my voice. I'm better than that.

Dane turns in the doorway and studies me. I press my lips together, refusing to care what he says next.

"You are," he says. "But I only planned on coercing you into staying for one meal." He picks up my clothes and brings them over to the bed. "We really do need to go grocery shopping now." He lowers his head until the tip of his nose touches mine. "Then we're figuring out when I'm seeing you next because I'm not waiting three months again."

And that's how you become addicted to someone.

– 9 –
Playlist

PORTLAND AND I PART WAYS on a rainy day in August. Marco stands on the sidewalk under his umbrella, watching me dodge puddles in the most inconvenient locations while I load my four boxes and suitcase into the car.

Last weekend, we took a trip to San Francisco. I'd already found work as a tour guide at a museum, and his cousin knew a guy who had a friend whose sister was looking for a roommate. Marco vetted her to make sure she wouldn't undo everything he'd taught me about life and love.

When I asked what lessons I'd learned in my time with him, he rolled his eyes and said, "We live by three rules. Be happy, be safe, be kind. We love by one. Be true to you."

I wondered if you were supposed to follow both sets of rules at the same time, but we'd already reached his eye-rolling quota for the day. I didn't want to give him a headache.

All packed up, I leap over a pool of water by the curb and join him under his umbrella.

"I got you something." He reaches in his jacket and pulls out a copy of *Darkest Desires*. "Just in case you change your mind about happily-ever-afters and want a few pointers. Daphne ends up being unbearable about halfway through, but we all deserve a Denton. The man gives new definition to the word *stamina*, and in chapter thirteen, he—"

"Spoilers!" I grab the book from him.

Marco cracks a rare smile, and despite our agreement to remain indifferent during our goodbye, he hugs me. It only lasts three seconds before he pulls away and gives me an annoyed look for getting him wet. "Your hair's going to be a frizzy mess when it dries."

I back away with my guide to love. "I'll post a picture, so you can judge me."

"Which I will," he says, heading back inside. "You never find your light."

Without him standing on the curb like Keaton, waving until she was nothing more than a dot in my rearview mirror, it feels less like I'm leaving him behind when I drive away. And I'm not. Unlike my role model growing up, I understand you can leave a place behind and keep the people. Then again, she might have known that and just not given a shit.

Rather than the radio, I listen to a playlist created by none other than Dane Masters. He titled it *Dear Bennett*. The songs range from unexpected choices to unbearable nonsense. One even sounds like monkeys screeching with jungle sounds in the background. I stop for gas and text him.

> *I'm holding an intervention. You have terrible taste in music. Horrible. Dreadful.*

> A picture of his abs pops up in response, followed by, *Who needs taste when you have these?*

> I laugh and reply, *Sorry, some of those songs are unforgivable.*

The dots appear and disappear before his name shows up on the screen. I crawl back in the car as I answer.

"Unforgivable," I repeat.

"Scroll through the list again," he says. "You might change your mind about that."

Cryptic.

I hit the speaker button and swipe through the playlist starting from the beginning. At first, I'm not sure what I am supposed to be looking for, but then I see it.

The titles of the songs on *Dear Bennett* read:

Why Can't I Stop
Thinking About You
Seriously
I Want You
All of You
All the Time
Everywhere
You Drive Me Crazy
I'm Losing My Mind
Over You
Baby
And
I Never Want It
Back

I smile a ridiculously huge, cheek-killer smile and sink back in my seat. "I'm going to make you listen to every one of these songs."

"It's worth it if you're smiling." He lets out a long, dramatic sigh. "I need to go pretend not to be obsessing over you for a while."

He hangs up without a goodbye, and I pull back onto the highway, pretending not to think about him too.

TEN HOURS IN A CAR turns out to be basically the same thing as twenty hours. Sun replaces rain, the scenery loses some green, trees give way to buildings.

I crane my neck, looking up at the old warehouse converted into apartments. It has curb appeal, shrubs, and is on a quiet street.

I shouldn't be able to afford it. I've done the math over and over. My rent times two means this is one of the cheapest two bedrooms in the city.

Out of habit, I take the stairs. The heavy metal door out front matches the one marked four that I knock on. It jerks wide open, and the grin of a crazed pixie meets me.

"You're here!" she squeals.

Aria maybe breaks five foot with a bit of a heel, but she drags me across the threshold like a bouncer. She pulls me through the large open space with a living room and kitchen, chattering away. We head up the steel staircase, past the warehouse windows, and across a suspended catwalk where a metal railing is all that keeps you from falling back down. While she flits her way to my bedroom, I clunk along behind, managing not to tumble over the side to my death.

When we stop at the door, she throws it open and finally lets me go by the bed. "What do you think?"

Mouth gaping, I look around. What was a stark white, minimally furnished room is now anything but. The walls are a soft blue to purple gradient, candles and café string lights blanket the room in a glow, and a fluffy down comforter covered with decorative pillows finishes off the transformation. It's like a personal sanctuary I never want to leave.

"You did all this for me?"

She shrugs with one shoulder, feigning innocence. "It's amazing what you can come up with on Pinterest."

If she ever meets Keaton, they will be an unstoppable force.

"Thank you," I say, still in awe. "This is incredible, Aria."

"I'm just so glad to finally have someone else around. Steve spends most of his time either up in his tower or napping on the sofa." She pokes her head out the door and looks up and down the catwalk. "Little Stevie?"

Little Stevie, aka Steve, is a massive, long-haired tabby with a perpetual scowl locked on its face. He tried to bite Marco several times during our short visit. Aria claimed he was acting out because the vet had recommended he go on a diet. Also, at one point, she mentioned something about him not wanting to interact with new people until Venus is out of retrograde. People are weird with their cats. The way she talks about him sometimes, you'd think he was a human sharing a living space with her.

Aria never finds the cat. She helps me carry my boxes up and leaves for a pottery class before he comes traipsing into my room. He stretches out on my bed, king of his castle. I never had any pets growing up. My mother was burdened with taking care of me. Why add to it?

I unpack, exchanging glares with him until he falls asleep. Over the next few days, it becomes a ritual. The cat appears on my bed, acts like a jerk, naps, and then disappears.

Other than him, I am in the apartment alone most of the time. At least, that's what I think.

It takes five days for me to learn that has never been the case. When Venus leaves retrograde.

-10-
Harmonious Vibes

ARIA WARNED ME SHE WOULDN'T be around much the first few weeks, and she wasn't kidding. I only see her in passing when I come home from work and never for more than a few minutes at a time.

During the day, she works at a tech company focused on security something and other buzz words. At night, she fills in at a community college, teaching an English as a Second Language class until the instructor returns from maternity leave.

On Saturday morning, the metal door bangs at the normal time as she leaves for work. It's tempting to stay in bed, but I want to spend my day off exploring the city. See something other than car bumpers and school kids on field trips. The life of a museum tour guide is not an exciting one.

I take advantage of not needing to rush through a morning routine, enjoying a long shower. Little Stevie perches on the dresser, staring me down while I get dressed. My presence in the apartment during the day clearly offends him deeply.

"Deal with it."

I touch his nose, and he swats at me before jumping down. I follow him out, shutting the door to keep him from lying on my bed all day. When my eyes scan the living room and kitchen below, I freeze. The guy in sweatpants and no shirt at the stove glances over his shoulder.

"Hey," he says, going back to cooking. "I forgot to ask Aria if you eat dairy, so I'm putting soy milk in the pancakes."

I stand there, unsure of what to do. The way he talks, I should know why he's in my kitchen, making me breakfast, and I refuse to repeat the psycho-stalker mistake.

"Shit, I used eggs." He rubs a hand over his shaved head and turns around. "You aren't a vegan, are you?"

Face on, I recognize him and relax a little. Pictures of him cover the refrigerator, arms tight around Aria, kissing her temple, smiling like Liam when he looks at Keaton.

I shake my head, descending the stairs, and he blows out a relieved breath, spinning back around.

"That would have been a terrible first impression," he says. "Then again, I probably ruined my chances at a good one by refusing to meet you until Venus finished fucking with my life. Ari says I'm a temperamental artist, but I think it's just a nice way of stating I'm a douche."

Steve.

The Steve who naps on the couch and spends his time in his tower and is *not* an overweight and moody feline but very much a human. Thank God I didn't attack him with the TV remote or something equally embarrassing.

He checks over his shoulder and grins, seeing me in the living room. "It's weird, having someone else here during the day. Usually, it's just me and Stephen."

"Little Stevie?" I ask. I need confirmation there isn't another dude chilling around the apartment I'm completely oblivious to.

"Yeah, Stephen is his given name—Stephen Cornelius Matterhorn."

People and their cats.

The topic of conversation struts past, giving me the kitty side-eye on his way into the kitchen. He jumps onto the counter, and Steve absentmindedly reaches over to scruff up the fur on top of his head.

"I fished him out of a gutter when he was only a few weeks old," he says. "He was so malnourished that I almost lost him a few times. Not that you'd know it, looking at him now."

Little Stevie lets out a harsh yowl and jumps down, not a fan of being fat-shamed.

"He's *your* cat?" I wander farther into the kitchen, my apprehension overruled by my latest realization.

Half of Steve's face perks into a confused grin. "Yeah. Why?"

"You named the cat after yourself?"

"Of course not." He tosses the dish towel from over his shoulder down and flips off the burner. "He named himself."

"Oh," I say, fighting off a smile.

He catches it and scrunches his face in response. "Yeah, it's another thing Ari claims is adorable, but I'm pretty sure it's weird as fuck."

I laugh and shake my head. "Unconventional, maybe, but he really does seem like a Stephen."

Steve points at me with the spatula. "Harmonious vibes, Bennett Ross. You and me, we've got harmonious vibes."

No one has ever complimented my vibes before. But I think it means more to me than any other I've received.

ARIA AND STEVE ARE THE oddest coupling I've ever encountered. And the most beautiful pair I could imagine.

Most of the time, they seem mismatched in body and personality. Aria—with her sprite build, rainbow-tipped black hair, and sayings tattooed over her skin—wears a business suit nine-to-five, Monday through Saturday, and carpools to the daily grind. Steve—built like a weight lifter, most often found in gym shorts and a cutoff tee with bro quotes—spends his days locked away in an attic with a canvas and paint that always finds a way downstairs or at The Daily Grind—a coffee shop down the street where he listens to smooth jazz on a cassette player.

When they're together, though, she pulls down her professional bun, letting her color show, and he talks about investing in a mutual fund to diversify their portfolio. They love each other madly, unapologetically. It's raw and undiluted, and after a week of witnessing them together, I'm digging *Darkest Desires* out of the drawer I tucked it into, curious if Denton and Daphne could possibly compare.

I won't let myself get caught up in the story like Marco, but I can understand the draw. Through the first few chapters, Denton watches her from afar. He smiles when she smiles, and when they finally meet and Daphne experiences the connection he has all along, a part of you smiles with them. You hate anyone who tries to keep them apart and wait for the second they're reunited.

But good Lord, I can only handle so much throbbing and a certain number of body parts awakening before I have to set it down.

A few weeks after the Steve/Stevie/Stephen realization, Aria calls from work.

"You have the day off, right?" she asks, sounding much too busy with the tap of a keyboard and answering questions for other people before I can answer hers.

"Yeah. Why? What's up?" I lay the book on my nightstand and sit up, embarrassed to have lounged around all day when she sounds so productive.

"I forgot to leave food out for Steve."

"Stevie?" I ask.

"No—hold on." She rattles off a bunch of numbers, then she's back. "Steve's up in his tower, tortured over a dream bridge he wants to re-create. I meant to set up a lunch for him in case he wanders down; otherwise, he won't eat. Any chance you can run a sandwich up to him? If he doesn't answer, you can leave it outside the door."

"Sure," I say. "Anything in particular he likes?"

"Honestly, he'd mindlessly chew on sand when he's craving inspiration, so whatever you throw together will be great. Thank you *so much*, Bennett. I'll bake you a cake or something."

With a click, she's gone, and I go to feed the human.

I've never been up the spiral staircase at the end of the catwalk. It ends at a small landing, the entire apartment visible beneath me.

I knock, and when Steve doesn't answer, I start to set the plate down as instructed. But then the door swings open, and a hand reaches out, jerking me and the sandwich inside.

Steve secures the door behind me. "I'm so close," he mumbles, taking the plate from me.

He walks back into the room. It's all very dramatic with the abysmal lighting and him pacing back and forth in his pajama pants in front of an empty easel. I squint to see the paintings lining the walls, floor to ceiling. As I reach one side of the room, the overhead lights illuminate, and my jaw falls open.

Brilliant color everywhere in graffiti-style artwork of everything from buildings to religious figures. The largest, covering most of a wall, is of Aria, the details so perfected that it leaves no question what emotion inspired every stroke.

"Steve, this is…" I have no words.

The should-be jock is a fucking artist. Anywhere I look only backs up the claim. I spin around, and he's staring at me so intensely that I swallow. Then, he drops the plate. It clatters to the ground as he starts toward me with a wild look in his eyes. I don't even have time to decide how I should be responding before he grips my shoulders, ducking down far enough so we're eye-to-eye.

"I need you," he says, "to sit the fuck down." He marches back across the room and sets a large canvas on the empty easel. "I don't need a bridge, Bennett. I need you!" Since I have yet to move, he drags me over to the stool in the center of the room, talking fast. "It's the colors. The blues and the grays and—it's not you now, but what you have been. Or what you could be again, and I know that sounds crazy, but I think you'll get it when I'm done."

I nod like I have the slightest clue what he's talking about as he pulls out brushes and paint.

"Look that way"—he points to the corner above the door—"and don't move."

"For how long?" I ask.

"However long it takes…" he says absentmindedly.

While I would love for a more specific time frame, his brow furrows, a deep focus overtaking him. I doubt he'll answer if I ask, so I sigh and resign myself to posing until he finishes. The room falls quiet around us. Not even the tick of a clock or swish of a brush.

It reminds me of when Dr. Andersen insisted I practice silent meditation in front of a mirror to help with *self-appreciation and acceptance*. Staring at myself never bothered me; as a kid, I would do it, even when not instructed, searching my face for any part that might have come from paternal genes. The lack of sound irritated the hell out of me, though, being alone in my head without distraction. I only ever lasted a few minutes, and then I would remember he'd also recommended I walk into the woods and *whittle away my emotions* and turn on music to drown out the thoughts.

But there's no music now.

Just me.

And the corner.

And the silence.

And a nagging feeling that however long it takes is going to last a hell of a lot longer than my record of five minutes.

FOUR HOURS. TWO HUNDRED AND forty minutes of absolute silence with one exception of the door squeaking when Steve opens it for Little Stevie. He perches on a cat tree in the opposite corner of where I've been directed to stare, overseeing and judging.

"You can move," Steve says, not looking away from the easel. "Just your head."

"Finally." I lower my chin and crack my neck, the muscles not sure they remember how to function. "What if I'd needed to pee?"

"We were going to get to know each other in a way very few people do." He glances up to wink, and I laugh.

"Couldn't you have just taken my picture? It seems a lot easier."

"Then it wouldn't have been you as you are but you as you were then. This way, I captured all the parts of you as they happened…" His eyes glaze over as he becomes lost in his work again.

Having experienced enough self-reflection for a lifetime, I check out the art on the walls. When I get a text, I reach for my phone without thinking. "Shit, sorry."

But Steve doesn't seem to notice I moved, so I check it anyway.

> Dane: *Did I say three months? I meant one.*
> *Which means I'm overdue to see you. Com'ere.*

With the artist still focused on his work, I tap out a quick response.

> *I'll be there for dress shopping in six weeks.*

> *Too long. I'm starting to forget what you feel like.*

Words that should send me running, but I smile at them. No matter how many times he drives my heart into a frenzy or doles out breath-stopping looks, we both know Dane has settled in the one place I never will. The promise of permanent distance offers us the perfect safety net to fuck around on the tightrope between hook-up and anything serious. He can dive off whenever he wants, and I don't worry about what will happen if we reach the other side.

Win-win.

"Who's that?" Steve flicks his eyes up.

Even though he doesn't seem bothered by my disobedience, I feel guilty for potentially screwing up his creative process and lay the screen facedown on my leg.

"A friend from Phoenix."

Reaching for a different color, he squints a little and goes quiet for a few minutes. "The one getting married?" he asks, bringing my attention back from a neon-pink-and-orange lighthouse hanging near the window.

"No."

He follows the arc of the brush with his eyes, an eyebrow imitating the movement. "Yeah, with a burst like that, I doubted it was her. Here. Come look."

I stretch quick to wake up my body and slide off the stool. Not used to playing muse, I get excited, floating on my way over to the grinning artist and his masterpiece. I imagine intense colors. Everything about me majestic as fuck and ready for a spot on the wall.

Except I round the easel to none of those things. Muted blues and grays and black swirl together, creating the image of—"A sad clown?"

I try to keep the disappointment off my face and out of my tone, but ... Steve painted a sad fucking clown that doesn't echo me in the least.

He stands, smiling despite my less than enthused reaction. "Give it a second."

He moves me to the stool and pushes down on my shoulders until I sit. As he steps beside me, I sigh and reluctantly face the painting.

"*Really* look at it. Find yourself, Bennett."

And the longer I look, the more I do. The blue in the eyes matches mine. The hint of doubt too. The lips are overdrawn and gray but mine, in a flat line of uncertainty. My hair is a dull beige, half-smooth and half-wavy, unable to decide which it wants to be or where, going in different directions. And I realize it *is* me. The way I felt while staring at the corner, stuck in my head with whatever wayward thought would trickle in. The constricting ache of the last several years in Phoenix and the restlessness of my last few days in Portland. All the discontent that swims around inside me spilled out in a few dark shades.

I point to the only part with vibrant colors. A tease of rainbow centered at the bottom, like a glow radiating from an object hidden off the edge of the canvas. "What's that?"

Steve crosses his arms and tilts his head. "A bright spot."

Little Stevie lands on the floor with a *thud*, jumping out of his cat tree. Steve steps away to open the door for him, leaving me with myself. I examine his work a little longer before I snap a picture with my phone and send it to Dane without a message, curious if anyone else will see what I missed the first time.

"Well," Steve says, coming over, "being the subject, you get the choice: sell it, hang it, or burn it." He stops next to me, his head tilting again. "Just know, if you decide to burn it, I will descend into an artistic depression and might never lift a paintbrush again."

I glance over, and his mouth has already curved into a smirk. "Temperamental artist," I tease.

He laughs and bumps his hip into me. "I'll hang it in your room after I do a few touch-ups."

Leaving him to it, I spiral down the staircase back to my room. Little Stevie has already occupied my bed. Much to his displeasure, I crash down beside him.

"Deal with it," I tell him.

While he shuffles farther over, my phone vibrates.

Dane: *It looks just like you.*

Also, Phoenix to San Francisco is a 10 day walk.

I smile and reply, *You should drive then.*

Nah, he sends, *I think I'll fly.*

-11-
The Maverick

ON SATURDAY, DANE BLOWS OFF a golf game with his father. He pounds on the metal door shortly after I crawl out of the shower, having washed the tourist off me from work. On my way through the living room, I toss a blanket over Steve, who's stretched across the couch in his briefs for what he calls a *creative recharge.*

So, a nap.

Dane stands across the threshold and sweeps his eyes over me. "You give me a clown fetish and don't deliver? Why do I even bother with you?"

"The painting's upstairs in my room if you need a minute."

Bag slung over his shoulder, he locks his arms around me. "I need *you*, upstairs. The painting will just be a bonus." He leans in, but his gaze redirects behind me. "Are you aware of the shirtless dude cuddling a furry blanket on the couch?"

"It's part of his creative process."

Dane nods, eyebrows drawn together. "I'll have to try that excuse the next time I fall asleep almost naked at my desk."

I laugh, and he backs me through the apartment, past the snoring artist. I try to turn around at the stairs, but he holds on to me.

"No, no, no," I say in a panic. "I'll fall."

"Well, we don't want that." He picks me up and climbs the stairs, wrapping my thighs around his waist. His lips twitch when I squeal and throw my arms around his neck.

At the top of the stairs, I wiggle to get down, but he keeps going across the catwalk. I clamp my eyelids shut even though I have less of a chance of plummeting over the side while clinging to him than anytime I traverse the damn thing myself. I never did take that yoga class.

I direct him to my room, his slate eyes amused at the sight of the clown looming over my dresser. He swings the door shut behind us and drops his bag on the floor, followed by us on the bed. I skim my hands to the back of his neck and tug him down to kiss me. With his weight on me, I sink into the fluffy comforter.

Pushing it away from our faces, he smiles against my mouth. "This thing is…"

"Like a cloud?"

He nods once before his tongue dives into my mouth, and neither of us cares about the plushness of the dream comforter anymore. His lips leave mine as I drag his shirt over his head. I nudge him onto his back and crawl on top of him. While I straddle him, stripping off my top, he scrubs a hand over his face.

"You okay?" I ask.

The answer comes in the form of him dragging me down and sealing his mouth over mine. "Never. Fucking. Better," he says between kisses. His hands go everywhere after that, jerking my hips forward, squeezing my ass, cupping my breasts, rubbing his eyes, thrusting into my hair.

He sniffs and flips us over.

"Are you getting sick?"

"Nope," he says, yanking my jeans off. But while shoving his own down, he wipes another hand over his face.

I sit up and feel his forehead.

"I'm not sick." He plants a kiss on my cheek, then one on my neck, and another on my shoulder, gently guiding me back down until a twenty-pound pile of fur jumps onto the bed, dipping the mattress where he lands. He must have darted in before Dane shut the door. For being overweight, Little Stevie can haul ass when he wants to.

As he rolls around on the comforter to claim his spot, Dane's eyes cut to him. His slightly red eyes, watering the tiniest bit.

"Oh my God." I sit up again, pushing him back. "You're allergic to cats."

He starts to shake his head but then moves it in a circle. "A little."

"Dane!" I bat at him as he crawls backward off the bed.

"I'll be fine," he says. "I can be around them. We even had one for a while when I was a kid."

Ignoring him, I collect Little Stevie. "Sorry, dude, but you are officially banished."

After a swipe at my hand when I set him in the hallway, he trots away with a little more attitude than normal. I toss the comforter out, too, over the railing and into the living room to wash later.

When I turn around, Dane grins on his way toward me. "You should do all activities from now on, dressed just like this, bra and thong only. We'll set up a live-stream to my computer, and I'll—"

I push onto my toes and smash my mouth against his to shut him up. Then he takes an antihistamine and fucks me on my top sheet, rubbing his face on my chest until the pill kicks in.

DANE BRACES ON AN ELBOW beside me, watching his fingertips drag across my skin, up my stomach, over my breasts, tracing the line of my collarbone.

"You're making me self-conscious."

"Sorry," he says, but he doesn't stop. "I'm memorizing. This has to last me until October." He looks up with a wolfish grin and splays his hand out across my rib cage. "Unless you'll let me take pictures."

I roll my eyes, and he falls onto his back, pulling me with him. We lie there, his fingers linking and unlinking with mine, my cheek on his shoulder. Other than Dane, I haven't cuddled with anyone after sex in a long time. Not since Bentley and I went down in flames for a second time last year. And I won't lie; I've missed the physical aspect. The warm body to sink into and lazy touches to remind you of what just happened. The part where the brain tries to trick you into emotionally bonding, not so much. Snuggle up and open up. Bleed all over the person who was just inside you to satisfy a hormonal need for connection. *Yuck.*

"Are you going to have any fallout from bailing on your dad?" I ask.

He twists my fingers until my wrist turns and then flips it the other way. "No. One of us usually cancels at the last minute."

"I take it you two don't share the same type of relationship as Liam and his dad?"

Weekend camping trips, father-son poker games.

"Not remotely," he says. "He and Shane genuinely enjoy one another's company. Greg and I tolerate each other for family events and business meetings."

I want him to keep going, show me his soft underbelly. No one enjoys being vulnerable, but we all love to be the one to bring it out in someone else.

"What about you?" he asks. He tips my chin so I'll look at him, ready to make me bleed. "Liam told me about your mom, but he's never mentioned anything about…"

"File six-two-four-nine-zero?" I shrug against his chest. "Straight brown hair, brown eyes, an inch shy of six-foot, athletic."

His eyebrows draw in. "Sperm donor?"

"My mother's choice in men was terrible. She outsourced for a chance at promising offspring, but like everything else, I failed to complete her. I ruined her body, soiled her life with sticky hands and requests for attention. And she was never going to forgive me for not being the answer for her."

I mess with the chain around his neck, examining the broken line etched into the bar.

"You talk about her like she died," he says.

I laugh once, scraping my nail over the metal. "I doubt it would feel much different if she did." The words bottom out in the pit of my stomach, and I push off Dane's chest, shaking my head. "I'm sorry. I shouldn't have said that."

Damn it, Bennett. His mom *actually* died, and I act blasé about mine's life.

But he sits up beside me and runs his fingers down the hair hanging over my shoulder. "You have nothing to apologize for. You should be angry with the woman who ran off and left you behind. I'm pissed, and I've never met her."

I lick my lips and look down. The room is too warm, even with the window open.

"Hey." Dane pushes his hand into my hair, and I turn back to him. "Let's get out of here. We can go on our fourth date in five months." He kisses me but draws back and raises his eyebrows. "Unless this is an out-of-state booty call. In which case..." Another kiss as he leans me back on the bed, following me down until my head lands on the pillow and he hovers over me. "We'd better make the plane ticket worth my while."

I smile, the breeze from the window reaching us again. "I don't remember my last booty call involving an overnight bag."

He presses his lips to mine one more time before he crawls off the bed. "This must not be one then."

I guess not.

DANE MEETS STEVE AND ARIA over dinner at a crowded restaurant a few blocks away. At least twice as many people cram into the space as capacity allows, leaving us all sitting on top of one another at a table for two. By the time we order dessert, he and Steve have all but declared their love for one another. The financial advisor and painter share almost every interest—music, movies, opinions on late-night talk show hosts. Steve's eyes when Dane offers a tip on investments compares to a man watching his bride walk down the aisle. Twenty minutes into a play-by-play of a football game that happened before either of them were born, Aria lays her head on my shoulder and sighs.

"I always tell him he should open up to people more."

"You regret it?" I ask.

Mid-yawn, she says, "Right now, I do."

She falls asleep shortly after, and Steve carries her out of the restaurant, never even considering waking her. Dane and I trail along behind, but halfway to the apartment, he tugs on my hand.

"We'll catch up."

"Have fun," Steve calls over his shoulder.

Dane turns me the other way down the sidewalk.

"And where are we going?"

He glances around us, lights and music coming from the different bars and shops lining the street. They all blend together, but he zeroes in on a horseshoe blinking in neon on the side of a building. "How do you feel about country music?"

"I hate it."

"Then I'll have your full attention." He hooks his arm around me and drags me toward The Maverick.

Peanut shells crunch under our feet as we slink past belt buckles and cowboy hats line-dancing to a song comparing a woman to a cornfield or something. We find a booth in the back corner, and he leaves me to go order at the bar. While he's gone, I watch the people like I used to in Portland.

The music switches, and the lines morph into couples shuffling across the wooden floor. They spread out enough that I see Dane on the other side. He holds cash up between two fingers, the bartender taking it with a smile. His hair's grown out, so the front brushes his forehead like the first time we met. I want to remember him holding the door for me the night of graduation. No beanie. His arm grazing mine like he wanted to catch me as I stumbled past.

When he comes back to the booth, he sets my beer down and slides in across the table from me. He sits sideways, his back to the wall and leg up on the seat. "I think the view's better from over here."

"Is that so?"

"More cowboys." He sips his beer and moves mine closer to him when I reach for it. "Come here and see."

I switch sides, crawling into the booth between his legs. As I settle back against him, he puts his arm across my chest and pushes his nose into my hair.

"See? So much better." His voice, low and smooth, melts me further into him, and I rest my head on his shoulder as the song changes. Something upbeat that floods the floor with boots, everyone singing along to the part where the music drops out. They dance, I watch, and he grazes his lips over my skin.

"Stay with me when you come back," he says in my ear. "Tell Keaton you're staying at her parents' and her parents whatever the hell you want, just … be with me when you're there."

I should take longer to respond. Think it over a few seconds or at least pretend to.

"Okay," I say.

Dane nuzzles my neck and sighs. "Okay."

-12-

Not long ago, if someone told me I would voluntarily spend my Saturday night snuggled into a giant comforter in my own personal sanctuary of a room, reading a romance novel, I would have cackled until I couldn't breathe. But here I am, wine-drunk at two in the morning and only a few chapters away from finishing *Darkest Desires*.

Ugh. Daphne.

Marco won't need any more context to know which scene my message refers to.

When my phone buzzes a few minutes later, I expect a catty comment about the voluptuous woman on the page in front of me. Instead, I see a sad yet incredibly sexy puppy-dog face. Dane pouts out his lower lip, his eyes glassy and begging.

Want you.

Two weeks, I text back.

Now.

He sends a shot of his T-shirt on the floor.

Your turn.

Drunk Dane strikes at the perfect time. The empty bottle of red on my nightstand agrees, and suffering the effects of GD Daphne and quaking body parts, I slip off my socks and toss them to the end of the bed, sending him the photographic proof.

Fuck yes, he replies along with a picture of his belt on top of his shirt.

I peel off my tank top and add it to the socks. He hits right back with his jeans, and I shimmy out of my sweatpants. His boxers next. Then my panties.

What now? I text with the last one.

Bra?

Not wearing one.

Prove it.

More heat floods my already-flushed cheeks, and I drop my head into my hands. *Shit.* But what did I think would happen once he got me naked from a state away? A *cool, see you in a few weeks* and a thumbs-up emoji?

Before I lose the nerve, I flip the camera around on my phone and send Dane a picture of my tits.

Who even am I right now?

The dots blink, my heart pounding way too hard for sitting in my bed, not doing anything. I down the last of the wine in my glass and consider chancing the catwalk for another bottle until the dots stop.

Jesus, you're beautiful. I'm hard, just thinking about what I would do to you if I were there. I want to touch you so bad.

I wish you could.

Yeah? Tell me how you want me to touch you, baby. How to make you come.

Better yet. Show me.

And I'm about to. About to answer his video call, flashing on my screen. About to do something I've never even considered doing with anyone else. *For* anyone else.

Until a message drops down from the top of the screen.

Marco: *WTF!*

Then another.

You see Insta?

Another.

Who's the bitch tagged with my Great Dane?

I blink at the phone a few times, my sloshy brain slow to process. When I open the app, I see a post from Dane, a picture of a beer bottle on the coffee table in his living room from thirty minutes ago. I tap his name, so I can go to his tagged photos. Marco used to check them in case someone caught an ab shot, always disappointed with a lack of flesh. Except the first picture that pops up does show bare skin. It just doesn't belong to Dane but the midriff of a blonde his arms happen to be around.

Dane tries calling again. I stare at the screen until it changes back to him and the girl. Six posts with them in the background, each a little more obvious about where their night heads. His nose against her cheek, lips on her jaw. Her body pressed into him, hands fisted in his shirt. The same shirt lying on his bedroom floor in the pictures he sent me only a few hours later.

Your turn, he said, but now, the words mean something entirely different.

85

Boulders slowly rolling over logs. My insides feel like the wood sounds. Cracking and splitting under the weight of the stone. I've experienced the sensation before and remember it well. Bentley screwed around a lot the first time we dated. The bowler, too, only he and his shoe ho barely blipped on my radar. With Bentley, though, it hurt every time he cheated, and finding out I'd been sharing him without my knowledge left me feeling exactly that—I gave him all of me, and he gave part. He cheated more the second time around, but I cared less. It spared my insides.

By the time Dane's name flashes on the screen again, I don't feel drunk anymore. On wine. Or him. But I feel sick from both, even though I shouldn't. Dane hasn't cheated on me. He can't because we're not together. So, why all the crushing?

What happened? he texts. *Where'd you go?*

I shove the phone in a drawer and slam it shut, wiping away tears I have no reason to cry. Angry over nothing and betrayed by someone who hasn't done anything wrong.

All the clothes I was wearing I bury in the laundry, and I dig through my dresser for something warm. Nights in San Francisco get so cold. The cool blue and purple walls in my room only add to the chill. Bundled up in a sweatshirt, fleece pajama bottoms, and two pairs of fuzzy socks, I crawl back under the covers. Not that the extra clothing helps, as I still shiver. Still need to curl into a ball. Still wish I could be anywhere else.

Anywhere but here, in a room that reminds me of him.

Turns out, a safety net under the tightrope only matters if you fall. It does nothing to save you from slipping and hanging yourself on the wire.

-13-
Taste My Rainbow, Bitch

A MUTED KNOCK WAKES ME in the morning. I've burrowed so far under the comforter that I exist as a lump in the center of the bed. How I prefer to stay for the day—pity myself before I pick it all up and push forward.

"Bennett?"

Aria lifts the comforter from the bottom of the bed, finding me in my lumpiness. She thoughtfully studies me, and when I don't say anything, she crawls in without asking any questions. We lump together until Steve pops his head under the blanket. He focuses on me, scanning over my face like he wants to paint me. Afraid I'll wind up stuck on the stool in his tower for six hours, I sit up and rip the cover off my head.

"I'm going to take a shower."

He nods, accepting my choice of cleanliness, and I dash into my bathroom before he changes his mind.

When I come out, they've both vacated. One thing about Steve and Aria is they never pry. I get dressed and go downstairs. He stuffs me full of omelet, and she curls up on the bench next to me at the table. Neither mentions how I spent my morning in hiding or push for the reason I keep ignoring my phone. It drives me nuts, and the less they ask, the more I volunteer.

"She's pretty," Aria says when I show her the post.

By the time I dug my phone out of the drawer, Dane had untagged himself from the pictures, but I remembered his friend's name who'd posted them. I tilt my head, looking at her from another angle. A high-voltage smile like Keaton's that would draw a guy in from across the room. Genuinely happy and not missing pieces.

"She is," I admit.

Steve pauses the old Giants game he watches and leans over from the other end of the couch. He tips the screen in Aria's hand, so he can judge for himself. His nose wrinkles as he relaxes back in his seat, not offering an opinion beyond that, except when he glances up, hitting play on the remote, and winks.

Good man.

She hands me back my phone. "So, now what?"

"Nothing." I fold my feet up under me. "I live my life, and he lives his."

"And when those lives cross?" Steve asks.

I glare at him for the reminder, not that he notices with his eyes glued to the TV.

"Well," Aria says, swiping through her phone, "with him out of the picture, I have a guy from work I'd *love* to set you up with."

I don't have a chance to say no before Steve asks, "Which one?"

"Noah H."

"Is that the one with the hydroponic tomato crop on the roof?"

"No. That's Noah T. Noah H. has the Tesla."

I have no interest in farmer Noah or car Noah, but while they sort out which one I'll refuse to meet, Liam calls. Since we only text each other, the sick twist in my gut from last night returns, saying the call comes on behalf of a certain cousin. I leave Steve and Aria on the couch and wander toward the kitchen to answer.

"Fiancée's best friend," Liam says in greeting.

"What do you want, best friend's future ex-husband?" I run my nails over Little Stevie's head as I pass the counter where he lounges. I get one of those surprised-kitty purr-meows that makes you warm on the inside.

"Switch your visit to next weekend, and I'll pay for you to fly first class."

"You have my attention." I lean on the countertop, more interested in his proposition than I'll let on. "Why?"

"Because spending her actual birthday with you will make Keaton do that little squeal thing she does. I love that fucking squeal, Bennett. I want to hear the fucking squeal." Then he adds, "Even if it means spoiling your ass to make it happen."

I smile at yet another one of his incredibly sweet gestures. "You know, if you weren't such a dick all the time, you'd be the perfect guy."

"Keep it in your pants, Ross. Yes or no."

I can't even feign annoyance with him. "Of course, yes. But what about our appointment for dresses? We couldn't schedule anything with the place she wanted any sooner." The only reason we decided to celebrate her birthday a week late.

"You're down for Saturday at one. I bribed them to bump another bride."

Such an asshole but for such pure reasons.

"I can hear her squealing already."

He sighs. "So can I. Thanks, Bennett."

"Hey, Liam." I straighten up, twisting at my bracelet. "Don't tell Dane I'm coming back early."

The request earns silence, a rarity for Liam. I know him; he's fighting the urge to ask why. Despite the incessant insults, we would do anything for each other. He has thrown down for me more than once. If he thinks his cousin wronged me, he would again, so avoiding details saves everyone the drama.

"I don't see why he needs to know," he finally says. "I'll send you your ticket info and pick you up on Friday—oh, and if you miss the flight, I swear to God, Bennett—"

I hang up on him. In all the time we've known each other, he's never finished the threat, and today won't be the day.

Aria has her manic smile plastered on when I head back into the living room. "Noah will meet you for drinks on Tuesday."

Steve glances up from the TV, ready for me to shut her down. *I'm* ready for me to shut her down. So, it surprises the hell out of all of us when I shrug. "Have him text me."

Maybe it will make the other texts—six so far—easier to ignore. One day, I'll find myself in a room with Dane Masters. It will happen, but until then, I'll do something I'm incredibly talented at. Avoid, avoid, avoid.

NOAH'S SWEET. A LITTLE NERDY, but he has an edge that sucks me in. Our drinks turn into a late dinner that leads us to a rooftop bar for more drinks. I only plan on staying for one. I have work in the morning. After three, I take up residence on the ledge of the fountain in the middle of the roof and send him off for another round. I just wander around, pointing at shit all day anyway.

Noah grins on his way back to me, a colorful drink in one hand and a beer in the other.

I squint at him as he hands me the alcoholic rainbow. "What?"

"Everyone said if I let Aria set me up, I'd end up wanting to jump off a roof."

"And do you?"

He tucks his black hair behind his ear. "Only if you tell me to."

When I purse my lips and pretend to think about it, he starts for the edge.

"Stop!" I tell him, pulling him back by the hand. "You're my ride."

He chuckles and settles in next to me. His glasses remind me of Liam's. Behind them, black lashes frame amber eyes. They almost distract me from what I wanted to do before his jumping-off-the-roof nonsense.

"Oh no." He groans when I pull out my phone. "You're going to hold a photo session with your drink, aren't you?"

"Shh. I need to focus." I set my drink on the stone between us. With my hand on the base, the light glints off my bracelet. All pretty and shit.

"So, I shouldn't do this?" Noah slides his fingers into my shot at the last second.

I press my lips together to hide a smile, pretending to ignore him, and so they creep farther, past the drink and onto my leg.

"You're cold," he says.

The truth provides him the perfect excuse to rub his hand over my thigh. It proves very distracting while I complete my obligatory drunk-girl post.

Once I've filtered a worthy picture and tapped out my less than witty caption—*taste my rainbow, bitch*—I look up. The nerd has all but disappeared, the tan skin and sharp edges taking over and ready to pounce.

I drain my drink. The colors numb my tongue, and I dangle the glass in front of him.

"So, take me home."

Not taking his eyes off me, Noah tips back his beer bottle until it empties.

BETWEEN LEAVING THE BAR AND Noah backing me into his apartment, I decide the point of my little date exercise is to prove Dane's not special. I can date. Form an attachment to someone, anyone.

While tiptoeing out the door a few hours later, careful not to wake him, I decide *anyone* might stretch it. I don't want to attach myself to a guy who drives a Tesla. It sounds like a lot of work, always finding charging stations.

The Uber driver cranks nineties hip-hop, earning her tip for not trying to engage with me. She bumps, and I scroll through my phone. I notice Marco commented on my photo from earlier. I check to see what insult he came up with because he always has one. He doesn't disappoint. *You need your nails done.*

Nothing but true. I chewed the shit out of them the other day. As I read the next part of his comment, I choke on the new-car smell permeating from the air-freshener hanging on the rearview mirror.

And who. Is. The. Man? You can't leave forearm porn to drool over and not show a face.

That's when I realize what a drunk-on-a-rooftop Bennett failed to. I posted the wrong fucking picture. The one I put up shows not only my hand on the bottom of the glass, but also Noah's arm reaching over, his hand stroking my upper thigh.

I deflate into the seat, willing the Kia to swallow me whole. With my caption, it looks like I want everyone to know he'll be *tasting my rainbow.*

What if Dane saw?

Do I care?

I delete the post, and for good measure, I deactivate my entire account and delete the app from my phone. Social media has turned on me. So, fuck it. I don't need that negativity.

I'm not about that life.

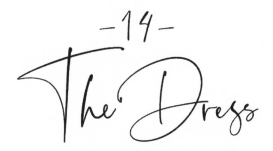

-14-
The Dress

SINCE I PLANNED ON BUYING Keaton a gift over the weekend, I meet Liam in the terminal empty-handed, other than my suitcase. She works until eleven, waiting tables to earn extra cash for the wedding. It gives me plenty of time to stash my stuff at their apartment and figure out a present.

I borrow Liam's truck and drive until inspiration strikes. The kitchen at one of her favorite restaurants closes at ten. I can order, and while they make everything she has ever said *mmm* to, I'll walk the few blocks to a boutique that screams Keaton. We tell people the only reason we stay friends is we're the same size. A fact that comes in handy when buying clothes. If an outfit looks decent on me, it shimmers on her.

After ordering half the menu, I ask for utensils for eight to stop the judgment radiating off the hostess. I head for the boutique with almost an hour before I have to lug a dozen sacks of food to the truck. Maybe if I act overwhelmed, the staff will take pity on me and help carry.

A few doors from my destination, I pass a bar Liam's dragged us to a few times. Cheap drinks and a smell of popcorn I never understood since they don't *serve* popcorn. People crowd the patio, the air cool without the sun beating down. I bump into someone on the sidewalk and laugh out an apology, having no excuse other than not paying attention, and when I glance at the patio again, I see him. Beanie. Teeth in his bottom lip.

Our eyes lock. He straightens up from the high-top he was leaning on, and I screech to a stop, my mind in a panic before I even register the girl. Dane's hand jerks off her arm like she grew spikes, every feature on his face confused. And ... relieved? He still hasn't looked away, the girl turning.

I charge down the sidewalk. I have no idea where I'm going anymore, just away.

"Bennett."

Maybe I'll walk back to San Francisco. Ten days, was it? I wonder what Patrick's doing tonight.

"Bennett!" His arm slips around me. Not just his hand tugging on mine, but his whole damn arm snaking around my middle and spinning me to face him.

We both freeze, staring at each other for a few seconds, maybe more; he has really pretty eyes.

"What are you doing here?" he asks, his hand still on my back. The other drags off his beanie. Maroon. "I thought..." He shakes his head and looks down, jaw tensed. "You've been ignoring me."

Not a question, but a fact. We both have the proof on our phones, the unread texts on mine and unanswered ones on his. I might not excel at much, but I mastered avoidance a long time ago.

His gaze comes back to mine. "If this is because—"

I step back when he tries to pull me closer. "Your date can see us."

He doesn't look back at the brunette on the patio where he left her, death glare lasered in on me. I thought Noah H. leveled our playing field, but it appears I have the rest of the Noah alphabet to go for that to happen.

"She's not my date." But he lets his hand fall away, and it hurts as much as if he'd said she was.

"Stay here," he says.

"Dane, I—"

"Damn it, Bennett." He reaches for me but stops and lowers his arm to his side, fist clenched. "I swear to God, if you aren't here when I come back, I'll tear this damn city apart to find you. Liam and Keaton's, her parents', everywhere you might be. So, stay here. Please."

I glance at the dagger eyes still waiting at the table and then up at him. He licks his lips, his gaze the soft one that makes it hard for me to breathe.

"Please," he repeats.

I cross my arms and nod.

Dane backs away, keeping me in sight like he doesn't believe I'll be here when he comes back.

Fair since I won't be.

The second he turns to push open the gate to the patio, I rush up the step and into the boutique. The door hits a bell hanging overhead on open and close. I relax on the second ding, the sound of safety. For now, anyway. He could very well beat me back to the apartment, and I have no clue what will happen then.

A candle burns on the counter. The jasmine and scent of new clothes purges my nose of him while I wander the store, shopping and avoiding. The salesclerk steps out from the back. She must deem my face trustworthy and ducks right back through the opening on her phone. I should steal the candle to prove her wrong.

I find a few outfits in case I need to distract Keaton with something shiny later. An all-black jumpsuit with a tie at the middle, cutoff jean shorts and an off-the-shoulder orange top, and a short red dress she'll purr over. Wearing the last one, I creak open the door to my dressing room and step into the larger area with angled mirrors to check the cutout in the back. She has a regrettable tattoo that I prefer not see the light of day—*I* regret her getting it, not her. Once I've assured the sunflower will stay hidden under the fabric, I face the main mirror and smooth my hands over the front.

"Buy it," Dane says from the doorway. I suck in a breath and glance over at him, his arms crossed and gaze tracing over me in one of the mirrors. "If you don't, I will."

"How did you find me?"

"I watched you trip up the stair as soon as you thought I wasn't looking."

I brace myself when he strolls over. The jasmine candle already loses out to him.

"The dress isn't for me," I say as he stops behind me.

"It should be." He slides up the strap that slipped off my shoulder. "You look fucking gorgeous."

I recheck the price tag, pretending not to care when he drags his knuckles down my arm. "I picked it out for Keaton. She looks better in red."

When I look up, he shakes his head at me through the mirror. "Not possible."

The words linger between us, his eyes searching my face.

"Talk to me," he says. "I know it's about the picture—"

"It really doesn't matter." I sound detached and unaffected, a cool bitch above the jealousy.

"If you're upset enough to stop talking to me, it does." A crease appears in his forehead. "I'm sorry. I was drunk, and ... I thought you were into it."

I stare at him blankly. He thought I was into— *Ohmytitsinthecloud.*

Dane's not talking about the pictures of his hands on someone else in a bar. He means the one I sent him and forgot all about after Marco's text.

"Delete it," I blurt out. "Delete the picture of me."

"I already did. That night after you stopped responding."

I blow out a breath, but the relief only lasts a second.

"That's not what you were mad about? Then what pictures..." Realization lights up like a flare across Dane's face, his fingers skimming over my forearm switching to a light hold. "Marco's still stalking my Instagram?"

With nowhere to go but head-on into the truth, I nod.

"Shit, Bennett." He spins me around and slides his hands up to cup my cheeks, so I can't look away. "I never slept with her. I didn't even leave with her. And if I had, there's no way in hell I would have been hitting you up the same night."

Out of everything, my mind sticks on the *if I had*, and the sense of betrayal returns. "So, you only text me on nights you can't get laid?"

"What?" He shakes his head. "No. I text you because I want to, no other reason." When I sidestep, he moves with me. "Would you quit trying to run?"

I stop and force myself to stand there, trapped by him and his words and the ridiculous threat of tears.

"I need you to tell me if I did something wrong. Am I not supposed to be with anyone else?" he asks with such sincerity, which makes the whole situation all the worse.

"No," I say, but I barely believe myself. "I don't know. Maybe? I don't want to make it complicated."

"Baby, *you* are complicated. I've been trying to figure you out since I caught you sneaking out of some other dude's apartment. And I think I'm further away now than then because I didn't think you wanted anything serious."

"I don't." I shake my head, as confused by myself as he is. "Or I didn't."

"But you do now?" More sincerity, genuine, and he's looking at me like he does, and I can't stand it anymore.

"I don't know, okay?" I practically yell it at him in the middle of an empty dressing room, wearing a dress that isn't for me.

Liam's right about the crazy, and in my case, it only gets worse with anything feelings related on the table.

Dane was supposed to be the *what could have been* if I'd stayed. Then he was the guy I hooked up with when I came back to Arizona. And now, I'm not sure what the hell is going on other than this fabric is becoming scratchier by the second. Although it could be my aversion to emotion physically manifesting. A therapist warned me about that once.

I shrug, frustrated with myself for the tangled mess I created. "I don't know what I want."

Dane lowers his head, so we're eye-level. "I know I don't want this to be over."

"I don't either, but—"

"No," he says. "Sentence done."

He has barely finished when his lips crash against mine. All the Dane-related chemicals flood back into my brain, shutting down all parts unrelated to him. Him. I definitely want him. My lips mold to his, and I back into the mirror, so he'll press against me, my needy showing. His mouth dips to my throat. I tilt my head back, letting him reclaim me. Erase every trace of Noah from my skin and any insecurity brought on by the blonde or woman a few buildings down.

He brings his face back to mine, eyes hooded. "You know what else I don't want?" he rasps, and I shake my head. "I don't want you to disappear on me anymore."

Our chests heave in sync.

"I don't want you texting me in the middle of the night when you're drunk."

"And I don't want you to pretend we're fine if we're not." He kisses me again, not reclaiming me anymore but slow and intoxicating. The type of kiss I've learned to crave from him with his lips too soft and tongue teasing mine. Pulling back, he grazes the tip of my nose with his. "What else don't you want?"

For some reason, don't-wants feel less constricting than wants. A request rather than a requirement. More breathable. And my next one comes without thought.

"I don't want you to ask me to stay in Phoenix. Ever."

It's one thing I've wanted from everyone and gotten from no one, but Dane doesn't miss a beat. "Okay, I never will."

He smiles when I do and drapes my arms around his neck, then he glides his hands back to my cheeks and rests his forehead on mine. "There's one more thing I don't want." He chews on his lip, hesitating while he cradles my face in his hands. "I don't want other guys anywhere fucking near you and your rainbow."

My heart trips worse than my feet ever have. He saw the picture. Noah's palm on my thigh and thumb hidden under the leg of my shorts.

"I was talking about the drink," I whisper.

"I'm not," he says. "Seeing someone else touch you…" He rubs his forehead back and forth across mine in a slow shake of his head. "I was so close to getting on a plane and kicking down your door. I don't want to feel like that again, Bennett. I might legitimately turn into a psycho stalker."

"Fine, but you have to stop picking up chicks at the bar."

"Fine," he mimics. He fights off a smile when I narrow my eyes and hovers his mouth over mine, but before they connect, hangers rattle outside the dressing room.

"We're closing soon," the clerk says, passing without so much as a glance inside at the two of us shoved up against the mirror. "I can ring you up whenever."

Once she disappears, Dane presses his lips to mine fast and straightens up. "Can I wait for you?"

I push off the mirror. "Only if you want to help carry thirty pounds of food from Solstice to Liam's truck."

"Sounds like exactly what I want to do." He kisses the top of my head and walks away but stops. "Oh and, Bennett?"

"Yeah?" I say, swinging open the dressing room door.

He turns around and looks me over, his gaze dragging down my body. "So we're one hundred percent clear, you're keeping that dress."

LIAM SHUTS ME IN A closet when I get back to the apartment. I read Dane's texts while I stand in the dark, the smell of him on my clothes and taste on my tongue. Apologies and confessions of missing me and an actual plea for me to answer him. Causing a man with so much self-assurance to beg for attention leaves me feeling guilty. And a whole lot empowered.

When Keaton opens the closet to toss her shoes in, she bounces, Liam gets his squeal, and I've earned my place in first-class. We empty the bags of food, filling the counters and arguing over what I forgot and should have brought. I miss Dane's entrance. His hand skims my side while reaching for a breadstick in front of me, and I jump. Without a word, he brushes the hair away from my neck to plant a kiss before he joins the other two in the living room. I grab a fourth glass out of the cupboard, following behind him with the bottle of wine.

I should tell Keaton. I should have told her about him from the beginning. But every time I think about it, I remember the glee in her eyes whenever she saw me with Bentley and how it crushed her when it fell apart. Maybe I'll slip it in tomorrow between the tulle and lace.

Keaton and I share an end of the couch with the other two in the beanbags. It shocks me to the core that Keaton hasn't insisted on buying more furniture. She finishes eating and disappears into the kitchen to reorganize the fridge, unsatisfied with the way Liam and I shoved all the leftovers in.

"So," Dane says from his bag to Liam's, "because you bribed Bennett to come back a week early to go wedding dress shopping, we now have to find our tuxes tomorrow instead of in January, like we planned?"

"Yep." Liam shovels a forkful of pasta into his mouth.

"Because it somehow messes with the timeline?"

Mouth full, he nods. "Mmhmm."

"Exactly how does the math work out on that?"

Liam points the fork between the kitchen and me. "Ca-ray-zay. Math doesn't have to math for them, dude."

Dane glances up at me and mouths, *Ca-ray-zay.*

I shrug.

If he hasn't figured out how right Liam is by now, there's no hope for him.

At midnight, I light the jasmine candle I spent forty bucks on from the boutique for Keaton to blow out. She squeals again at the *two* outfits she pulls out of the bag. Dane wipes a hand over his mouth, hiding a smile. He leaves shortly after when Liam starts heavily hinting that he wants Keaton to go to bed. Once their bedroom door latches, I sneak out to the hallway where Dane is leaning against the wall. I say we should go inside, he says his truck, so we split the difference. We stay there and make out like a couple of high schoolers. It's one of the better days I've had in Phoenix in a long time.

WHEN KEATON AND I FINALLY begin functioning as humans in the morning, we have enough time to lunch and make our appointment at the dress studio—studio because *every dress is art.* I snap a picture of one of the mannequins, lipstick drawn on a featureless face, no arms, and in an ivory dress with gold threading throughout. I send it to Aria.

Haunting, she texts. *Beauty in the incomplete.*

I smile, deciding I like that.

A few minutes later, I get a slightly different take on the subject.

Steve: *Dafuq? They call that art? Delusional.*

The dresses are beautiful though, only a few of each made. Keaton seems intimidated, so I offer myself as a sacrificial lamb and try on a variety of bridesmaid dresses. She chooses a few different styles and settles on a color, and once she's warmed up, there's no stopping her from sorting through rack after rack of bridal gowns.

I watch her twirl on the riser and help hold up different veils, but when she walks out in *the* dress, I don't even bother getting out of my chair.

"That's it."

"It is," she whispers. Then she starts gnawing at her fingernails. "So, I only pulled dresses in my budget at first, but when I saw this one, I grabbed it, thinking if I liked it, I could find something similar—"

"How much?" I ask.

"Hmm?" She has a wild look in her eyes like she might bolt with the dress on. Being her best friend and maid of honor, it will fall on me to block for her if any bitch tries to stop her, so I'd rather she not.

"How much out of budget, Keats?"

She hesitates, nail between her teeth. "Two thousand."

Silence. So quiet she hears my swallow.

"OhmyGod, Bennie, it's perfect though." She picks up the skirt and rushes to the dressing room.

I catch up as she digs her phone out of her purse on the bench.

"Liam built in some wiggle room in case we need it, but I'm not sure how much." She holds the phone up to her ear, chewing her finger again.

I give her a few minutes to sweet-talk him and pretend to look at jewelry.

It turns out, I give her a few minutes too long.

I duck under the curtain into the changing area, and she's fully dressed.

"He said no?"

"Technically," she says, "but we're going to change his mind."

"And how are we doing that?"

She holds up a white strapless bra in one hand and the top of the gown in the other.

Oh God.

"No way," I say, shaking my head.

"It's only bad luck if he sees *me* in the dress."

"That doesn't sound remotely accurate."

"Please, Bennie. I know when he sees it, he'll love it. The dress is our size and everything, so it will look just like it will on me, and he'll get the full effect."

I stare at the ceiling. "Except it's not the woman he loves, so not at all the same."

When she doesn't say anything, I bring my head up. She smiles sweetly to lull me into a false sense of security, and then she attacks.

"Three years ago, when I pretended to be you on that blind date with the guy who ended up being arrested. Mid. Dinner."

Fuck.

"HOLY FUCKING SHIT."—LIAM WHEN I walk out of the dressing room.

His fiancée is hyperventilating in the restroom, praying to the bridal gown gods, while my thong rides up.

"Is that it?" he asks, circling me as I climb onto the riser. "The dress Keaton wants?"

I follow him with my head. "No, I picked it out for *our* wedding. Maybe you'll leave her. We'll give it a real shot."

Still walking, he ignores me, and judging by his face, he's running numbers through his head to rearrange a wedding budget. But while he focuses on the dress, I have no intentions of seeing myself all white and fluffy and look everywhere but the mirror. Which means I immediately spot Dane rounding the corner with two glasses of champagne in his hands.

"Dude, they get to drink over here while—holy fucking shit." He stops short when he sees me, the complimentary bubbly sloshing over the side of one glass and onto the carpet.

You've got to be kidding me. Less than twenty-four hours ago, I told him to stay away from other women while in a dressing room, and now, I'm wearing a wedding dress in another? Keaton's six hours at the police station answering questions after they hauled that guy away in handcuffs fails to compare.

To spare myself the shock on his face, I close my eyes, already gathering up the train when they open. "You good, Liam? Great." I stumble off the pedestal and mad dash for the curtain.

Once hidden, I sink onto the bench in the corner and press my palms to my hot cheeks. The drape next to me rustles, and Dane's hand pokes through with a flute.

"Hey, Bennett," he says.

I sigh and squeak a, "Yeah?"

"Maybe don't keep that dress."

I snort out a laugh and swipe the glass, draining the champagne before I set it back in his hand.

-15-
Birthday

I THOUGHT I'D MOVE ON from San Francisco before the holidays. Spend a month driving from place to place or head east. But the itch to leave stays at bay, my mind and body content where I am for now.

With my most recent trip to Phoenix only a month ago, I spend Thanksgiving in San Francisco. Aria and I burn dinner. Utterly destroy every biscuit, sauce, and pie we come in contact with, while we laugh at our inability to Martha Stewart past setting a badass table with a runner and painted dishes, courtesy of her pottery class. The smoke-laden air tips off Steve when he descends from his tower. He sniffs once and is calling for delivery by the time he reaches the stairs.

I'll spend my birthday—two days before Christmas, which meant the few people giving me gifts growing up lumped them into one—in Phoenix, so the three of us celebrate the weekend before. Aria bakes me the cake she promised. The inedible turkey should have prepared me for the first bite.

I swallow fast, so my taste buds won't have to suffer long. "So good!"

She smiles and feeds a forkful to Steve, who nods, chewing.

"Mmm, babe. Best you've made."

Once she leaves the room, a terrible accident happens in which Little Stevie jumps onto the counter and knocks the rest to the floor. We press his paws into the mess to back up the story, and since he gets to lick frosting from between his toes, he takes no issue in being framed.

The three of us wander around, viewing street murals for the day, and spend the night watching their friend's band perform at a dingy bar only using oil lamps for lighting. I keep waiting for the dust particles in the air to combust, but they never do.

They give me a camera. A real one with film and a real weight to it.

"Since you've shed the engineered persona created with our culture's obsession with social media," Steve says. He plants a kiss on the top of my head on his way to feed Little Stevie.

I bite back a smile. He has a secret Instagram where he posts cat pictures on a semi-regular basis, but I don't mention it.

And then I'm walking through the gate in Phoenix again a few days later. No bubbly-blonde ambush or annoyed Liam waiting for me but a familiar smile and outstretched arm.

"There's my girl." Patrick tucks me in for a hug. "Happy birthday, sweetheart."

I smile against the pocket of his shirt, always soothed by his embrace. Patrick's gruff, but underneath the beard and naturally furrowed brow lie three soft spots, one reserved for me. He keeps an arm around me. We stroll through the terminal, indistinguishable from the families reuniting for the holidays.

The house smells of sugar cookies, even after I pass the plug-in in the foyer. Keaton and Joyce flip through magazines at the counter. Both lean on an elbow, their chins resting on a hand. The rest of the flat surfaces are covered in containers filled with decorated desserts. Tomorrow night, we'll have the annual Reynolds' Christmas—this year at Aunt Peg's—and no one shows up empty-handed.

Today, though, we're celebrating my birthday and nothing else. A cake sits on the table alongside brand-new candles ready to be lit. It took until I turned twenty to convince them to stop throwing a full party. They seemed set on making up for all the ones I'd missed before I moved in with them. The simple fact that they cared meant more than the streamers and balloons.

We've switched to a family dinner the past few years. The four of us at first, and then Liam joined the fold. But as we settle into our chairs at the restaurant, he's still a no-show.

"Where's the man?" I ask.

Keaton frowns across from me. "Didn't you see my texts from earlier?"

I dig my phone out of my purse. Dead. *Shit.* And I was doing so well.

I hold up the black screen, and she shakes her head at my inability to adult.

"They rushed his grandfather to the hospital this afternoon. Heart attack."

"What? Is he okay?"

"They're performing more tests, but he should be able to come home in the next day or two."

Under the table, I continue pressing the button on my phone to turn it on. Nothing happens, of course, but I try anyway. If Dane texted about his grandfather, I don't want him to think I'm ignoring him again. Or worse, that I don't care. We haven't seen each other since my last visit, and he's been working so much that he texts at random intervals. He spares me the details, unlike a blabbering Liam would, but the end of year seems busy for them. Usually, the messages consist of pictures, him dramatically sprawled on his desk or the clock with a *FUCKIN' REALLY?!*

"Liam's at the hospital with the rest of his family then?"

Going vague with an overall Masters inquiry is the only way to ask about Dane since after she shoved me in a bridal gown, I decided to put off telling her about him. Again. *God, I'm a shit friend.*

"He and his dad and Dane are still there," she says, checking her phone for any updates. "Everyone else has either gone home or back to the office to finish up before the holidays."

"Let them know I'm thinking about them?"

She gives a small smile, and I force one in return.

Halfway through dinner, Liam sends her a text, asking how my flight was. He's never shown an interest before, so I don't question who really wants to know.

BACK AT THE HOUSE, I plug my phone in to charge while Keaton and Joyce set candles on my cake. They sing, and I open gifts. A planner from Patrick, a set of canvas shopping bags from Joyce, and a classy mug from Keaton that says, *It's vodka, and no, you can't have any.*

She leaves when Liam calls to tell her he's heading to the apartment. I'm staying at the house to help Joyce with last-minute wrapping in the morning, so I give her a squeeze just outside the front door.

"Let me know if anything changes."

She nods, pulling back. "I'll see you tomorrow." She steps down onto the sidewalk before she pivots back around. "And I've already done recon. Ford said he and Lincoln are the only two going tomorrow night."

I sigh out a, "Thank you," to both her and the universe. No Bentley for at least one more family function.

Once her headlights disappear, I go to my room and finally turn on my phone. I check the messages I missed. Both Dane's and Keaton's relaying the information about his grandfather. He lost consciousness at the office. They called the ambulance, doctor ran tests, and he should be released in a few days.

The last text from Dane is from a few minutes ago.

Come back outside.

I smile and grab a hoodie from my bag. Joyce and Patrick are watching a movie in the family room. Neither shows interest as I walk past to the front door. They're probably just grateful I've stopped crawling through windows at twenty-three. *Growth.*

The sweatshirt hangs past the bottom of my skirt when I pull it on, and I hide my hands in the baggy sleeves on my way off the porch. It takes a second to notice his truck, parked in the shadows a few houses down. I'm almost there when the driver's door slams shut. Dane steps around the hood and into the yellow cast of a streetlight.

"You need to hurry up."

"*You* need to learn patience."

"I have plenty, just not when it comes to you." He runs his hands over my hips when I reach him and kisses me hard. "See," he mumbles. "No restraint." But he finds some after he backs me to the truck. He jerks open the passenger door and picks me up to set me on the seat. "Scoot over."

I slide toward the middle, and he crawls in.

"How's your grandpa?"

"Shh," he says, shutting the door. "He'll be fine, but right now"—he moves closer and reaches past me for something—"we have business to take care of."

When his hand reappears, he's holding a cupcake with a single candle in the middle. I get one more kiss before hearing the flick of a lighter. He tosses it on the dash once the candle burns. The cab illuminates, shadows dancing across his face, and I smile.

"This is so—"

"Cheesy," he says. "It's disgustingly cheesy, and I'd hate myself for it if not for that fucking smile."

I shake my head and touch his cheek. "Sweet. It's so incredibly sweet."

The stubble on his jaw scrapes against my skin as he turns to kiss my palm, eyes reflecting the flame when he looks at me again. "Happy birthday, Bennett."

I lean in, and right as I blow out the candle, his gaze drops to my mouth. I have no idea what happens to my cupcake once the cab darkens. Dane's mouth slams into mine, both of his hands tugging me over to him. He lifts me—not on top of him, but to the other side so that my shoulders press against the door—and he moves across to where I was a second ago, breaking his mouth away from me.

"What date are we on?" he asks. "Five? Six?"

"Does it matter?" I try to pull him closer, but he won't budge from his spot in the center of the cab.

"I thought since you don't fuck on the first date, you'd require at least half a dozen before spreading your legs for me in the truck."

My feet are on the seat between us, and when his hand skims up from my ankle, I wait for it to reach my knee and drop it to the side. His gaze flashes to mine. "Sixth date it is."

He doesn't even slide my panties off, just tosses my legs over his shoulders and nudges the material over like both are in his way. But I guess they are. He dips his head between my thighs, and I hiss out a breath, his mouth grazing over me.

"Fuck," I say.

"Yeah?" His eyes glint, staring up at me. "Tell me how you really feel."

I press my lips together, taking it as a challenge, but my plan goes to hell the second his finger slips inside me. One, then another, and I moan. His tongue flicks, and I drop my head back on the window. I lift my hips, seeking more friction he gladly supplies. A screen door slams somewhere, but my mind is in a desire haze, not concerned we're parked in a residential neighborhood while I grind against his face.

"Oh my God." I whimper, grasping at his hair.

"Come on, Bennett." His voice is raspy and pulses through me. "End your birthday right."

I arch my back as he speeds up his movements. His fingers and mouth work in unison. Harder, faster, licking, sucking until my legs tremble, and I tighten my thighs around his head and cry out. Dane reaches up his free hand, covering my mouth as I come.

I'm boneless, a panting mess on his bench seat, as he looks up at me, teeth digging into his lip. Before I can fully recover, he glances at the clock on the dashboard, a grin spreading. "And ... midnight."

– 16 –

We Are

DANE STRETCHES THE LENGTH OF the cab, his knees bent, feet up, and head in my lap.

"My father was on the phone with the lawyer before the EMTs even had my grandfather in the ambulance." He reaches up and grazes his fingertips over my lips. "Everyone else was worried about the old man, and Greg was concerned about getting his hands on the fucking business."

I run my hand through his hair and let him talk about his family. I have nothing to contribute, so all I can do is listen. No father, my grandpa died when I was two, and my grandma moved across the country shortly after. I met her once when I was eight. She called me Kendall the entire visit. My mom never corrected her, so neither did I. A year later, she died in a car accident. We didn't go to the funeral and never talked about her again.

"I think that's why the old man was so adamant about me moving back," he says.

"Because of your dad?"

He nods, his eyes scanning the roof of his truck. "My family is so dramatic. I'm talking daytime TV–worthy. Backstabbing, scheming—" His gaze shifts to me. "You know how my father met his current wife?"

Aubrey, the clinger.

"How?" I ask.

"I took her to homecoming our junior year."

"What?" My mouth falls open when he nods, and I gasp. "No!"

He chuckles at my reaction but then goes serious again. "And before the question creeps into your sweet little head, no. I never fucking touched her. Anytime she opened her mouth, I wanted to swerve into traffic. I ditched her the second we walked into the school's gym."

I shake my head and push the hair off his forehead. "I don't know if we can be together now. I mean, I'm used to winning the worst parent award."

"Is that what we are?" he asks. "Together?"

He chews on his lip, studying me in the way that sends my mind racing in every direction. My gaze averts out the window to Mr. Sully in front of his house with his dog. A mix between one of those breeds with the stubby legs and some larger one that gives it unfortunate proportions. Buggy eyes and an off-balance head.

"It's late," I say, looking back at Dane. "We should go."

"Nah." He shifts to his side, pushing an arm behind me and burying his face in my belly. "I'm good right here," he mumbles.

Heat from the deep breath he exhales flows through my sweatshirt. I wonder if he doesn't want to go home. If after spending most of his day at a hospital, the memories of his mom are too fresh. It happens to me whenever I drive too close to my old neighborhood or catch a glimpse of my reflection and notice the resemblance. Until it fades, I try to stay away from anything else that might trigger memories.

"Hey." I nudge his shoulder, and he grunts. "Come inside with me."

He angles his head, half of his face still covered. "What about Keaton's parents?"

"They'll be asleep on the couch. You can leave when Joyce goes on her power-walk in the morning."

"From sneaking out to sneaking in," he says, sitting up. He hands me my cupcake off the dash and kisses me on the nose as he leans over to throw the door open, scaring Mr. Sully and his dog in the process. "We've come a long way, Angel."

As he crawls out, I smile. Twenty-three, my year of personal growth it seems.

DANE STILL SNEAKS OUT BUT only after waking me up and giving Patrick a reason to suspiciously stare at me over breakfast. I guess cleaning my closet at five in the morning wasn't the best on-the-fly excuse when he asked why I was moving around so early.

After spending the day wrapping gifts for a horde of Reynolds members, Joyce, Patrick, and I load box after box into the car. Keaton decided to wait for Liam to get back from visiting his grandpa before meeting us at Aunt Peg's, so I'll need to practice evasive maneuvers without any backup.

Easier said than done.

I've barely stepped through the door when the first question about San Francisco hits me. My smiles stay small, and I back out of conversations after a few minutes. The trick is to keep a plate of food in your hand, always chewing so that answers are short with nods and *hmm* and *mmhmm*. But for every step I make toward the kitchen, another relative catches my elbow.

I shouldn't complain. Everyone in Keaton's family treats me like one of their own—a minority excluded, who have either been in my pants or still hope to be one day. Speaking of the latter, Ford walks in. He immediately ducks out of a hug, his eyes searching for what I can only assume is me. I'm mid-lecture from Aunt Patty about the liberal leanings of my current city, so I throw out a closed-lip smile and clear my throat.

"Excuse me, I need some water."

A few feet from the kitchen, Peg intercepts me. I prepare to choke out a cough and double down on my water excuse when an arm hooks around my neck and drags me away from her.

"Sorry," Lincoln calls over his shoulder. Then he rests the side of his head against mine. "Food, Lex. You have *got* to get to the food!"

Lex.

Despite his drudging up the nickname, I laugh and push away from him once we're safe in the kitchen. Ford and Bentley's baby brother holds his arms out, his wingspan easily the length of my body. When I don't run into them, he pouts out a lip. I roll my eyes and step into him. He wraps me in a hug. I've missed him.

"It's Bennett, by the way," I mumble into his flannel shirt. "In case you forgot my name."

"Nope. Bennett Lexus Reynolds-Ross. I remember it perfectly." Lincoln steps back and gives me a wink, and I can't help but smile.

While I dated Bentley, they dropped the A from Alexus, so I fit the car theme. Ford stopped when I asked, but Lincoln and Chevy refused. With or without their brother, they consider me family. How can I be upset by that?

Lincoln zeroes in on the two tables of food and pushes me out of his way. He fills two plates, tossing a few extras on my plate when he runs out of space. I let him clear the way back into the living room. We both bite the top of our cups, carrying them in our mouths to deter anyone from talking to us.

It's an art, not getting trapped in conversations, and we've mastered the craft.

Ford catches up with us at the couch. With the plastic cup still in my teeth and my hands full, we exchange an awkward half-hug. By the time Liam and Keaton show, I'm wedged between the brothers while they pick over my food. She plays barrier to Ford, inserting herself in the inch gap by my leg until he moves to the arm.

"How's your grandpa?" I ask Liam.

He finishes chewing a sugar cookie he popped into his mouth while passing Aunt Patty. "Should go home the day after tomorrow." He wipes his hands on his khakis. "He kicked Dane and me out about an hour ago."

Keaton grabs my wrist and brings my cup to her mouth for a drink. She pulls back fast, making a face. "Cherry vodka, soda, and Jägermeister?"

"What?" Jäger and I have a sordid history. We've been on a permanent break, so when I tip the cup and taste bad decisions, I whip around to Lincoln. "I looked away for two seconds, asshole."

He yuks it up through a proud grin. "Two seconds too long."

I elbow him and go for a drink that won't land my head in a toilet. With everyone in the living room, I hang around the kitchen a few minutes before wandering to the *sitting room*. Peg fills the space with expensive furniture for a more formal area, but I've never known her to use it. Leaving the light off, I sit on the ottoman and check my phone.

Dane texted a picture a few minutes ago, feet up on his coffee table, next to an open bottle of wine and two glasses.

Are you trying to lure me to your house? I reply.

He answers right away.

One thousand percent yes. Is it working? Are you here? I'll open the door.

More than a little tempting. Maybe after Keaton and I exchange gifts later, I'll *go for ice cream*. Or tell her I'm going to see Dane and watch her head explode in visions of sugar plums and tandem bike rides.

"You used to hide in here and wait for me to find you."

I might not have been moving much before, but all of me—outside and inside—stills at the voice, deep and gravelly across the room. Then, it all kicks back on at once, my heart hammering out of control and my head snapping up to the darkest shadow hovering beside the piano.

"Probably not why you're in here now, huh?" Bentley steps in front of the window. The moonlight streams in silver on the side of his face, and he cocks his head to the side. "Hey, Lex."

My hands shake, and I stand up fast. "Ford told Keaton you weren't coming."

"The exact reason I told Ford I wouldn't be."

As he steps forward, I back into the ottoman. I stoop to regain my balance and straighten up. I have nowhere to go. Bentley stops in front of me, the two of us face-to-face for the first time since the last time. When I was screaming and he was shouting.

"Tick-tick, Lex. You gonna hug me or hit me?"

I thought I knew the answer, but with him here, I can't decide.

Bentley cracks a rare smile. "We'll go the nonviolent route then."

Regardless of how much I've tried to forget, my body remembers him when he pulls me into a hug. My arms automatically go around him, my cheek to his chest, and my shoulders relax when he rubs the nape of my neck. While he sighs into my hair, I have a perfect view of the couch. I flash to him shoving up my crushed velvet skirt when I was sixteen. Considering it a warning shot, I back against the ottoman again to get some space.

"Let's bail. Go somewhere to catch up." He reaches out to move my hair back from my face, but I dodge.

"Shouldn't you check with your girlfriend first?" I'm baiting him. I have no idea if he has one.

"Come on," he drawls. "Don't be like that."

"Be like what? The girl who won't mess with a guy who has a girlfriend?" I throw enough bitch behind it that he rubs his jaw. Right hand, left side.

"You think, out of the two of us, I don't have more of a reason to be pissed? You threw my shit in a pond."

"Lake," I correct. "And only what you left at my apartment."

After catching him texting yet another girl—four was apparently my limit—I left him on the side of the road in the middle of nowhere. By the time he caught up with me, I'd set most of his stuff adrift. Liam was my accomplice. We'd only met a few minutes earlier, so the experience really bonded us.

With my brain re-boarding the anti-Bentley train, I scoop down for my phone and drink, and when he doesn't move to let me through, I open my texts. "Who do you think will get here first, your brothers or Liam?"

"Liam." The voice comes from behind Bentley, and my eyes dart to the front of the room. Liam presses his shoulder into the archway leading to the hallway. "Everything good, Bentley?"

Bentley passes over his jaw again before he spins around. "Yeah. I was just saying hey."

Liam pushes off the wall, his expression neutral. "And now, you can go say it to everyone else." He walks farther into the room and holds out a cup. "Mind taking Keaton her drink?"

"Sure." Bentley glances back at me and gives a smile. "You look good, Lex."

I pick at the case on my phone until he looks away.

The two of them meet in the middle of the room, and as Liam hands him the cup, Bentley pats him on the back.

"Congrats on the engagement, man."

Liam gives a tight smile in response. He rotates his upper body to watch Bentley leave the room, then turns back to me. "You okay?"

I shrug, still looking at the hallway. "Nothing I haven't handled before."

The first time we broke up, we saw each other a week later at a family reunion. He brought a date. I sobbed in the park restroom for an hour with Keaton's arms wrapped around my heaving shoulders and a weird sludge in the floor drain a few feet away.

Liam waits while I gulp down my drink and extends an elbow. I hook my arm through his and let him lead me into the hall. "You wouldn't happen to know what Lincoln did with the Jäger, do you?"

"Not happening, Ross."

We round the corner into the kitchen as Keaton barrels in from the other side. "Bastard," she says, beelining for us. "Did he touch you?" She grabs my face in her hands to search for signs of impending waterworks. "Just say the word, and I'll lose his wedding invitation."

"He's an usher. Do you even send him an invite?"

Her eyes drift up in thought. "I have no idea."

"All right"—Liam catches Keaton by the middle and drags her backward—"enough drama. Let's get back to evading slightly inappropriate questions from fourteen thousand relatives."

She keeps hold of me as he hauls her out and pulls me with them, straight into a night of awkwardness. A state of being to which I've grown quite accustomed. But with bodyguards all around me, Bentley keeps his distance. Our group hovers around the couch with him staying on the opposite end. I keep glancing over—a filthy habit reawakened.

Other than the obvious ex tension, we Christmas with the best of them. The closest we come to an issue is when Ford holds on too long while telling me goodbye. Bentley stands and clears his throat, siblicide in his eyes. Ford and I share an eye roll, and to stick it to his big brother, Lincoln swoops me up and swings me around the living room.

By the time we're leaving, Liam has enjoyed himself enough that I need to help Keaton shove him into his truck.

"I'm sorry about the gift exchange." She rushes to the driver's side. "We'll come over early tomorrow."

"Great. Hungover Liam is my favorite type of Liam." No sarcasm. I find him the most tolerable in that state.

She snorts, climbing in. "I swear, he's the only person who becomes nicer when he's miserable."

I wave as she pulls away, and I walk to the car. Joyce and Patrick are standing in the doorway while he makes one of his epically long goodbyes to Peg. While I wait, I text Dane to take him up on his invite.

"And then there were two."

I look up at Bentley striding down the sidewalk. And here I thought, I'd get out of here without another one-on-one.

Silly, Bennett.

I'm finishing my message as he leans back on the car beside me and peeks at my screen. I tilt it away but not fast enough.

"Dane." But he says it like *Daaaayne.* "Sounds like a douche."

"You would know." I scrape my shoe over a crack in the sidewalk. "What's your damage, Bentley?" I ask, feeling his gaze on my face. "Are you expecting a fight or an easy lay or—"

"I love you."

A laugh bursts out of me. Joyce looks over, and Bentley gives her a smile, so she'll go back to minute seven of the farewell. I shake my head and close my eyes. I've drunk myself into oblivion or unwittingly consumed hallucinogens. There is no other explanation for what is happening right now.

"You don't love me," I tell him.

He audibly sighs and drops his head back. "And why's that?"

Dane replies, *I'll open another bottle of wine.*

I tuck my phone away. "For one, you don't call someone you love a 'cold-hearted bitch incapable of genuine emotion.'"

"I didn't mean that," he says to the sky.

"Two, how many times did you cheat on me? Three, we haven't seen each other in almost two years and haven't had a real talk in much longer." I pause the extensive list and face him, resting my hip on the door. "The only reason you're saying you love me is because I'm with someone else."

"You're *with* him, huh?" He lifts his head and stares straight ahead.

I shrug and fidget, and why am I feeling guilty right now? It's not like I'm dangling Dane in front of him like a *screw you*. Even if I were, Bentley never hesitated to flaunt hook-ups in my face after we broke up, not to mention actual relationships. Then, at the first sign I might be moving on, it was all, "*We're meant for each other, Lex.*" And, "*I've always belonged to you.*"

So, we're right on schedule when he turns toward me with a dangerous look of determination in his eyes. "Bennett…"

I shake my head, ready to cut him off, but I never get the chance.

Bentley doesn't play fair. He slips between cracks, and you don't realize you're under siege until he's already infiltrated. The arm I failed to notice creeping closer along the side of the car encircles me, and I'm up against him, his mouth on mine and the hand not cupping my ass locked in my hair. For a split second, it feels right. Familiar lips and the soft groan escaping him like he'll never get enough of me. It's what I know better than anything else. I could easily fall back into it—into him—except I don't want to.

I shove him off. "What the hell, Bentley?"

When I push him again, in case he missed my point the first time, he steps back and smirks.

"What's wrong, Lex?" He glances at Patrick and Joyce, finally on the move, and looks back at me. "I'm just saying goodbye."

119

I bite the inside of my cheek to keep from screaming at him as he brushes past me. He stops on the sidewalk to wish them a merry Christmas and pecks Joyce on the cheek, and then he throws one last grin at me over his shoulder before he walks away, hands in his pockets.

Welcome back to the Bentley-Bennett shitshow.

Price of admission: my peace of mind.

DANE'S DOOR SITS WIDE OPEN when I walk up the sidewalk hours after he joked about it. As if he wasn't tempting burglars enough, he's passed out on the couch. I sip from the glass of wine he left for me and kneel on the floor in front of him. When I lay my head on his arm, his eyes slit open, heavy with sleep. His mouth perks up on one side as he brings his other arm down from under his head. I let him trace my jaw and cheekbones and lips with his fingertips, lost in a moment with him. Quiet, calm, simple.

Maybe I should tell him about what happened, but once I do, Bentley's here. I don't want him crawling between us, wreaking havoc where he doesn't belong.

"We are," I say after a while.

Dane nods, agreeing without knowing. "Okay, we are…"

"Together."

It feels like a confession, difficult to admit and weighty to say aloud. Of all the things I didn't want, this one topped the list. But I don't want to lose it more.

He hasn't said anything, leaving me exposed, emotions bared to him. I can't take the silence anymore and go to look away when he catches my chin, keeping me there with him.

"We're together."

-17-

M.E.

IT HAPPENS ON A WEDNESDAY. Nothing special or monumental triggers it. I step out of my bathroom, and the purple and blue look different. The walls closer, the air stale. I'm late for work because I rearrange the furniture to find more space. The bed and dresser scrape over the floor as I drag them from one side to the other, but everything ends up where it started, and I feel on edge the entire day.

Aria curls up on the couch next to me that evening. I don't know if she sees the computer screen or notices the change as much as I do, but she sighs. "You're leaving."

"Not right away," I tell her. "I'll wait until you two find another roommate."

"Don't worry about it." She waves it off. "We knew you were a flight risk when we took you in."

"Me, a flight risk?" I drop my jaw, feigning offense.

She laughs and moves the laptop from my legs to hers. "So, where are we going?"

The question I've been asking myself for the last few hours. Financially, it makes sense to stay no more than a state away from Keaton and my wedding duties. In the next few months, I'll need to travel for two bridal showers, a bachelorette party, and a final dress fitting. Plus, any unforeseen emergencies, which I anticipate at least one of when reality strikes Keaton that she is, in fact, getting married in five months.

"Have you ever been to Nevada?" I ask.

"You're not moving to Nevada," Steve says from behind us.

I tip my head back as he walks across the catwalk. "Why not? And how did you know I was moving?"

"Harmonious vibes, remember?" He jogs down the stairs and jumps over the couch, landing on the cushions on the other side of me. "And you're not moving to Nevada because you'll think it's too much like Phoenix."

"So then, what about Colorado? It touches Arizona, and I haven't been there before."

He juts out his chin, thinking it over. "I thought you hated the cold."

I shrug. "Only because I don't know it."

A down jacket, wool mittens, I could steal one of Dane's beanies. I'll rock the winter look, build a snowman, and then watch the world melt into spring.

"Here." Aria moves the computer between us, already having found several Roommate Wanted posts. She clicks through, giving me enough time to scan them. "This girl is our age," she says. "And here's one with a cat."

After my adventures with Little Stevie, I don't consider it a selling point and let her move on. Post after generic post. Respectful of privacy. Clean. On-site laundry. 420 friendly. Recycled words off a How to Write an Ad site.

She speeds over one that's, from what I catch, different than the other listings. A fresh flash on the screen that snags my attention.

"Wait," I tell her. "Go back."

Aria stops on a two-bedroom in Durango with a roommate who enjoys LARPing on the weekends.

"One more."

"You won't like that one," she says.

I pull the computer onto my lap to read the description anyway. "*Compassionate young lady wanted for housemate. Only kind souls will be considered. Furnished west-facing room with tranquil sunset views, ample space, private bath—*" I cut off, turning to her. "What's not to like?"

"It's in the middle of nowhere." She points to where I left off. "*Must commute for work/shopping/play.* What if it snows?"

One of a dozen points I should consider—road conditions, a job, the length of the lease.

But it's too late for me once the images load. A cottage settled in a grove of trees along a river with mountains in the background, a legit field of wildflowers outside the back door, and two wooden rocking chairs I can hear squeaking. Goose bumps dance across my skin, my mind already on the stone patio in a mental parka.

It feels right. Where I want to be.

I grab my phone to check the distance from Phoenix and text Dane.

> *It's only a six-day walk to Colorado.*

His answer pops up fast.

> *Now we're talking. Just let me stretch first.*
>
> *Because, baby … I would walk anything under five hundred miles.*

I smile through my eye roll at his Proclaimer's reference.

> *Cheesy,* I text.

> *Worth it,* he sends back. *Now leave me alone, so I can get my shit done and see you this weekend.*

Steve leans over and nudges me with his shoulder. "Well, is it Colorado?"

My eyes drift back to the computer, to my little cabin of solitude. *Colorado.* Not somewhere I've pictured myself before, but I can't imagine going anywhere else now.

I send a message to the poster. With the deal they're offering on rent, the room won't last long. The young lady requirement I have locked down, but the rest is subjective, so along with the basics, I toss in a hefty dash of sweet-talk. Then I hit send and wait. My fate is now in the hands of one M.E. Stanton, and for the first time all day, I relax.

"A COFFIN," DANE SAYS. "M.E. Stanton wants your measurements to build a coffin."

The email hit my inbox yesterday. A cryptic response involving an almost-poetic invitation to an interview for the room. Along with the rather odd request involving my bust, waist, arms, and neck. I'm rereading it, stretched out on the couch between Dane's legs, my back to his chest and head on his shoulder. He was already here when I got back from work, watching a sports recap show. Steve had taken the liberty of filling him in about M.E. Or what we know anyway.

"What if she—"

"It's a he." He shifts behind me, a tension in his tone. "Some sicko waiting for a sexy-ass woman to show up who he will then murder and bury in his backyard."

Steve said the same thing, minus the sexy-ass part. Maybe they're right. Flying to meet a stranger who lives next to a river on the outskirts of civilization could set me up to become a statistic. But any time I see the email that gives directions using landmarks and minutes instead of street names and miles, I want to follow them. Go to the picturesque house surrounded by nothing but trees and air.

Dane slides the phone out of my hand. "I'll rearrange my schedule."

Already smiling, I flip over, so I can see him. "You're coming with me?"

"I can shuffle things around on Thursday and drive up. We'll find a sketchy motel for the night and visit your potential killer in the morning." He sets my phone on the end table over his head and sighs, resting his hands on my back. "You know what this means, right?"

"I owe you?"

"Absolutely. But also…" He hangs his head, so our noses touch. "We'll be together for Valentine's, which requires me to spring for a less skeazy place. Maybe even take you to a dinner we don't order at a counter."

"Sounds rough."

"I know. I don't even like you that much."

I wrinkle my nose, and he kisses me.

Except he does like me that much, and when I get off the plane the following week, he's waiting for me—a man with a smirk and a plan. A dinner reservation first, then a real hotel with an ice machine on every floor he insists on showing me. I've never understood the draw of Valentine's Day, but after all the complimentary champagne and strawberries at the restaurant, I come around on the idea. Or it could be him. Probably him.

SINCE OUR DESTINATION GIVES NEW meaning to middle of nowhere, the most convenient place to meet was New Mexico. Anything else would have required a connecting flight for me and an extra few hours of traveling for Dane. Our morning drive will take over an hour, so Dane stops for coffee before we abandon society.

He looks suspicious as he crawls in and hands me my drink, and then I see *Angel* printed on the side of the cup with a halo over the A.

Oh no. I sip and grimace. All milk and sugar with an accidental splash of coffee underneath. The same thing I ordered the morning we met.

"Your favorite, right?" he asks, lips twitching.

I down the entire thing out of spite.

The scenery is sparse for much of the drive. Then, halfway there, a dusting of white covers the road. More snow falls, hitting the windshield before sliding off with each pass of the wiper blades.

"Have you ever driven in snow?" I ask.

Dane cranks the heater because I am not yet a winter goddess. I've been shivering since waking up and have on one of his hoodies over top my own.

"Plenty," he says. "I lived in Minnesota for a minute. Connecticut, too, but it only snowed once."

My forehead scrunches. "I thought you lived in LA the two years you were gone."

"Only the last six months. I bounced a lot before I landed there." He glances over, his mouth turned up. "It takes a drifter to recognize another drifter."

"So, why go back?" I bury my freezing hands in the sweatshirt.

Dane shrugs. "It was always the plan. Spend a few years traveling until Liam finished school and then show up like expected." But his jaw tightens for a split second, the tension gone as fast as it formed.

"You didn't want to," I say.

He readjusts his grip on the steering wheel, not answering right away. A remixed pop song fills the space between squeaks of the blades, scraping over the glass, and he focuses on the road with a faraway look in his eyes.

"It was more that I hated it wasn't on my own terms," he finally says. "If I had a little more say in the timing, it might not have felt like a noose tightening."

I understand the suffocation more than most. I stayed in Phoenix for my family, and Dane returned for his. The difference seems to be the reason—mine a choice and his an obligation.

"Although"—he relaxes in his seat, stroking his chin in thought—"the old man summoning me to Phoenix when he did has had a few perks." His gaze flits to my empty coffee cup and then to me, holding longer than it should, considering he's driving.

"Dane," I warn, but he won't break eye contact, a grin forming as I shift around. "You're ridiculous," I say, looking away first.

"You're beautiful ... and about to drive in snow for the first time."

My eyes snap back to him. "What?"

He slows and pulls onto the shoulder.

"You're serious?"

Shifting into park, he turns to me. "You have to learn some time."

"But right now?"

"It is snowing," he says. He unbuckles his seat belt, and when I don't move, he clicks mine. "My truck will handle far better than your car, which will need new tires before you move."

I check up and down the highway, no other cars in sight to save me. Even if there were, it wouldn't matter because Dane's out of the truck, *skating* his way around the front end. He slides the last several feet, catching the handle of my door to stop himself and swinging it open. He climbs in and nudges me to the driver's side.

"Shit, it's cold."

As he brushes off the snow, I lower the steering wheel so that I can see over it and move the seat so that my feet aren't comically far away from the pedals. We strap back in, and Dane sinks into the seat, not offering the least bit of guidance.

"I thought you were teaching me."

He points straight ahead. "Drive."

"Helpful," I say, shifting gears.

Once I ease onto the road, I quickly decide it's not so bad. The yellow line appears intermittently to keep me on track, and with the wiper blades, the windshield stays clear.

"Stop!"

Dane lunges forward, and I instinctively slam on the brakes. The tires lose traction on ice hidden by the snow, and the truck slides sideways, no matter how far I turn the wheel to keep it straight. I wasn't going very fast, so after a few heart-wrenching seconds, we skid to a stop in the other lane.

I whip my head toward him, still in a panic, but he's slouched in the seat again like nothing happened. "What the hell, Dane!"

"Next time, do the opposite of everything you just did, and you'll be fine. Lesson complete."

I close my eyes, exhaling, and drop my forehead to the steering wheel. "I hate you."

"Well, we both know that's not true." When I look over, skin still pressed into the leather, he smiles. "I warned you I was impossible to stay mad at."

"I'll prove you wrong," I tell him.

"Maybe one day," he says, reaching over to rub my back. "But not today."

A FEW MILES DOWN THE road, we find our first landmark—a white barn with a large metal T anchored to the side. I follow turn after turn, weaving through back roads until we reach a mailbox with *Stanton* etched in the wood post. The driveway snakes us past barren trees, missing the green from the pictures but not the serenity. My pulse races when the cottage comes into view, six-pane windows, blue trim, and a porch swing.

As I park near a rock garden with a birdbath in the center, Dane side-eyes me.

"What?" I ask, doubting I want to know.

"That's a lot of rocks to hide a body under."

I roll my eyes and climb out. We meet at the front of the truck just in time for me to slip on the slick gravel. I gasp, sure I'm going down, but Dane's reflexes prove faster than gravity. He catches me at an angle, one arm behind my back and the other wrapping my waist.

I stare up at him, my eyes wide in shock. "Colorado might be rejecting me."

"You'll win it over." He rights me but keeps me held against him. "Unless a Dahmer-Bundy mountain man answers. Then I'm carrying your ass to the truck because if anyone gets to lock you in a basement, it's me."

By the time I laugh, he's already kissed me on the nose and started for the porch. The steps creak, which I, "Awww," at, and Dane shakes his head.

Even if we end the day murdered, what an adorable place to die.

When I lift my hand to knock, he adjusts so that he stands slightly in front of me. The protectiveness sends a jolt of nerves through me, like I really do need defending. M.E. is dangerous.

The entire trip has been a colossal mistake. I'll never find out if the rocking chairs squeak or see butterflies in the wildflowers.

The lock turns, and I latch on to Dane. He curls his fingers around mine, but once the door creeps open, both our grips loosen. M.E. smiles from the other side of the threshold, and Dane chuckles.

The toastiest brown eyes I've seen warm even more as I slip around him.

"You must be Bennett." The old woman reaches out a hand for me when I nod. "Goodness, my dears, come in before you freeze." She steps back, bringing me with her.

I glance at Dane, following us in, and mouth, *Told you so.*

He bites back a smile and holds up his hand in a silent admission of defeat. We both know it right then, walking into a cozy room with a fireplace on one end and blankets thrown over the backs of both recliners and the couch.

I'm moving to Colorado.

-18-
The Look

My HEART HURTS, CROSSING THE border back into New Mexico.

Maggie Elizabeth—she uses her initials for all correspondence, telling us, *"You can't be too careful about who knows you're a little old lady, living alone."*—sent Dane out the door with a plate of cookies and promises of a home-cooked meal the next time he visits. She also double-checked my measurements, concerned the arms of the *sweater* she's knitting me would be too long.

That night, I find a few jobs I could potentially talk my way into.

Dane snorts when I mention one for record-keeping at a body shop. "Because when I think Bennett Alexus Ross, I think cars and math."

Not a point I can argue, so I fill out the application for an assistant to a realtor instead and send my résumé. They want a people person with photography skills, and I've perfected small talk and I own a camera. The employee pool must be shallow because an office manager has emailed by the time I arrive in San Francisco the next day.

With everything set and the countdown on, the apartment feels breathable again. A few days before the move, I pack with Keaton on speakerphone. We did the same thing when I was leaving Portland. I don't think I ever want to load myself into boxes without her.

"I can't believe how close you'll be," she says. "I can drive to see you whenever I want."

I smile, taping the first set of flaps shut. "I can't wait."

"Are you sure you don't want me to fly in and ride with you? I hate you driving so far alone again."

Another thousand-mile trip, only this time will be a little different.

"Actually…" I hesitate, stretching another line of tape across the box. "I won't be alone. Dane's going to be with me."

I brace myself for the squeal of all squeals, but it never comes. She doesn't say anything. One second passes, two, three, four.

"Keats?"

A rush of breath comes through the speaker. "God, *finally*! I thought you were never going to say anything."

"What?" I drop on the bed, bumping the box off and not trying to stop it. "You knew?"

"Since the engagement dinner."

I sigh and hide my face in my hands. "Liam told you?"

"Only after I asked him. I mean, it wasn't hard to put together, Bennie. Dane popped out of the house with one more button done than when he showed up, and you looked guilty as sin."

"How have you not said anything?"

Keaton can barely contain herself when I go out with the same guy twice, let alone seeing someone exclusively for close to six months.

I sit up, glad I'm not holding the phone or I'd drop it. Six months. *Is that right?*

"I didn't want you to spook," she says, but I'm barely paying attention, counting months in my head.

Each person has their moment in a relationship—whether they recognize it or not—that changes the way they perceive it. For some, it comes with a specific milestone, the first holiday spent together or when they stop feeling the nagging need to only be seen in full makeup with a fresh blowout. They either want more from the other person or less of them. My moment hits shy of the six-month mark and is always the second option. Or it has been. I wait for the realization to crawl up and lodge in my throat, except nothing happens. No panic. No urge to delete Dane from my life.

If anything, I miss him more than a second ago.

I force myself to the closet before I overanalyze my lack of a freak-out and, therefore, freak out.

"Forgive me?" I ask Keaton.

She hums it over for the sake of drama. "Only if you promise not to hide any other love affairs from me."

"I'll shove all future ones in your face."

"Oh," she says, "speaking of stealth missions, I found a frog in one of my first graders' backpacks today."

"Ew." As gross as the change of topic, at least she's attempting to avoid berating me with Dane questions—Liam's influence, no doubt. I pull the hangers off the rod and carry them to the bed. "Dead or alive?"

"Dead. Or so I thought."

By the time she finishes her harrowing tale of the Jesus frog, I've finished packing. The only things left are what I need to survive the next few days and the clown painting screwed into the wall. She looks less sad today, the bright colors at the bottom lightening her mood. And mine.

Later, I'm cross-legged on the bed with my phone on my lap when Steve pokes his head in long enough to say, "Remind him he owes me twenty bucks from last week's game."

"You just assume I'm texting Dane," I call after him.

"Nope." His voice drifts in from the hallway, heading toward his tower. "I know you are."

I am, and I smile at the message he sent before Steve's interruption.

Friday. You and me and not a damn soul I have to share you with. Just us.

No constriction in my chest or feelings of being trapped.

Can't wait, I reply. *But I'm picking the music.*

MY LAST MORNING AT THE apartment feels nothing like goodbye. Since Steve has found a steady buyer for his work, they've decided not to rent out the room again, and Aria promises, as long as they live there, it's mine. In fact, they both insist I'll be back to the point that I start to believe them. So much so, I leave the painting behind, wanting it to be waiting if I do.

Little Stevie plants himself on my lap after breakfast, biting whenever I try to move. His stonewalling ends the second he hears his food dish. He bounds off, as disinterested in me as ever. Before I leave, I boop him on the nose one last time, smiling when he swipes at me.

Aria hugs me at the curb—Steve, too—with a kiss on the cheek. When we pull away, he scoops her up and tips her backward, her rainbow hair brushing the cement and him appearing more in love than yesterday. I snap a picture, already missing them. Then I turn and take one of Dane. The first I've taken of him, but by the time we leave California, I have a roll of him. Of us.

Because I own no winter clothes—the closest I come is a lightweight jacket and a few sweatshirts—Dane and I wind up in a department store at one in the morning when the temperature dips. As I turn for the dressing room with an armful of long-sleeved shirts and sweater dresses, he tosses skimpy lingerie on top. I give him a look, and he shrugs.

"I need something to think about when I'm stuck behind a desk. It might as well be stripping that off you with my teeth."

"Such a romantic," I say dryly.

"Only with you, baby." He slaps my ass as I pass.

The slats in the door show him leaning next to it after I close it.

I've tried on most of the pile when he asks, "What are you doing for Keaton's bachelorette party?"

I peel off a rejected knit top. "We're taking a dance class she's always wanted to try."

Close enough to the truth. Technically, I booked a strip class at a local club to surprise her, but I prefer not to dangle the exotic-dance carrot in front of him.

"What about you? Any crazy plans for Liam?"

"Just a little karaoke. About as exciting as a dance class."

I stifle a laugh with a wool sweater. "Is most of the guest list his friends from the frat?"

"Yes," Dane groans the response. "A night full of L-Dogs and Master-bater jokes."

Liam's friends are nothing if not stereotypical, dragging him down to near caveman status when they get together.

"My best friend from the engagement party is also on the list."

"Ford?" I go rigid, arm half in a sleeve and half out. "You're inviting Keaton's cousins?"

"Only a few of them. Mustang and Buick and—"

"Bentley?" I cringe at how the name sounds out of my mouth, wrapped in history with familiarity dripping from each syllable. And yet, I say it again. "Is Bentley invited?"

Worse the second time. A gritty feeling left behind.

I have yet to bring him up, in general or the specific stunt he pulled at Christmas. My reasoning has been Dane and I see each other for such short periods. I hate losing any of it to a game of trade the exes. In all honesty, I don't want to learn about Dane's. I'll stumble into the trap of comparisons like a newborn fawn.

When he doesn't answer right away, I pull on the shirt I came in with. He's looking at his phone when I step out, his head resting against the wall. He rolls it toward me as a less than enthusiastic lady on the loudspeaker tells Kelly to go on break.

"No Bentleys," he says once she finishes. "The only vehicles Liam texted are Ford, Lincoln, and Chevy."

My insides unclench. I should have known his cousin wouldn't put him through an awkward night out with my ex.

"Is there a reason you look so relieved?" he asks, straightening up.

Dane has this look, a slight narrowing of the eyes, brows raised infinitesimally. I've only seen it directed toward me whenever he wants more than what I'm giving him. Right now, it hones in, asking for the missing pieces.

I play with the door handle, wondering if Kelly gets fifteen minutes like I used to. It never seemed like enough time to do much of anything.

"Bennett," he says, bringing my focus back.

"You know how you went to homecoming with your dad's wife?"

Great lead-in.

"Forever trying to forget"—he crosses his arms—"but go on."

"I went to mine with Keaton's cousin." The knob turns clockwise and counterclockwise in my hand, and I watch it rather than him. "We dated for over two years in high school and another six months in college."

"That's a long time." His voice stays even, not offering any indication of his reaction. "So, it was serious?"

I peek, but his expression matches the tone. "As serious as it could be with him screwing anything that moved." I go back to studying the metal, gold paint flaking off. We keep having these moments in dressing rooms, and I make a mental note to avoid them in the future.

"I take it he wasn't at the engagement party, or I would have known."

"He's stayed away from family functions since we broke up, but he showed at Christmas, and…" I peer up, and *the look* awaits, drawing the rest out of me. "He tried to kiss me."

"On Christmas Eve?" His stare hardens, the indifference gone. "Before you came to see me?"

I swallow, realizing Dane considers this a bigger deal than I gave it credit for.

He waits for my nod before he smirks and shakes his head. "And you waited until now to tell me you kissed him?"

"I didn't kiss him," I say fast.

The irritation in my tone isn't expected but sounds right, and he responds to it with his own.

"Fine," he says, voice harsh but hushed, "I'll rephrase. Your lips were on your ex's in the same night they were on mine. Is that a more accurate description?"

I bite the inside of my cheek, trying to stay calm. He's twisting the situation into me cheating on him, and as someone who's been on the receiving end of that conversation, it takes a lot.

"It was *nothing* like you're making it out to be. Bentley tried something, and I shut him down."

"We're together." He steps toward me, a disdain in his expression I haven't experienced before. "That's what you told me that night, Bennett. We're fucking together."

"We were. We are."

"Did you bother telling him that?"

The accusation is like a slap in the face, and I have to suppress the urge to actually slap his. "How can you ask me that?"

He heaves out a breath, followed by a single, annoyed laugh. "Why wouldn't I? You only now told your best friend about us, so what would make me think mentioning it to an ex while he—" He stops and holds up his hands. "No. You know what? I'm not doing this."

"Doing what?" I ask as he brushes past to grab the clothes off the bench. "Dane," I say.

But he's already stalking away through the abandoned clothing section, leaving me with the sudden threat of tears. I have no idea what he's not doing, but it sure as hell feels like anything to do with me.

I catch up with him at the only open register, the cashier starting to scan the clothes. I mentally vetoed half of them, but I doubt now is the time to mention it. Just like it wasn't the time to talk about Bentley.

"You can't just walk away like that," I tell him on our way across the parking lot.

He ignores me. The last time we left a store together, he wanted everything to do with me. Now it's the opposite, and nothing feels right. Anxiety digs its claws in when he starts the car, still not looking at me. I don't need to refer to any therapy sessions to explain the ache in my chest. We're reenacting the last few minutes I spent with my mom. In the car in the middle of the night, bags in the backseat, the air thick with words that need to be spoken. But neither of us says them, the next few hours driven in silence.

THE HOUSE IS DARK WHEN Dane parks next to the rock garden. He follows me onto the porch with two boxes and our bags, and I balance one, unlocking the door. I use my phone to light the way to my room, and while he goes for my other two boxes, I find sheets to make the bed. Before he comes back, I shut myself in the bathroom. I'm exhausted—physically, emotionally—but I unpack what I can from the box I brought in and my travel bag.

Stalling at its finest.

Dane and I haven't fought before. Unless you count the bar blonde and lettered Noah, which I don't. Some people thrive on the arguments and the make-ups. I've been one of them, driven by the drama. But that's not who Dane and I are together. We're validating, understanding of each other. At least, I thought we were.

When I come out, he's not there. My last two boxes are by the closed door, the overhead light off and the pink lamp with white flowers on instead. The dim room fits the mood. More shadows than light.

I wait a minute, five, then ten.

Where are you? I text him.

His answer takes just as long: *Needed air.*

Please come back.

We need to talk about this.

I'm sorry.

Every response I start, I delete until I give up altogether. I change into sweatpants and a T-shirt, and then I go through his bag to find a sweatshirt. I crawl into the bed he's supposed to be in with me, the hood over my head, the drawstring pulled so tight that it closes in around my face, only the tip of my nose out, and

I hide my hands in the sleeves, so as much of me is covered with him as possible. Self-inflicted torture. Dane is in every breath and thought, thoroughly consuming me. It hurts, but it's better than him not being here at all. The harshest truth I've had to admit to myself.

A LOT OF BREATHS PASS before the sound of my bedroom door. I'm still buried in the hood, but I hear his shoes hit the floor. He climbs into the bed, the blankets moving as he adjusts them over us.

All goes quiet again until his soft voice asks, "You in there?"

I tug at one side of the hood, loosening it until I can see him. His eyes trace my face for a second before he pulls me to him. His hands are cold and his lips, too, when they first touch me, but they warm fast against mine. He kisses me, shaking his head as he apologizes against my mouth. "I'm sorry. I'm so sorry for acting like a dick." More head shaking, his lips pressing to mine again. "I'm not a jealous person—or I haven't been until you. It scares me. *You* scare me."

"Why?" I whisper.

"Because you make me want to fly two hours every weekend and buy cupcakes for your birthday and lose my shit thinking about anyone who's ever touched you or might think about it." He pauses, skimming his fingers along my hairline and down the side of my face. "I have no idea who I am since I met you."

Same. I don't lump for men. I don't start talking to them again after I stop. I definitely don't hide in their clothes, counting my breaths and missing them.

"I'm sorry for not telling you about Bentley sooner."

He stares into my eyes, the way I only let him do. "I need to know you won't keep things like that from me anymore."

I nod, running the pads of my fingers over his jaw and down the chain on his neck. From don't-wants to needs, and again, mine comes easily.

"And I need you not to walk out on me again." I blink through tears, another confession pushing to the surface. "I can't deal with you leaving and not knowing if you're coming back."

His brows knit while he studies me, really looking until the understanding I'd hoped for earlier floods into his eyes. "Oh shit." He pulls me closer, his arms tying tight around me, and I press my cheek to his bare chest. "I never meant to make you think I wasn't. I couldn't stay away from you if I tried."

I sink as far into him as I can. I want to believe him beyond all doubt, but it only goes so deep. Trust runs shallow in my veins. People who shouldn't leave do and ones who should stay. They care, then they stop. Love until they don't. You can't predict which way someone will go.

Ourselves included.

-19-
Gettin' Sticky

LIFE WITH MAGGIE IS AN experience. She times her life around the sun. For a frail woman in her late eighties, she accomplishes more in a morning than I do in a day, sorting boxes or reading or baking. After the first snow, I wake up, and the sidewalk has already been shoveled and my car cleared off. I start setting an alarm to beat her to it.

"No, no, no," she says when I bring back green bananas. "Only ripe ones. And only three at a time. Otherwise, I might die before they're ready to eat."

The same with all other produce, which means I become a household name at the tiny grocery store across the street from the realtor's office.

The work is easy, unlocking doors and guaranteeing open houses don't run out of snacks. By the end of the first week, I've walked through every for-sale house in a twenty-mile radius of the office. I snap pictures, doing what I can to disguise problem areas that could deter someone from looking.

Katie Sayer, The Home Slayer, claims if she can get someone in the door, her charm can, "sell a barn without a roof." She proves her magic when two couples enter into a bidding war over a house with more holes in the drywall than outlets and light fixtures combined.

I quickly adjust to the cold. After a few weeks, I stop putting on a coat when I dash out to start my car in the mornings to let the engine warm.

The day before I fly to Arizona for a weekend filled with bridal showers, I help Maggie move a box down from a shelf in what was her husband's office. George worked on custom jewelry, engravings, and bending spoons to make into bracelets. The room is untouched from when he passed away ten years ago, his pliers and reading glasses still on the workbench he used.

Back in the living room, she plops on the couch and pats the seat next to her. "I have something for you to take with you for your friend."

"Keaton?" I ask.

She gives me a look, saying, *Who the hell else?*

"You don't have to give her anything."

"Have to and want to ain't got nothin' to do with one another." She starts digging. "I have no use for most of this stuff anymore, but nostalgia tricks the mind into keeping things long after they've served their purpose." A pleased expression appears on her face when she finds whatever she's searching for. "Here it is. George gave me this the morning of our wedding."

She hands me a yellowed piece of paper, black ink faded but legible. I suspiciously eye her after reading the bold print at the top—*Why you'll be a terrible wife.*

"No offense, Mags, but I think this could very well push Keaton over the edge."

"Ohhh," she says, tapping me on the hand. "Read before you sass."

I reluctantly settle back on the cushions. "*Number one: you are your own person.*" I immediately question the type of marriage Maggie endured but continue, "*If you want to be fully devoted, get those silly ambitions and dreams out of your head. Focus on your future husband and not on the desire to become a better person. Self-actualization never put dinner on the table.*"

Maggie nods along as if reciting it in her head.

"Two: you question your future husband. The vows include the word obey *for a reason."* Annoyance cakes my tone the further I go. *"Whether the command comes out ill-tempered or demeaning, never you mind, just fulfill the promise made. Number three: you refuse to settle for what he gives you, pestering him to better himself—"* The awfulness continues, but I stop. "I can't read any more."

"Then skip to the bottom." She taps a finger on the page, the smile lines on each side of her mouth deepening.

With a sigh, I scan down. Then I smile, seeing the final handwritten line. *"And this, my love, is a list of ways you'll make a terrible wife, but all the reasons you'll be an incredible partner to share my life. My equal, my best friend, my everything—I love you and choose you. George."*

"The man's sense of humor drove me mad," Maggie says, eyes on the fire but far away. "But he loved me selflessly despite my stubbornness and independence and a barrel's worth of flaws. And he gave me a reminder, so neither of us lost sight of who he'd chosen. If Keaton finds the slightest bit of herself in here, and any part of Liam at the end, they have the love that sticks."

"Sticky love sounds dangerous," I say, folding the paper along the delicate creases.

She pats me on the leg and grunts, pushing to her feet. "Only if you're determined to get out of it alive, my dear."

Keaton laughs, reading the letter. As she wipes under her eyes, careful not to smear her mascara, she says, "Do *not* show Liam this. He'd tag the apartment walls with a list of ways I'm terrible."

I tuck the paper back in my bag when she hands it over. We snuck off from the bridal shower for a moment of peace and are lounging on the swings in the backyard of her parents' house. Joyce's side of the family is a notch down on the decibel chart from the Reynolds side, which we'll deal with tomorrow, but still rowdy for a bunch of women on a Saturday afternoon.

"You want to do Greek tonight?" Keaton twists her swing toward mine. "Or maybe we could go to that Thai place down the street?"

I nod. "Yes to both. My restaurant choices have been limited to pizza, pasta, and fried chicken for far too long."

We both pretend not to watch Aunt Donna dip behind the gardening shed to smoke.

"Then we can watch a movie that involves no explosions," she says.

I'm staying with her for the weekend. Dane and Liam went out of town for, what his cousin called, a work conference. Dane claimed the real reason is a golf tournament his grandpa wanted to hit in Miami and offered to pay for them to go on the company credit card.

I consider it a chance to spend time with my best friend sans boy drama.

After the party wraps up, we do eat at both places, bringing leftovers back to munch on during our movie marathon. Halfway through a rom-com, I think of Denton and Daphne for the first time in months. I can't even remember packing *Darkest Desires* when I left San Francisco.

SHE DRIVES ME TO THE airport after the bridal shower on Sunday.

"I'll only see you two more times before you're here for the wedding," she says, hugging me before I go through security. A crazy thought that sticks with me the entire flight.

And then, a few weeks later, her arms wrap around me again, but now I'm lugging my bag off the plane for the bachelorette party.

As she lets go, she gives me a longer look than usual. "You look different."

"Really?" I ask, searching for a window reflection.

She glances back for Liam to weigh in, and he smirks at the opportunity.

"Yeah. Older. Paler. Bitchier."

I flip him off and purposely drop my bag on his foot. He flings it into the backseat of his truck when we get outside, aiming for me, but I block it while checking my phone.

"I thought Dane was coming with you," I say after he climbs in the front.

"Grandpa threw him the entire Willis portfolio out of nowhere. It's one of our biggest clients, and he needs to catch up before a meeting on Monday. He's been buried in balance sheets and earnings reports, yelling, 'Fuck me,' from his office all day."

Sure enough, a text says something similar, but in Dane.

Fuck. This. Shit. No chance I'll be at the airport. Or dinner. Or my own funeral.

I wilt into the seat. We haven't seen each other in over a month, since our fight about Bentley. The morning after, I thought we were back to normal, but our goodbye felt off. The time apart different.

"I'll assume you won't throw a fit about stopping there real quick?" Liam eyes me through the rearview mirror. "I need to drop something off."

Glancing out the window, I shrug and say, "Whatever."

He starts the truck, and I bite my lips together to keep the smile off my face. Because the face-cracking grin on Keaton's is enough for both of us.

THE LOBBY OF THE BUILDING is quiet, except the trickling water of a fountain in one corner. The lady behind the panel with Masters Financial Group etched into hazy glass gives a small perk of her lips and goes back to her work. Keaton loops her arm through mine as we follow Liam across. We pass a small kitchen and a conference room before he ducks into one of the offices.

"Dane's is the next one," Keaton says before she goes in. She sits in one of the chairs in front of the desk, Liam on the other side with a stack of papers.

I hover outside a few seconds and then stroll farther down. When my knock on the half-open door is met by a low growl, I push it the rest of the way. He doesn't look up, on the office phone with his elbow on the desk, head in his hand, and fingers in his mussed-up hair. The few people I've seen were in suits and skirts, Liam in slacks and a dress shirt. Dane is in jeans. The sleeves of his button-down are rolled up and the tie around his neck loosened.

Propped in the doorway, I watch him glance between the papers in front of him and his phone off to the side. I slide mine out of my back pocket and text it.

Waiting for something?

The phone vibrates on his desk, his attention trained on the screen right away. He checks the message, and a smile curves on his lips. "If you're not the one in my doorway right now, we're going to have a problem."

When I don't say anything, he looks up. Nothing is wrong or different once our eyes meet.

His entire body relaxes back in his chair, and he dangles the office phone away from his ear. "So fucking beautiful."

"Important call?" I ask, stepping farther in.

He drops the phone onto his desk and presses a button, so hold music streams through the speakers. "Not anymore." He hooks a finger at me, mouthing, *Come here.*

I shut the door, and on my way over, I scan the room. It's bigger than I imagined from the pictures he'd sent. Art prints on the walls match those hanging in businesses across the country. The chairs are the same as Liam's, and Dane has a leather couch under the window. But the desk, the desk I recognize. Black and sleek.

"I was wrong," he says. He rolls his chair back, and when I'm close enough, he pulls me onto his lap. "We have a problem *because* it was you in my doorway."

I drape my arms around his neck and lean back on his arm. "I could go. If you want."

"I don't want." His hand pushes into my hair, loosening the sloppy updo I threw together in the airport bathroom. "And if you try to leave, I can't be held responsible for what will happen."

He brings my lips to his, letting out a gruff sound when they connect. I wonder if he would have kissed me like this at the airport. In front of Liam and Keaton. A terminal full of strangers wouldn't matter, as we've been all over each other in various bars in San Francisco and a few tourist stops along I-80, but people we know in the real world?

"Mr. Masters?" a man says through the phone.

I missed the music cutoff, but Dane seems unsurprised by the interruption. "Still here," he says.

"We've moved the reservation for Monday ahead two hours, sir, and scheduled your tee time for eleven a.m. As always, we're thrilled to have you dining with us, but we're sorry your father won't be able to join—"

"Uh-huh. Thank you." Dane slaps at the buttons on the phone, hanging up on him.

I tug at the knot of his tie. "Liam said you have a lot of work to do this weekend?"

"Thirty years' worth of investment history the old man expects me to know by Monday at eleven. But"—his eyes drift down from my face to the desk—"I could spare some time to knock out one or three of the fantasies I've had about you being in my office."

I laugh, but it chokes off when the door flies open. I leap off Dane's lap, more in shock than anything else, as his dad charges in, red-faced and finger pointed at his son.

"You took on Willis?" he shouts, a vein in his neck bulging. He's far from the cool, collected man I met at the engagement dinner. "You ungrateful—" Greg cuts off, noticing me for the first time. His furious gaze burns over me before flicking back to Dane.

Unaffected by the glare, Dane eases out of the chair. "You remember Bennett." He snakes an arm around my waist, tugging me against him. "From Liam's engagement party."

Greg adjusts the cuff of his suit coat and unclenches his jaw enough to say, "Of course. How are you, lovely?"

Dane curls his fingers into my side at the pet name. "Bennett," he repeats.

Greg forces a smile, his eyes still locked in a standoff with his son's. "Yes, right. Bennett, *lovely*"—he refocuses on me, all the charm from the first time returned—"would you mind giving me a minute alone with my son?"

It's not a real question, a command in sheep's clothing.

147

The hold on me tightens. Dane exhales slowly before he looks down at me. "I'll meet you at the house later?"

More than ready to slink away from the family drama, I nod.

He grabs his keys off the desk and unhooks one. "Here," he says, closing my fist around the key. His fingers slide under my chin, tipping it up so that I look at him. "There's a bottle of red waiting for you."

"Luring me with wine again," I say.

He smirks and, ignoring the set of eyes on us, brushes his lips over mine. "It has yet to let me down."

As I back up, I smile at him and keep the expression held when I turn to his dad. "Nice to see you, Mr. Masters."

"A pleasure," he says, his head following me as I pass to the door.

I think of his wife. How, right now, Aubrey would be clutching his arm or chest in a desperate attempt to either scare me away or remind him that she existed.

The second the door latches behind me, Greg's voice booms from the other side. Walking to the office next door, I decide to save the wine for Dane. It sounds like he's going to need it. Half the bottle anyway.

I FALL ASLEEP ON THE couch around midnight. The last message Dane sent said he was leaving the office, but after twenty minutes, I stretched out, and the cushions sucked me in. When I open my eyes, I'm in his bed. A border of light surrounds the curtains, illuminating the room enough to tell me I'm alone.

My face rolls onto something smooth, bright pink, and stuck on the pillow. A mini-mem but with small, blocky letters instead of Keaton's usual frill. I yawn, reading it.

> *Stole these from Liam's the morning you left. Keaton had a drawerful, so I doubt she noticed.*

I laugh and see another stuck on the book on his nightstand. It's different each time I'm here, always a slip of paper sticking out as a bookmark. I peel the note from the cover and turn the lamp on to better see.

> *You weren't supposed to have been someone I couldn't stop thinking about, but you were. Page 208.*

Flipping the book to the marked page, I find a different sticky note. One with my handwriting—*Two messages.* He kept it. Even more, he keeps it close to him. Keeps me close.

My message is stuck to his bookmark, so I lift it to see the white paper underneath and find more writing but not mine or Dane's.

> *Go, go, go.*
> *Fly, fly, fly.*
> *Then come home.*

She signed it *Mom* with two *X*s. I swallow back the lump in my throat and tuck our messages to him back in the book. When I crawl out of bed, I notice my next mini-mem, waiting on the bathroom door.

> *Smiling when I replayed your laugh in my head, wanting to stare into your eyes again, I was hopeless.*

And when I close it, I see another.

> *Still am.*

Stuck on the mirror over the sink:

> *Snake + Angel*

After my shower, I notice the heart he drew around it in the steam.

The others left to find while I get ready apologize for him not waking me and say he needs to finish a few things before Liam's bachelor party.

The last one is on a milk carton in the fridge.

All I'll be thinking about tonight is you. Expect drunk texts. Lots of them.

He left the pad of sticky notes on the counter with a pen. I write on the top one, leaving it there for him.

I'll be waiting. Don't disappoint.

-20-
Cherry Pit

Strip class.

It was a risky choice, but one that pays off.

Keaton glances over as our party bus rolls up to Cherry Pit, her eyes bulging. "Bennie…"

I hold up the container of body glitter I've been hiding in my bag all night and brace for the tackle I know is coming.

She lunges, and I fall back on top of the padded seat, taking the full force of blonde curls in my face as she says, "Thank you, thank you, thank you!"

One thing most people don't know about my best friend is she's always been in love with strippers. And once we get her near a pole, you can hear Def Leppard's "Pour Some Sugar on Me" playing in the background. Like, it's what actually plays while she whips her hair and crawls over a practice stage.

Our instructor, Candy—her real name's Millicent, but who wants to toss bills at the feet of someone with the same name as their great aunt Millie?—wisely keeps me away from the pole after seeing me trip on my way in. I am a natural for the lap dance though. Another skill to add to the résumé. Small talk, owns a camera, can point to things and shake my ass. And the career counselor worried about me. How do you like me now, Miss Greene?

The room for the class is in the back of the building, so rather than going through the padded double doors on our way in, we veered into a hallway. Not that we could have gone in if we wanted since the sign taped up said they were closed for a private party. One that's in full swing as we leave. A bass beat pulses through the walls, and employees mill around backstage.

When a side door opens and floods the corridor with music, Keaton latches on to my forearm, bringing me to a stop.

"Oh my God," she says.

"What?" I wiggle my arm, so her nails stop digging into my skin.

Keaton's hand falls away as the door slams shut. "What was Dane planning for Liam's party tonight?"

"Karaoke. Why?"

Before she answers, another girl walks through the same door, and more music pours out. Unless they have a super-rare recording of the Poison song playing, it is *not* Bret Michaels singing about roses and nights with dawns. The lyrics are off-key and slurred together like the singer's drunk.

She narrows her eyes, an unimpressed look on her face. "Because I hear that voice every morning in the bathroom."

The second she says it, I recognize it too. Liam sings in the shower—if you can call it singing—and right now, it is without a doubt him butchering a classic inside.

"Just a little karaoke," Dane said. "About as exciting as a dance class."

Poles and all apparently.

I catch the door before it closes again. A chance to crash Liam's bachelor party, *plus* strippers? I can admit, the night I planned pales in comparison to the perfect Keaton bachelorette party we just stumbled upon.

"Well, bride-to-be," I say to her, "bar-hopping with the girls and an ever-escalating game of Truth or Dare or…" I cock my head toward the club.

She snorts, already on her way past me. "Like you had to ask."

If any of our group of crashers was worried about sneaking in, they shouldn't have been. None of the employees blink an eye at us. Not that we'd leave even if they asked us to once we see Liam on the main stage—cowboy hat, a leather vest without a shirt underneath. Keaton cackles so hard beside me that I have no idea why it takes so long for any of the guys to notice us.

Lincoln's the first, relaxed in an oversize chair. "Hey, Keats," he shouts around the set of tits in his face. Then he leans over, so he can better see me and nods. "You workin' tonight, Lex?"

I mime a laugh and flip him off.

At the sound of my nickname, Ford jumps up from a chair. The girl previously on his lap hits the floor, and he starts toward me to stake a claim. But a different brother beats him there.

A tree trunk of an arm slides around my shoulders as Chevy steps between Keaton and me from behind. "These jackasses make it easy for me to be your favorite."

I smile up, and he grins down. The last of the garage and the youngest by three minutes, Chevy is my favorite. He has a calmness about him Lincoln lacks, confidence Ford needs, and the heart Bentley will never possess. My ally, even when I probably didn't deserve one.

Our attention jerks to the stage when a loud thump travels through the speakers, followed by a short burst of feedback. Liam has dropped the microphone, eyes set on Keaton. He walks straight to her. And I mean, a straight line that leads him right off the front of the stage, over a chair, the table, another chair.

"My woman!" He dips her almost to the ground, and Chevy and I sidestep before we're a part of the sloppy-drunk reunion suddenly taking place.

Our group has started dispersing through the club. Most know either Liam's frat brothers or the few cousins from Keaton's side. People watch the dancers on the smaller stage and lounge around, catching up with each other. I scan them all, searching for one in particular but not seeing him anywhere.

By now, Ford has reached us. I expect to be handed off from one brother to another, but before it happens, my feet leave the ground. Dane swoops me up, coming from I don't know where.

In the same motion, he hitches my legs up around him and crashes his lips down on mine. My curiosity about him at the airport? Gone. Dane will kiss me how he wants to kiss me without any concern about anyone else's give-a-damn. Except for mine. But I don't care near as much as I thought I would. He tastes like bourbon, and I'm drunk the second his tongue plunges into my mouth.

As he carries me toward the bar, I cradle his face in my hands. His lips leave mine, and his teeth immediately dig into his bottom one. "Filthy party-crasher. How am I supposed to bachelor with you here, tasting like a fucking dream?"

"It's not my fault you left out the details of your night."

"Two words, baby. Dance class." He nips at my jaw and sets me on a stool. Barely half-open, his glassy eyes gaze into mine.

"You're trashed."

His head bounces in something resembling a nod. "Wasted."

"I've never seen you drunk before."

"Well then"—he reaches for a drink beside me—"you're in for a treat because I'm a delight."

"I can tell," I say.

A smooth smile forms, and he tips the glass toward me in offering. "Be drunk with me. We'll get fucked up, and when we go home, I'll hold your hair and let you have the toilet while I puke in the bathtub."

I laugh, taking the glass from his hand. "This is a terrible proposition."

"Oh, it will be awful," he says, waving at the bartender for another. "We'll wake up in the morning, tangled up on the bathroom floor, absolutely miserable and swearing we'll never put ourselves through it again."

"Why do it in the first place then?"

He grows serious, skimming his hand over my arm. "Because it's what should have happened a year ago. But I showed up too late, and you were in too much of a rush to go."

It feels like something I should have remembered without him telling me. That one year ago I walked out of the bar as he walked in. Our lives passed without either of us realizing they were already intertwined.

"I sip whiskey," I say. "If you want to get me drunk, you'll want tequila."

"I want." Dane swipes the glass from my hand and finishes it. "And this time, you're not leaving this fucking bar without me."

FOUR SHOTS INTO OUR NIGHT of redemption, Dane disappears on me. Chevy has taken over his barstool and is surprisingly on board with someone he only just met plying me with booze.

"You're supposed to watch out for me," I say, playing with the tiny straw in his drink. "My brother-cousin or some shit."

He laughs once and shakes his head. "The second he steps out of line, I'm there, sister-cuz. Until then, I'm going to enjoy the show."

"Show?"

Chewing on the straw, Chevy tips his head toward the stage. The girl ballad cousin Stephanie was singing has faded out, and I spin my stool around. Dane's onstage, swinging the microphone around by the cord. Suspicious, I squint at the guy wearing an ugly olive beanie in May.

He winks. And then the music kicks on. A chord everyone knows accompanied by drum hits fills every corner of the room, repeating to the opening *da-da-dada-da* of "Bennie and the Jets."

Oh no.

"Fuck yes!" Lincoln shouts, moving from underneath a dancer.

He dashes for the stage along with Liam and Keaton.

The burn should rise in my cheeks when Dane brings the microphone to his mouth, but I can't stop smiling. I blame the alcohol and not the way he looks at me with every, "*B-B-B-Bennie.*"

In the middle of his performance, he hands the microphone off to Liam and jumps off the stage. He drags me off the stool and holds me close, swaying to the rest of the song. I never want him to let me go and blame the alcohol for that as well. It has nothing to do with any of it though. Every shiver and moment since we've met has belonged to him. Even when I didn't want it to.

"You've never called me Bennie before."

He chuckles, gliding his hands further down my back. "I've never made an ass of myself on a regular basis for someone either, but here we are."

LATER, WE'RE AT A TABLE with half a dozen other people. They talk while Dane and I stare at each other. I've tasked myself with remembering him from the bar even if I have to make it up. I looked up and smiled a thank-you. His gaze slid down me, and his teeth worked into his bottom lip by the time it returned to mine. Our eyes held longer than they should have, and when I stumbled from not paying attention to where I was going, he caught my arm.

My mind loses focus on the task then, filling in what would have happened if I'd stayed. More extended looks, his hand on my thigh, the two of us leaving together and screwing in his truck because neither of us would have taken the other home.

"When you look at me like that, it makes me hard," he says.

I lay my arm on the table and my head on my arm. "Convenient since I was thinking about you inside me."

Again, Dane finishes the drink in his hand, only instead of telling me I'm not leaving the bar without him, he proves it.

WE MAKE IT THROUGH HIS front door before undressing each other. His keys skid across the counter when he tosses them, jangling to the floor. He collapses onto the couch and pulls me on top of him. I straddle him, on my knees with him pressed between my legs.

"Condoms are in the bedroom," he says, not taking his mouth off mine. "Nightstand. Drawer."

"Okay."

But our movements mismatch the conversation. I lift onto my knees, and Dane drags me back down, letting out a groan as I sink onto him, all the way down.

"I missed this last night." His arm wraps my waist as I start to move against him. "I missed you—fuck, I miss you every night," he says.

I miss him, too, but it comes out in a moan.

He thrusts up into me, slower than I thought he would, each drawn out like they mean more. The same more that he slips between words unlike anyone else can. The more in his eyes when he looks at me sometimes. The way he's staring at me now with my palms against his chest and his heart beating wildly beneath them. He grabs the back of my neck, bringing my face to his. Our lips rub together, not kissing but sharing air and drinking each other in.

"I love you," he rasps.

As if he feels the panic race through me, his grip at the nape of my neck tightens, so I can't pull away. He cups the side of my face with the other, and I can't run, even though every instinct inside me surges to do so. All I can do is be there with him, his hips pushing up to fill me and his eyes pouring out the more.

"You shouldn't. I'm a train wreck." It's a warning, albeit a short one part of me wants him to ignore.

"It doesn't matter," he says. "I love you anyway."

Breathing through what feels like my hardest confession yet, I rest my forehead on his. "I love you too."

We're both panting when I smash my lips to his, afraid of what else might spill out of me. I brace on his shoulders with my hands in his hair and ride him faster. He growls in response and grabs my hips. When he flips me over onto the couch, I gasp into his open mouth. He reclaims control and slowly thrusts so he can watch me come undone beneath him. My body curls around his. I hold on to him inside and out. As I cry out, he drives into me harder before he shudders and buries deep.

I'm shaking as he relaxes. We stay quiet while we recover, him breathing hard against my neck until my chest rises slower. After a minute, his lips find mine, kissing them and then smiling against them. And then he tightens his hold on me and rolls us off the couch and onto the floor.

"Dane!"

But I'm laughing as I land on top of him. He drags a blanket down to spread over us, and I cuddle into him. I fall asleep with my face nuzzled against his neck. We're drunk and tangled in each other's arms on the floor, like he said we'd be—how he thinks we were meant to be all along.

Last year, I walked across the stage, stripped out of my cap and gown, and declared myself a week away from freedom. Nothing else stood between me and leaving—no more reasons to stay.

That's what I was celebrating the night I was supposed to meet Liam's cousin. The man Keaton had claimed I would fall in love with and who would make me want the white dress and a house full of belongings I wouldn't want to ever move again. Dane Masters is the real reason I left the bar early, desperate for none of those things to happen.

But here we are.

-21-
Rehearsal

A PIPE BURSTS IN THE realtor's office a few days before I'm supposed to leave for Phoenix for the wedding. I make sure to get Maggie an extra few brown-spotted bananas and drive down early to surprise Keaton. It gives me an entire week in town to help with last-minute preparations. Dane fully approves of the change of plans and kidnaps me not long after I get there. Five days straight of each other will be the most we've gotten, and I think we're determined to become sick of each other.

The day of the rehearsal I spend with Keaton at the venue. We walk in with our overnight bags, leaving the other six bags of makeup, hair supplies, tape—both Scotch and body—and everything else we could ever need for Liam to carry. The bridal suite is enormous, an entire room for Keaton and a pull-out couch in the living room for me.

Liam will be in a series of cabins with the groomsmen and ushers and an assortment of other wedding guests. Dane has already devised a plan to scale the building. I'm not mad at the idea, but I think the pull-out will get a little crowded when Keaton has a moment of panic in the middle of the night.

We unload our bags and lie on her bed for a twenty-minute meditation in which she repeats her mantra for the weekend, "I am a classy bitch and won't slap anyone."

Then we head to the garden where she'll say her vows in twenty-four hours. As breathtaking as the sight was a year ago when we visited, to see it in all its pre-wedding glory is divine. The arches wrapped with vines and flowers and a white fabric runner laid down the aisle with white padded chairs on either side.

Our afternoon consists of wrapping ribbon around candelabras and putting bows on the end chairs. When we head inside, we have another moment of shock at the ballroom. The tables are set, stemware perfectly spaced. Accents of deep purple and black dance around the room in the table runners and napkins, and even the potpourri in the bathrooms matches her wedding colors. We add in the centerpieces we put together at Christmas, the fresh flowers on their way in the morning.

It's only as we're standing in the center of the dance floor with a gorgeous chandelier above us that Keaton sucks in a deep breath, holding it until I think she'll pass out. When they met, Keaton told me she hated Liam. He was a sexy Clark Kent in glasses, and she wanted nothing to do with him. She told me the same the second time she saw him. But now, she blows out the breath and smiles, looking around at everything he put together for her.

"He's kind of perfect, huh?" she says.

"No," I tell her. "He's completely perfect for you."

I tug her toward the door and shut off the lights as we leave. I don't think I'm supposed to, given people are still running in and out, but it feels symbolic, so I do it anyway.

With Patrick and Joyce helping the grandparents on their side settle in, Keaton and I are free to go back to the suite to change. I've been saving a specific red dress for rehearsal.

Keaton eyes it when I pull it on. "Since when do you do cutouts?"

I twist to see the bare skin on my back and shrug.

"Well, do them more often." She runs a finger along her lip line to clean up her lipstick.

When she's nervous, Keaton turns into a little old lady. We need to rush down to the gardens with her insisting we're late even though we arrive half an hour before anyone else. Except for Liam. He's perched on a chair, tapping his brown loafer on the grass.

"Where have you been?" he asks. "I was getting worried." His lips twitch, giving way to a smug smile when she checks the time.

Ugh. Disgustingly perfect.

We spend the extra time moving things a few feet over one way and adjusting them back. If Keaton needs to work off her nervous energy with mindless organization, the least I can do is shift things around a few dozen times. By the time she has everything perfect—and precisely the way it was when we started—a few people have wandered in.

I, as always, search for Dane's face. Unlike Keaton, he has a tendency to show up whenever, so I check my phone. The text waits for me.

> *So late. Don't let Keaton kill me when I get there.*

Given Liam's frown, he received a similar message.

Keaton walks over a few minutes later, repeating her mantra with an extra edge to her tone. "The best man can't even make it on time."

"I'll stand in."

We both turn at the sound of Ford's voice.

"Unless you think I need to practice walking Grandma up and down the aisle more than once."

When she hesitates, giving a quick look to check with me, I nod. "We both know if I don't have someone to steer me the right way, I'll get lost."

Ford smiles and offers his elbow, and I grab hold, letting him lead me away. We hang around the archway at the back of the garden while everyone else is organized and instructed.

"So," he says, "Colorado? What on Earth prompted you to go there?"

"Hey, I can Rocky Mountain with the best of them. I learned to fish a few weeks ago when Dane visited."

Technically, I only held the pole. He put the worm on the hook, cast, and reeled in when I squealed and dropped the pole at the first tug on the line. So, when Ford quirks a questioning brow, I pretend to adjust the strap on my heel.

As we're being told to line up, Keaton bounces her way over. She squeezes my hands before she rushes back with Patrick to hide behind the archway for authenticity. The other bridesmaids and groomsmen start down the aisle, but before our turn, Ford glances over his shoulder. My skin prickles when his smile slips. I don't need to look to know why, but I do anyway. Bentley strides in, late for his usher training, his hair pushed back and focus on me from the first step through the arch.

I drag Ford down the aisle, not keeping the spacing between us and the others. We part ways at the end, and I take my place off to the side. After Keaton and Patrick join us at the front, the officiant requests we practice the entrance again. She squints at me, probably having labeled me the troublemaker, but I own it, giving a hair flip on my way past.

By the time we get back to the starting point, Chevy has steered Bentley in the other direction. Ford and I reset with everyone else, and once again, we wait our turn. He's keeping his distance now. I contribute it to a death glare issued by his brother, but then I catch a glimpse of Dane walking through the parking lot. He combs a hand through his hair and hugs Keaton's shoulders on his way past, saying something to charm her scowl into a half-smile.

Ford steps aside when he reaches us. The bachelor party must have bonded them because they exchange a nod, and Dane slaps him on the back.

"Thanks for keeping her upright for me."

"Careful," he says, backing away. "She pulls to the left."

Being the bad girl of the wedding party, I start to back-talk, but Patrick clears his throat as our cue to go. Dane cocks his elbow out for me, and we head down the aisle.

"Where were you this time?" I ask.

"With the old man." He glances to the side where his grandpa is pacing, on the phone. "I needed to run a few things by him."

We're walking too slow, dragging out our time together. If that isn't enough to earn me another chastising look from the officiant, when we reach the end, Dane dips down to kiss me.

"I've really missed that dress," he says. His eyes lower to my cleavage, one side of his mouth perking, and then he kisses me again before he goes to stand beside Liam.

Dane Masters, the gray-eyed rebel to my blue-eyed badass, breaking rules left and right.

-22-
I Do

AFTER WE'VE RUN THROUGH THE ceremony once and practiced walking until I'm rid of my defiant ways, we head for a veranda set for dinner. Not all of Keaton's family is in attendance tonight, but the core group of cousins she grew up with is representing. Liam's sister flew back from North Carolina. Her little girl is an absolute doll and completely in love with Keaton, mirroring her every gesture.

"I could never do that," I say. "Raise a human."

Dane rests his arm on the back of my chair, his hand rubbing my shoulder. I like how he always touches me. No matter where we are, some part of him wants to feel a part of me.

On the opposite side of the room from our table, the entire garage is seated together. Bentley rubs his jaw. He's been watching us since we sat down, his brothers doing the same to him. They won't give him a chance to pull anything, a promise reinforced when Chevy looks up and winks at me.

"I can get on board with that," Dane says, bringing my attention back. "I've managed to keep from screwing myself up, but put me in charge of an entire life? They'll be fucked."

With him being one of the stablest people I know, I disagree. A house, a career, secure in himself—if anyone should be reproducing and bringing up the next generation, it's someone like him. I think about telling him such but stop myself. He might agree.

The servers clear the plates, and people begin migrating toward their rooms for the night or to the bar, which is staying set up for a while longer. We intend on a stop at the latter after he drops his suit off in his cabin. He's sharing one with Liam. When he flips the lights on, the place is a disaster. Neither of us bats an eye, though, having seen Liam's apartment before Keaton got her hands on it.

"The guy is serious about living one last night of the single life." Dane hangs his suit in the closet while I uncover Liam's from the floor.

I hook the hanger next to Dane's, and he catches me before I turn. He runs his hands around to my backside, grinning down at me. "How long before you think he'll come back from walking Keaton to your room?"

I drape my arms over his shoulders and purse my lips, pretending to think it over. "Long enough."

"Impossible," he says. "I never get enough." He drags the tip of his nose over mine, his hands creeping lower. "Weekend trips and even the last five days…" His brows draw in, his voice a slow rasp that travels through my core. "I always want more time. More you." His mouth covers mine, the feeling behind it matching his words.

But his lips stall, and he groans, letting me go to fish his phone out of his pocket. "Keaton's looking for you."

"What?" I grab my phone out of his other pocket, where I stashed it earlier. "Why didn't she—"

Dead. Which means she'll more than likely have a stack of notes waiting when I get back.

"Well, I guess we're back to me sneaking onto your balcony later," he says, leading me out of the cabin.

"You could come in the normal way, and we'll just be quiet." I wait for him to lock the door before we head for the main building.

He walks down the path behind me, slipping his arms around me and holding me against him. "Normal. Quiet. No part of that sentence sounds fun."

I laugh, and he sighs into my hair.

"I love that sound."

That sound cuts off when the outline of the person coming toward us slows. The posts lining the path emit enough light I recognize the shape. Bentley is alone. No brothers. No aunts or uncles to put on an act for. And his hand is running up and down his jaw.

"Shit," I mutter, straightening up.

Given the way Dane's hold on me tightens, he knows who it is too. He spotted Bentley with his brothers during the rehearsal, and we shared a look. His eyes asked, and mine answered, but neither of us said anything.

Bentley stops in front of us, taking up the center of the path. It makes him the gatekeeper, an interaction with him required to pass. "Hey, Lex."

"Where are the others?" I ask.

He shrugs. "Around." He's far less interested in what I have to say than he is with the person behind me. "You forgot to introduce me earlier."

"*Forget* isn't the right word," I say, but then I act like a civil human being despite my better judgment. "Dane, this is Keaton's cousin, Bentley."

I glance over my shoulder, but Dane's locked in on Bentley. When I look back at Bentley, he's widened his stance. The two show down, no words, just hard stares and clenched jaws.

"Keaton's waiting," I say, my hand finding Dane's.

Bentley's eyes drop to them, then shoot back to mine as I start walking again. I step off into the recently watered grass to avoid going any closer to our roadblock, but Dane doesn't bend, walking straight on. His shoulder bumps Bentley's. I think it will set him off, the night erupting into flying fists. Bentley sidesteps, though, offering Dane all the room he wants to pass.

It shouldn't be so easy. I know this, and yet I relax when Dane pulls me against his side. He presses a kiss to the side of my head, calmer than I expected him to be. At least, he is until the strike I should have been expecting.

"What," Bentley says from behind us, "no kiss goodbye this time?"

Dane's arm drops from my waist as he turns. "What the fuck did you just say?"

"Dane." I grab his hand again, but he's not listening.

He jerks away from me, already stalking toward Bentley. "You want to try that again?"

Dane stops with only an inch between them. Bentley's slightly shorter, but he tips his chin up to make up the difference, a cocky grin in place.

I've broken up plenty of fights between the brothers over the years. With them, they still needed to put up with one another at the end, so after a few hits, they would stop with or without interference. But when I reach Dane and Bentley, I realize it won't end with back slaps and splitting a six-pack.

"My girl—"

"Not your girl," Dane says. "Not at Christmas and sure as hell not now."

Bentley's eyes dart to me as I latch on to Dane's arm, urging him to take a step back. He looks surprised I told Dane about his asshole move, like I would have wanted to keep the moment for myself, and a hint of torment clouds his eyes. Hurt with Bentley means he lashes out, and when his gaze shifts back to Dane, I notice the fist clenched at his side.

The next few seconds give me mental whiplash. Bentley draws his arm back, and Dane pushes me out of the way, and then all three of them are on the ground even though there should only be two. The extra body belongs to Ford, throwing himself in the mix out of nowhere. He tries to separate them without much luck. Then Lincoln is behind me, gripping my shoulders to drag me away from the mess of punches, while Chevy yanks his oldest brother up by the shirt collar and ducks one last swing.

"You done?" he yells, shoving him backward.

Bentley swipes the back of his hand over the blood dripping off his lip and holds out the other palm in submission but keeps his attention chained to Dane, helping Ford off the ground. Fighting out of Lincoln's hold, I run to them and throw myself at Dane. He has a red lump on his cheek. Nowhere near as obvious as Ford's already-swelling eye. Still, he checks me over like I was the one in the middle of the brawl.

I look back for Chevy, but my gaze meets Bentley's. It holds until he smirks, and I fucking lose it. I tear away from Dane to unleash every ounce of aggravation I've bottled up toward him. Less than a step and I leave the ground, over Dane's shoulder and being hauled away.

"Good call," Lincoln says as we pass.

While I agree that it would have ended badly, I kick at him to prove the point not to fuck with me in the future.

As we gain distance, a wall of brothers surrounds Bentley.

"You can let me down," I tell Dane, watching them go toward the cabins.

"No. I can't."

I sigh and wiggle in protest. "I won't go after him, I swear."

"Yeah," he says, readjusting his arm to better cover my upper thighs, "but I might."

My attempts to get down stop. If he needs to haul me off to keep from murdering my ex, I shouldn't be difficult.

We reach the veranda where we ate, and he lowers me to the ground. In the patio lights, I see the bruise forming on his cheek.

"Keaton's going to freak," he says, stretching out his knuckles.

My stomach sinks. I didn't think about what their fight would mean for tomorrow. Three members of the wedding party will have bruised faces with hundreds of pictures to be taken.

"You okay?" he asks.

I nod, forcing a smile. "Hope you don't mind wearing cover-up."

"Marco once messaged me that contouring would bring me to an all-new level of hot. About time I test his theory." His mouth perks up, and my smile turns genuine.

When we stop at the suite, he grazes the pad of his thumb over my bottom lip before he bends down to kiss me. "We still on for the balcony later?"

"No, but you can text me when you're at the door."

He hands me my phone out of his pocket. "Better charge it. Otherwise, I'm Romeo-ing."

Doubting he'll hesitate if I don't answer, I beeline for my charger when I get into the room.

Keaton marches out of her bedroom and smacks a stack of sticky notes on my forehead. "Of all days, Bennett Ross."

I pluck them off, sorting through a list of reasons to panic that she de-escalated on her own. "I'm sorry." I collapse onto the couch and toss the mini-mems onto the table on one end. "Bentley picked a fight with Dane."

"What?" She pulls her feet up under her, sitting on the cushion beside me.

I wince, looking over at her. My best friend, ready to get married now having to deal with the results of someone else's bullshit. "Ford has a black eye, Bentley has a split lip, and Dane's cheek is going to bruise."

Her face falls, and her throat bobs in a hard swallow. "Oh."

It breaks my heart to see the tears welling in her eyes, and I pull her into a hug. "We'll figure something out. Who knows? Maybe they won't look so bad in the morning."

"Yeah, Bennett." Liam stands in the doorway, shaking his head with a look of disgust. "And maybe you won't fuck anything else up between now and then."

"Liam," Keaton says, her tone short.

"You think it's my fault?" A jolt of irritation spikes through me, and I push off the couch. "Bentley was being an ass."

"Bentley is always an ass."

Unarguable.

"So then, please enlighten me. How exactly am I to blame?"

"How?" Liam steps farther into the room, the usual joking undertone he carries with me gone. "Dane's not the guy who lets someone like Bentley get to him. He knows who's worth a fight and who's not. At least, he did until you decided to play relationship with him."

"Play relationship?" The words come out in a shocked breath, and I blink at him, more hurt than I'll let on. "You think I'm *playing*? I love him."

He scoffs, shaking his head again. "Do you even know what that means?"

"Liam," Keaton warns.

After a second, he glances behind me to her on the couch. "No, she needs to hear this." Then he's back to me, and I want to shrink, smaller, invisible. "You had no problems running off after graduation. You left Keaton, Joyce, Patrick, me—everyone who's been there for you—and you never even blinked. If not for the wedding, how many times would you have visited?" He only pauses a second. "Once?"

I should defend myself, but I can't. Once might be pushing it if I were given more time away, more chances for excuses. Instead, I pinch my thumb between the nail of the other and my index finger until it dulls his lashing.

"She missed you every fucking day, Bennett, and when the wedding's over, you'll abandon her all over again. Leave her here to wonder if she'll see you again. And what about Dane?"

He lowers his gaze for the first time, and I swallow back the tears that have been stabbing for a chance at air. Real concern paints his face when he looks up, but it's not for me.

"He'll follow you. Maybe not at first, but it will happen. He'll give up everything for you. But we both know, you won't give up a damn thing for him. You won't settle down or stop living out of boxes. You're selfish and blind to how it affects everyone around you." He pauses before he says, "You'll break him and then leave him behind. Just like your mother did to you."

The last one hits like a brick to the face, the regret on his instantaneous.

"Bennett, I—"

"Get out." Keaton shoots off the couch and runs at him while the blow seeps through me. "Get. The fuck. Out!" She shoves him toward the door, her hands on his chest, driving him backward. "You don't get to talk to her like that. She's nothing like that woman. You have no idea who she is!"

Liam lets her push him all the way out with minimal resistance. His panic-ridden face disappears when she slams the door, and Keaton presses her forehead to the wood, her shoulders heaving. I imagine him in the hallway, doing the same with only a few inches between them. Maybe I should be mad at his words, but he was being honest. Hurtful and blunt but more honest with me than I ever am with myself.

"He's right." My voice is quiet, weak with truth, but it's enough that she turns around. I breathe, trying not to choke on what I've been avoiding the entire week while the tears freely fall. "I won't be back for a long time. Maybe I'll come for Christmas, but…" I trail off.

I don't need a reflection to remind me that I'm my mother's daughter. She left to find a missing piece, and I've been seeking the same one since then.

The closest thing I have to family stares at me for the longest time, and then she shrugs. "So?"

I open my mouth but close it without a response, confused by her chill.

She notices me struggling and rolls her eyes. "I've known you were going to leave since we were kids. But I've also known you'll always be there if I need you. I mean, look at the last year. Anytime I asked, you were here." She passes me to my phone on the cushion and plugs it into the wall charger. "And if the roles are ever reversed, then I'll fly to Maine or Spain or wherever you are because you're my forever-bitch."

When she faces me again, I throw my arms around her. "I'd never go to Spain," I say.

"Right. You hate sangria."

I laugh-sob into her shoulder and squeeze her tighter. "I'm sorry. For Bentley and Dane and ruining your wedding."

"Honestly"—she pulls back—"I've been hoping for a disaster all day. I read something about how if nothing goes wrong for your wedding, it means you'll have a bad marriage."

"That's ridiculous," I say.

She nods. "Probably, but now, I won't have to worry about it for the next fifty years."

The soundest logic I've ever heard.

She sighs, her gaze drifting toward the door. "What are we doing about my asshole fiancé?"

"We forgive him." I swipe my fingers under her eyes while she does the same to me, clearing the tears and smudged makeup. "He's put up with a lot of crazy so far, and he was bound to snap eventually. And now that I've blown the chance for the marriage imploding, he has a lot of years left to endure."

"I kind of want to make him sweat it out for a while."

While I respect her methods, I shake my head. "Torture the guy for your first anniversary, Keats."

I step out of the way, and she marches for the door, a little fast for someone who, a second ago, wanted to make him suffer. But a thump turns us both around. A Liam-sized shadow stands on the balcony. Fucking Masters men. Dane and Liam might be cousins, but they sure as hell think like twins.

AFTER A MUSHY APOLOGY FROM Liam, I give him and Keaton space to make up however they so choose. She's very specific about him leaving before midnight, so I don't go far. I follow a different path to a man-made lake where water shoots from a fountain in the middle, the streams dancing before they splash onto the otherwise still surface.

The sky reflects in the water. The stars remind me of the Reynolds' living room, my safe night sky.

"Couldn't stay away?"

I smile at Dane's voice. "You're the one sneaking up on me."

He steps behind me, and I spin around. He's changed into a T-shirt, his sweatpants hanging low on his hips, so a gap of skin shows. I run my hand over the trail of hair disappearing under the top, and he presses me against the stone wall I was leaning on. His hand creeps to the bottom of my dress, inching it up my thigh.

"We doing this?" he asks.

I tip my head in question, and he pushes the fabric higher, his eyes flashing to the lake behind me.

"No," I say, but he steps back and drags his shirt over his head. "Dane."

He pulls me to him, cupping my face when he kisses me. "I love it when you say my name like that. Now get in the water, and I'll make you say it the other way I love."

Leaving me shaking my head, he heads for the water's edge and strips off his sweatpants and briefs. When he glances back to grin at me before walking into the water, I shiver—another one that belongs to him.

I am selfish. I run away and avoid. I'm a broken mess with little chance of anything sticky holding me together for long. But I am in love with Dane. I know I love him.

I do.

-23-
Don't Want

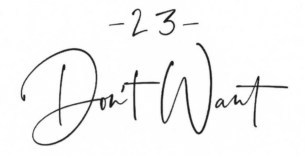

Dr. Faulk was my favorite therapist. She listened and gave thought to every answer and recommendation. During one of our sessions, she asked me the last time I had told my mother I loved her. It took a minute to remember. The memory wanted to stay buried with the others. Avoid, avoid, avoid, and whatnot. Then she asked the last time she'd told me. The rest of the session passed in silence while I tried to come up with not just the final time, but also a single instance.

A week later, I randomly remembered while in a checkout line. I wanted to tell Dr. Faulk about it, about how much it'd hurt. She wasn't in her office when I got there for my appointment, but the crime scene tape was still on the sidewalk out front. She'd taken an early lunch and walked off the roof. I cried on her overstuffed couch for an hour, wondering the last time someone had said those three words to her.

I still think of her now and then. Once, when I was having a particularly terrible day, I went to her grave, hoping she'd listen to me one more time. Hours later, I left. I felt lighter than I had in a long time.

I haven't been to therapy since.

THE MORNING FLIES BY, FULL of smiles and tears and pictures. I consider reactivating my Instagram. I don't, but I really mull it over for a second.

Keaton turns in front of the mirror half a dozen times, the dress more perfect than any other time I've seen it on her. She wears her hair up with a few curls framing her face, a pearl necklace draped around her neck, and the smile of a woman as ridiculously in love as the man she's marrying.

With her superstitions holding firm, we won't have pictures until after the ceremony, and since her nerves are keyed up, she finishes getting ready an hour before the ceremony. I set her up in a chair with her phone so that she can text me if she enters into a last-second spiral of panic. Then I slip out, in search of Dane.

Cousin Steph offered to track down Bentley and Ford to hide the results of last night's after-hours activities. With enough concealer, we should be able to keep the family speculation train from picking up speed.

As I step off the elevator, I see Dane and Liam's grandpa in the hall. Other than what Dane's told me, I know little about the man. We met for a split second at the engagement dinner, exchanging a few words. Last night, he spent most of dinner in and out on his phone. Passing him, I smile, only for a scowl to cut through me—harsh and pointed. I don't remember much from our interaction before, but I doubt I did anything worthy of him serving a look like that.

I'm almost to the double doors that lead to the veranda when a hand grabs my wrist from behind. Dane turns me, his mouth seeking mine.

"What if you ruin my lipstick?" I ask, not caring in the least.

"Then I'll get to watch you put it on again." He backs us in the direction I came from.

"Where are we going?"

Checking up and down the hallway, he pushes open the door to the ballroom. He keeps me close, both of us unsure of my footing in the dark room. We weave through tables to the far side, our destination one of the bathrooms.

"I thought we were doing this in your cabin."

"Too many people in there," he says on our way in. "I wanted you all to myself."

I turn around at the sink and hold up my concealer. "Ready to become next-level hot?"

"Are you ready?" Dane sets me on the counter. He pushes my legs open to stand between them and leans down, so I can reach his cheek. He looks incredible, his dress shirt open at the neck where he's missing his tie. His hair is in a sexy, tousled mess I can run my fingers through.

I work quickly to touch up his cheek, his palm gliding over the bare skin of my leg the entire time.

"As much as I like the red, I dig purple too."

"Wine," I correct him on the dress color. "Finished."

He straightens to see the mirror, then drops back to my level. "I look exactly the same."

I shrug, setting the makeup next to me by my bouquet. Keaton insisted I not let it out of my sight until after pictures. "I can't have you outshining Keats on her big day."

He smiles, bringing his lips to mine in my favorite type of kiss, his mouth lazy against mine. I hitch my legs around him, pulling him with me until my back hits the cool mirror. Tomorrow, I'll leave, putting five hundred miles between us. The rest of our day and night and most of the morning is spoken for, so I want whatever I can get of him now. Dane shows no objections, rubbing his erection against me through his suit pants. He moans, kissing across my jaw.

"Stay longer," he says, his voice husky. "A day, a week."

I tilt my chin up when his lips move to the hollow of my neck. "I can't."

"Then ask me to go with you."

"*You* can't," I remind him. "You have work."

The way he grinds against me is driving me crazy.

I grasp the back of his hair while he whispers in my ear, "Fuck work. I'll throw my shit in the truck, and we'll go somewhere new. Wherever you want. I already told the old man I'm leaving."

He stops pressing into me as he reaches for the fly on his suit pants. It gives my love-drunk brain time to process what he said, and my eyes flutter open.

"Why would you do that?"

I got lipstick on his collar, a print of rose pink on a harsh backdrop of white. I want to wipe it away, but my arms are heavy, all of me really.

"Because I'm tired of not getting enough." His lips leave my skin, and he looks up, cupping my face in his hands. "I don't want the company if it means saying goodbye anymore. I want you and me. Us. This." There's that sense of more in the velvety pause he takes to kiss me with too-soft lips, more in his eyes behind long lashes, and in the touch of his thumb brushing my cheek. "I want it all the time," he says. "Every day."

I feel a warmth in my chest from him, but then a tightness takes over. Liam's words from last night replay in my head an impossible number of times, given the single breath I've taken. Everything is moving too fast, and I shake my head, trying to understand what is happening right now. Dane has deep roots holding him here—family, a promise to his mom, their memories on a mantel.

"What about your house?" I ask.

"I'll sell it," he says, his lips turning up. "It doesn't make sense to keep it, so once we—"

"No." My voice sounds dry when I cut him off, the air dragging in and out of my body, but I can't let him leave for me.

Dane's brows draw in, his mouth dropping at the corners. "No what?"

"I don't want you to."

And then it all slows to a crawl. He studies me, like maybe I haven't finished, but the seconds draw out without another word passing between us. The hint of confusion in his eyes gives way to something else. Hurt, irritation, and then the look.

"You don't want me to sell the house, or"—he steps back, so no part of him touches me anymore—"you don't want me to move to be with you?"

His breath stays smooth and even while he waits for an answer, mine struggling to find a rhythm. Dane has kept his word by not asking me to stay, but his offer to go feels worse. Unexpected. A reckless choice for the heart.

"He'll follow you."

"He'll give up everything for you."

Liam warned me. His timeline was just off. Dane's willing to tear apart the life he has, only to build one with me that won't last. And it won't. I'm too broken to make those types of promises, and when he realizes what a mistake he's made, he'll have nothing to go back to. Then he'll be broken, too, missing pieces of his own. What kind of a person would let that happen to him?

I've kept my eyes on his as long as I can, and I have to look away. The florist missed a thorn on one of the dark purple roses in my bouquet, a single spike, poking through the black lace wrapped around the stems. I press the pad of my finger onto the point and watch the indent deepen, the pain gradually becoming too much.

"Bennett." Dane pulls my hand away before it punctures the skin, and I look up, burying the tears. "Tell me which one you don't want."

We're back to don't-wants, but this one is the most difficult to say.

"Both," I tell him. "I don't want any of it."

Part 2

Dane

-24-
Just Visiting

SHE SMILES AS THE PHOTOGRAPHER zooms in.

Click.

The bouquet of dark purple flowers, roses and lilies that she threw at my head not even an hour ago, rests by her hand as she signs the marriage license.

Click, click.

Liam and Keaton's ceremony was flawless. The year of groans from his office and him rushing into mine to ask which color swatch he liked better is officially at an end. If only it were the only thing over.

Once finished, Bennett hands me the pen. Our skin meets, followed by our eyes, and then she looks away. She always looks away first. I fell in love with how her eyes divert mid-blink and the blush that creeps up her neck after. I was all the way down before I even realized how hard I could fall.

Click.

I lean over, signing my name and ignoring the brush of my arm over hers. Last night, I was inside her, making her eyes roll back in her head while she came on me in the lake. And now...

One more *click*, and I drop the pen.

"We done?" I ask.

The photographer frowns at my tone but nods.

"Great," I say. Then, under my breath, I mutter, "Now get me the fuck away from her."

Not Even an Hour Ago...

"YOU DON'T WANT ANY OF it?"

I stare at her, Bennett Ross, the frustrating woman who crashed into my chest, then burrowed the rest of the way in. She set a record pace, more of her in my head than myself at times, and now, she claims she doesn't want *any of it*.

"Why can't things stay the way they are?" she asks. She reaches for the rose stem again, screwing with a lonely thorn. "You come to visit often enough. We could—"

"I don't want to be a visitor in your life, Bennett."

I want to be it.

A drip from the faucet beside her is the only thing cutting through the intrusive feeling of everything she's refusing to say. I wait, willing her to let me in. Sometimes, it works. She'll glance up, and I'll see the thoughts winding through her, and then she'll open the gates to everything behind the doubt and cautiousness surrounding her. But right now, she keeps her eyes down, not chancing a connection between us.

"I don't want to do plane tickets and six-hour drives forever," I tell her. "I need to know if this is going somewhere. If there's more."

Another few drips pass with us locked in a moment between here and there before she looks up. "I don't know."

I blow out an exasperated breath, raking my hands through my hair and tugging at the roots. I've always been left as the one to move us forward, dragging her along. And I'm damn tired of forcing her in a direction I'm not even sure she wants half the time.

"Well, maybe it's time you fucking figure it out."

Her eyes narrow, the words sharp before they leave her mouth. "Maybe you shouldn't assume you know what I want."

"Should I wait for you to tell me instead? Because if that were the case, I'd probably still be getting laid on a regular basis by bar chicks instead of stuck, jerking myself off."

A ball of flowers launches at my head. I duck, letting them crash against the wall behind me. They hit the floor, and Bennett's off the counter, on her way to retrieve them. Worry overshadows what I imagine is the urge to slap me.

I scoop down, beating her to the bouquet, and when I stand up, she grabs for it. I keep ahold of the bottom, the fucking thorn jabbing my palm.

"Show me this hasn't all been leading up to you walking away and not coming back," I say.

Her brilliant eyes glisten. "I can't," she says. "I'm so sorry, Dane."

Sorry. The way it sounds with a slight crack in her voice cuts deep. I have to resist the urge to close the space between us and hold her, to tell her there's nothing to apologize for and push away how I feel so I can keep her.

I shake my head, scrubbing a hand over my face. "So, where does that leave us, Bennett? Because I'm done pretending to be okay with you walking away from me."

Her answer takes too long, her feet already pointed at the door when she looks up at me.

And I know. I know right then we won't leave the bathroom together. She won't be sleeping in my arms tonight in my cabin after the reception. I won't write her sticky notes or drive to Colorado anymore.

A year ago, I was trying to screw her out of my system. Now I'm hopelessly in love, threatened with watching her leave yet again. Only this time, for good.

Seeing if a reset will change the tone—stop us from shifting back, back, back to a point I can't recognize us anymore—I try the words I started with. "Ask me to go with you."

And then Bennett ends it with one.

"No."

-25-
Cheers

THE NIGHT I WAS SUPPOSED to meet Liam at the bar, I smoked a cigarette before I went inside. I'd quit a few years back, but the liquor store across the street carried my old brand, and I was in no hurry for what felt like a forced setup with my cousin's girlfriend's roommate.

After I lit the only one I'd planned to smoke, I handed the rest of the pack to the homeless man sitting outside. We chatted until I fished out a couple bucks for him and headed for the bar.

The guy pushed open the door first. I sidestepped out of his way, grabbing the handle before it swung shut on the blonde following him. Even with her head down, I could safely say she was out of his league—the legs, the hips, the tits. She tripped, her heel catching on the metal strip of the threshold. I reached for her arm to help right her as she found her balance. A hand flew over her pouty mouth, her face tipping up enough to see how right I was.

And then she laughed, a little wild and sexy as hell.

I smiled for the first time since moving back to Phoenix. The second time was the next morning, watching her program her number into my phone. Third when I crawled out of the shower and immediately recorded the message to tell her what had been killing me not to say when she was in front of me.

Bennett Ross owned my ass before I knew her goddamn name.

MY HANDS ALREADY MISS HER skin by dinner. I wish she were seated closer. It would be torture but better than having Keaton and Liam between us. I'm next to my cousin on the happiest day of his life, contemplating kidnapping the maid of honor.

Psycho stalker. A term we've thrown around since the beginning, but the further I sink, the more viable the option. I once joked I would keep her in my basement. My mom's house doesn't have one.

I drain the champagne in front of me before I search listings in the area.

The DJ is eyeing our table from his booth in the corner of the ballroom. We're well on our way to the toasts. I drafted my best-man speech on my first plane ride to San Francisco. After my weekend with her, I rewrote it on my return flight. Every time I saw her, I added or tweaked it with new thoughts on love or ideas of what it means to want to share your life with someone. Not topics I typically pondered, but then again, I didn't think about a lot of things until Bennett.

Reaching for the bottle of Dom in front of Liam, I casually glance down the table, past Keaton, to the woman draining her own glass. She asked at least a dozen times to read my speech, but I couldn't bring myself to let her. And now, the paper in my front pants pocket feels like fire, seeping through the material and the skin and muscle and into my bone.

When the DJ brings over the mic, I stare at it like he's trying to hand me his dick, and his gaze shifts to Liam.

"Oh," my cousin says, "we're starting with the maid of honor."

The DJ apologizes for his mistake, even though Keaton explicitly told him time and time again that I would go first. While he moves down to give the mic to Bennett, Liam leans over, his teeth clenched in a forced smile.

"You look like you want to flip the table. Bennett's scanning for exits like she's planning a bank heist. Do I want to know what's going on with you two?"

"Nope," I say.

He has enough to deal with today without me loading on our drama.

I finish off another glass and refill both our flutes, pouring mine all the way to the top. I'll need to teeter on numb if I want to get through the next few minutes because I've just realized, after an opening joke, my entire speech is basically a fucking love letter to the woman who just told me to fuck off with my ideas of having *any of it*. Yeah, I can't let that one go.

Bennett pushes her chair back, putting forth an actual effort not to look at me when she stands. Keaton's giving me a wary glance sideways. People don't give her credit for how perceptive she is, and the tension in her face says she's pieced together enough.

"I never wanted a sister." Bennett's voice trembles. "And I definitely never wanted a brother." She shoots a narrow look at Liam, and a few guests chuckle when he flips her off. "But somehow, I wound up lucky enough to find both."

Even at the rate she's drinking, her cheeks are more flushed than they should be from the champagne. I follow her line of vision to a table toward the center. My grandpa gives her a patented Miles Masters warning glare, blaming her for my disinterest in the company he built from scratch. Across the table, my dad watches like a hawk, which means his wife does, too, the jealousy swelling.

Despite the unwanted attention, Bennett continues the speech I've heard a dozen times over the past week. It's on brand for her. Awkward pauses, a dry delivery that adds to the quiet humor hiding in the words, and all of it borders on emotional without fully diving into the feeling. The last one's her specialty. Almost there but never quite. Even saying I love you, she found a way to hold something back—hesitating like being loved by her was a threat.

Holding up her glass, she recites the last line and ends with a, "To Liam and Keats."

Everyone sips while she gulps it all down. Keaton wipes away another round of happy tears and stands to hug her, and Liam passes me the microphone.

"One down…" he mumbles.

I want to tell him no worries, but he might need to. I feel very little, slipping out the paper, unfolding it, and giving it a look. The first sentence sticks in my throat. It's a joke about Liam's unhealthy obsession with Amelia Earhart when we were kids and how Keaton dressed as her their first Halloween together. The easy part.

Clearing my throat, I scratch my head with the hand holding the mic, still staring at my speech in the other. Then I make the mistake of looking to my right. Bennett is watching, waiting with everyone else in the quiet ballroom.

Fuck it. I've thrown enough of myself at her feet tonight.

"Keaton said she'd end me if I wing my best-man speech, so…" I make a show of tucking my well-crafted words into my pocket. "Let's find out if she meant it."

Liam drops his head onto the table in front of him. His groan is too low for most to hear above the round of laughter coming from anyone who's ever met his new wife. I clap a hand on his shoulder and stare straight at Bennett, who's messing with the stem of her glass.

"A lot of people think of Liam and Keaton as the perfect couple," I say, my voice bouncing out of the speakers at the opposite end of the room. "Maybe they give off that impression, but I've experienced what few others have. Between the sweet moments and them going the extra step for each other is the ugly side of their relationship. And trust me, it's not something they want getting out there. They yell, pick at insecurities. I can't tell you how many times in the past year Liam has shown up at my door with a six-pack, begging me to give him shelter from her storm."

A tension floats in the air, no one brave enough to react. Keaton has settled back in her chair, arms across her chest.

I wink at her and continue, "But I've also seen the make-ups. The second one of them misses the other. The tears and forgiveness and promises to be better to one another. And they really work to follow through on those promises."

I drag my teeth over my bottom lip, trying like hell not to look at Bennett again. "Liam and Keaton are far from perfect, for each other or to each other, but they do have a relationship we can all learn from." I lose the battle and meet her gaze. "They don't run from the ugly or try to bury it. Instead, they love through the flaws and discover ways to make them fit. For Liam and Keaton, their ugly side only strengthens them, giving way to more sweet moments, more going the extra step … more of what makes this love worthy of the fight over any other." I look away from her first, for once, and lift my glass in the air to finish. "And because of them, I can't wait to find someone to be ugly with. Cheers."

I knock back my drink, toss the mic to the frat brother next to me, and head for the bar, in need of something stronger to get me through the rest of the night.

-26-
Pretending

I WAIT FOR THE BARTENDER with my back to the head table and thus the majority of the reception. He looks flustered by a gaggle of Keaton's cousins, all ordering cocktails at once. When I reach over for a bottle of scotch, he gives a nod. Permission to serve myself.

"You can't wait to find someone, huh?"

I close my eyes. After all these years, I would still consider jerking the wheel into oncoming traffic at the sound of Aubrey's voice.

I turn around with my usual greeting locked and loaded. "Why, Mrs. Masters, have you had work done?"

She has. Her lips are fuller than when I saw her at the office yesterday.

Aubrey cocks her head to the side. "Your speech made it sound like you're having girl trouble."

Uncorking the bottle, I shake my head. I might not have kept the undertones of the speech as subtle as I'd have liked, but fuck her for being the one to call me out on it.

"And you care?"

She shrugs, turning around to prop her elbows on the bar ledge behind her. It pushes her tits out, her three-year anniversary present to herself. "We are family."

I take a long sip after that one. "Last time I checked, family doesn't send each other nudes."

"That was once," she snaps.

My relationship with Greg has been abysmal since he left my mom after her cancer diagnosis. Early on, Aubrey thought she could use it to her advantage. Pit us against one another to keep his affections. Because what could be more embarrassing than your wife sleeping with your son? If only I'd shown interest in fucking a woman who'd gone down on my dad. Now and then, she'll test the waters, but they remain ice cold.

As the speeches wrap up, she rushes to her table when the hubs shows too much attention to a server. Staking her claim is a must at events like these, too many places to disappear to. I scan the crowd gathering to watch the bride and groom cut their cake. With so many people in the way, I almost miss a peek of deep purple. Bennett's sneaking out a side exit. I'm right behind her. I want to see if a change in location matters. Outside, in a wide-open space without walls closing in on us, maybe we can find new air, new perspectives—compromise.

Someone beats me to the door. Her asshole ex glances around before he follows her out. I've all but forgotten my injuries until I see the split lip I gave him, and the reason feels as justified as ever. I meant every word about not being a jealous person. She turned me into one, slowly and without my consent. Even if she hadn't, I wouldn't trust Bentley near her. He looks at her like a toy. Something to play with whenever the hell he wants.

"My girl," he said.

As if Bennett would ever let herself belong to anyone.

The door bangs shut behind me, and he spins on his heels to face me. Bennett holds her arms over her chest. They fall away when she sees me, her eyes big enough to reflect the string lights surrounding us. She almost steps toward me, a forward sway that never develops. Like she remembers not to.

"Dane..." She trails off, checking on Bentley to see if we're picking up where we left off last night.

He's too interested in her reaction to worry about me. His head bounces between us, a smirk forming. "Looks like I'm not the only one chasing you, Lex."

I flex my jaw at the nickname. The others call her that, too, but it only bothers me out of his mouth. Another reminder of the object he thinks of her as—a toy, a car.

"Trouble in paradise?" he asks, more to me than her. "You screw it up already?"

He pushes hard but not enough for me to cause a scene. I look past him to Bennett, who's shrinking and eager for an escape.

"It's almost time for the first dance," I say. "Keaton's looking for you."

I hold out my arm for her. A test to see which of us she wants to run away from more. Him or me. She nods, giving Bentley a wide berth on her way to my side. I'm the lesser of two evils. I don't know what I would have done if it'd gone the other way.

As we walk inside, she leans into me, my arm around her shoulders. I've always been aware of how well she fits, tucked against my side, in the palm of my hand, in a place in my life I didn't know needed filled. I hesitate to let go once we've returned to the ballroom, but curious eyes fall on us from my family, hers, anyone who has noticed the change between us since yesterday. Each estranged minute, we've gained followers now interested in the reverse in direction.

While I couldn't give a shit, Bennett tenses under my touch and pulls away. I consider tugging her back, deciding for both of us that she is wrong and stubborn and needs to get over herself.

The DJ directs attention to the dance floor. The song Liam's been humming for three months while we shower at the gym floats through the speakers to start their first dance as husband and wife. Bennett heads for the bar when she hears it, but I stay in place. Let her breathe, find some wine. In three and a half minutes, she'll be back in my arms with nowhere to go.

WHEN I STRIDE TOWARD HER on the dance floor, I have no idea what song plays or any awareness of the other couples from the wedding party around us. I just see her. We danced at the ridiculous cowboy bar in San Francisco, and I pull her against me like then, taking advantage of the situation. The excuse to touch her and feel the warmth of her on my skin.

Until the music stops, we can pretend.

Her cheek presses against my chest, and I rest mine on top of her head.

"Ask me to go with you," I say into her hair.

It's not a plea but a last chance to rewind to before the bathroom. Before she decided to push me out of her life and rob me of what I truly want. Not a job someone chose for me or the house I've hated every minute in, except the ones she spent there with me.

Her.

Bennett buries her face in my shirt, and I won't get an answer. I won't ask again either. We hold on to each other until the music bleeds into something else, and our moment of pretending ends. The words and conflict return, pushing us further and further apart until I can't reach her anymore.

And whatever this was…

It's over.

-27-
One Month

BENNETT DUCKS OUT OF THE reception with Keaton's cousin Chevy shortly before the DJ stops. Keaton and Liam hold hands on their way out the doors, heading to their room. And I head to the cabin. Alone.

I don't see her at breakfast in the morning. Her car isn't in the parking lot when I take my bag and tux to the truck. No one says anything when she's not at the apartment later to help carry in gifts.

She's gone, and she's not coming back.

As I leave, I pass Ford in the hallway, the cousin I thought I'd have to fight off with a stick at one point.

With his arms full of wrapped boxes, he gives an empathetic half-smile. The expression says, *Welcome to the Bennett Club, my dude.*

But I refuse to learn a handshake. She'll change her mind. A lie I'll hold on to as long as possible.

Monday passes, then Tuesday, and a number of other days. I go to work, I go home, I obsessively look at my phone. When she does come to her senses, I don't want to miss any more time with her than I already have. It becomes a habit after a week. Park the truck, glance at the screen. Hop off the rowing machine, check for a text.

Liam starts taking the temptation away whenever he's around. He'll walk into my office and swipe my phone off the desk or throw it in his bag in the locker room. I appreciate the intervention. I wasn't a jealous person before her, and I sure as hell wasn't this fucking guy. Shadow Dane, waiting for a goddamn notification that I can have my life back.

He and Keaton held off on a honeymoon. They're saving for a house—white picket fence, a dog that barks when the doorbell rings. She shared a Pinterest board with him. I've seen it from over his shoulder, helped him pin a thing or two to balance out the fluffy pillows and matching *His* and *Hers* towels overtaking his virtual dream life.

Keaton and I tread water at first. We avoid eye contact, keep sentences short, and stay away from anything remotely related to her best friend. It occurs to me, she's been through it before with Bentley.

"It's different," Liam tells me while she's in the kitchen one day. "Bentley fucked Bennett over. He deserved her fury and expected it, but with you…" He sinks into the couch, pinching the bridge of his nose below his glasses. "She has no reason to hate you, and it pisses her off more than if she did have one."

"Ca-ray-zay," I say, mimicking his usual cadence.

My cousin nods, but I get it now. I find the crazy beautiful and irresistible, too.

I keep my distance for a while, not pushing Keaton, and one day, we re-sync.

She pops her head into my office, an irritated look in her eye. "I'm pissed at Liam. Take me to lunch?"

And I do. Like Bennett and I never happened.

It's the same day I stop checking my phone, but Bennett finds a new way to haunt me.

MY MOTHER DIED SUDDENLY. TO me anyway. She'd known the cancer was back for months. She'd kissed my forehead on her way to bed one night, and I'd found her unresponsive in the morning, her breathing shallow. She never woke up again.

I was furious with her for not warning me, for abandoning me and stealing my rights to a goodbye. I think the brain has trouble accepting losses like those—when someone's there and then they're not. Especially with people we love so deeply. We can't understand a world without them in existence. Just gone. So, the mind fills in the disjointed reality with something understandable. At least, that's what the dreams feel like.

Every now and then, I'll have one about her walking in with a bag of groceries or showing up at the office with a Cheshire cat grin and the latest carpentry bill for Greg. She'll sort through mail at the counter or roll her eyes at Aubrey. Neither of us acknowledges that she's been gone for seven years. I just know she's back with no concern for where she's been or how she came back.

I'm used to her invading my dreams, but then one night, it's Bennett throwing open my office door. She sits in the chair across from my desk, her wild laugh distracting me from whatever task I'm failing to complete. Then, just as fast as she appeared, she's gone, and I'm awake.

"Witchcraft," I mutter, reaching for my phone again, re-kick-starting the whole cycle.

MY GRANDFATHER WAS ELATED TO hear I'd be sticking around. My father, the opposite, but that was to be expected. He has the idea in his head that Miles is using me to nudge him out of the company. A complete possibility, given how the old man shoved the Willis portfolio my way and the furious reaction to my plans to leave. I've seen disappointment ooze from my grandfather on many occasions, but I've never been the reason.

The weeks creep by with minimal drama in the office, a rarity as of late. Of course everyone behaves now that I need the distraction. But when Miles drags me out to the golf course, midday in August, I know something is going down. For one, my grandfather has been under strict instructions to stay out of the heat. The big giveaway, though, is his sons and Liam aren't invited. No clients, just the two of us and the caddies.

I watch him, trying to suss out what the old man is up to while his caddy sets his ball. He stays seated in the shade of the golf cart until he's ready to tee off and strides over, driver in hand.

"So," he says, bringing the club back, "I'm cutting Greg out of the will." He swings while I choke on my beer.

"The fuck you say?" I wipe my chin, convinced the ten minutes in the heat have done him in. "You can't just—"

"I can." He lowers his arm once he sees where the ball lands and turns. "And I have. The minute you told me you were staying on, I replaced every instance of his name with yours."

I'm shaking my head on my way over to him. "What about Liam? We were supposed to take over together when Greg and Shane retired."

Circumstances have changed since last month when I planned on leaving to be with Bennett. Walking away from the family legacy for a chance at happiness, I could justify. Choosing love over business. But bailing simply because the thought of working behind a desk and schmoozing at the club for the next forty years makes me restless, I can't.

Waving me off, Miles hands the club to Richie—the kid has caddied for him since I was in high school, but he still calls him Ricky. "His turn will come in time. Shane has enough squirreled away. I'd be surprised if he doesn't take an early retirement within the next ten years."

"You gonna hold out that long?" My tone is light, but the question is serious.

He claims he'll die at his overpriced executive desk, but after the close call at Christmas and traipsing around for conspiratorial rounds of golf in hundred-degree heat, his wish might come true. I could deal with the fallout of taking Greg's place in the will. A final nail in the father-son coffin would be closure if nothing else. It's the possibility of owning half the business before my uncle Shane retires that worries me. I couldn't handle being Liam's boss, even in title alone. It wouldn't feel right. He's always wanted the business, and at this point, I'm only along for the ride.

"You'll be begging me to step down before I do."

My grandfather claps a hand on my back, heading toward the golf cart and effectively ending the conversation. I follow him and cast a glance at the green, the trees with the club in the background. I thought I was waiting to get back to my real life with Bennett. Turns out, it's been here all along, ready for me to wake up from yet another dream.

BY THE TIME I SHOWER and get back to the office, only a few stragglers remain. I have an afternoon's worth of work to catch up on. At least, that's the excuse I use when Liam asks why I'm still hanging around. The truth is, I've been staying at work later, the gym longer. At the end of the day, everyone goes home, but I don't have one. Home is warm and inviting, the place you want to be above all else. The house I live in is someone else's revenge incarnate. Nothing welcoming about wood floors placed after Greg flaunted around a twenty-year-old at the Christmas party. No heartfelt memories attached to the marble overnighted from France when she gave him a second chance and he screwed his secretary a week later.

I should have sold it years ago. The only reason I've held off is the flash of joy it will bring Greg and Aubrey. My mother taught me well in that regard.

If I wanted to, I could be out in under an hour. In a completely furnished house with every drawer and closet full, my belongings could fit in fewer boxes than Bennett used to move to Colorado. Drifters know drifters; drifters fall for drifters.

When I run out of shit to do, I flip off lights on my way out and set the alarm. My phone lights up as I walk to my truck. I stop and stare at the screen. It's a reminder I set months ago. Bennett and I had planned a trip for my birthday next weekend. Well, *plan* might not be the right word. We'd agreed to find the cheapest plane tickets available at the last minute and go wherever they took us, so long as neither of us had been there. I scheduled the reminder, so I could have extra time to talk to her into extending the trip. Four days instead of two.

I dismiss the notification and say, "Fuck you," to my phone for the taunting, but once I start my truck, I look at the calendar again.

The day celebrating my birth will also be an exact month since the wedding. One month since Bennett. Since the last time I saw her blue eyes blinking up at me, heard her sigh out my name, touched her skin—tasted it too—and fuck, she always smelled like candy. The five senses of Bennett, and I miss them all as much as I did the other times she was gone. Only now, there's no next time to push toward.

On my way to the house, I stop to buy a six-pack. I recline on my couch, thinking about where we might have ended up. If it was just somewhere she hadn't been, it could have been almost anywhere. She's only lived in four places. But I covered a lot of ground in my two years without a leash. I would pick up whenever, drive until I stopped, and figure out shit when I got there.

As I twist off the last bottle's top, I decide to go. Get the hell out of Phoenix, even if it's only for a few days. Except I won't be booking some random ticket or driving aimlessly. I know where I'm going and who I'll be seeing when I get there.

-28-
Matchmaker

TWO DAYS BEFORE MY BIRTHDAY, the door with a four swings open. A doofy grin waits for me on the other side, and I give one right back.

"My fuckin' brother," he says, his arms spread wide. "I've missed you."

I drop my bag and walk into those waiting arms—and not for one of those quick back-slapping-'cause-we're-dudes hugs, but a meaningful embrace. Aria rolls her eyes from the couch, and I give her a wink over her boyfriend's shoulder.

Steve Spires and I are in a full-fledged bromance; I will shamelessly admit it. Our relationship started simple enough. One of those situations where you see another human passed out on a couch, mostly naked, and think to yourself, *I like him*. The guy holds player stats like a computer and has better intuition for rebalancing a portfolio than most advisors I've met.

Once he releases me, I give Aria a proper greeting. She pushes onto her tiptoes so that she can hug me around the neck. Greens and blues have replaced the rainbow at the bottom of her black hair, the new colors providing a mermaid aesthetic. She holds on a little longer than I thought she would, a little tighter, too.

I sigh, pulling back. "Ground rules for the weekend: no pity, no asking if I'm okay, and no tricking me into talking about Bennett. Staying in her room is one thing, but I'd rather not think about her beyond that."

Aria's eyes bulge and dart to Steve and back before she breaks into a wild grin. "Sure. Great. How about I bake you a birthday cake?"

She rushes toward the kitchen, and I turn to a guilty-as-fuck Steve. He half-winces, half-smiles. "We might not have mentioned to Bennett that you were coming this weekend." I shrug, not seeing why it would matter until he adds, "She'll be here in the morning."

"Bennett's coming here?" I ask, needing confirmation I heard him correctly.

He nods, and I tense, glancing around the space she shared with them. As a child of divorce, I know how it works. Only one of us gets them at a time, and technically, I'm on her turf, visiting the friends she introduced me to.

"Should I leave?"

"What?" He shakes his head. "No. We left it out on purpose."

Undecided whether to hit him or hug him again, I raise my eyebrows. "Please tell me you're not playing matchmaker with me and my ex-girlfriend on the trip I took, so I *wouldn't* think about my ex-girlfriend?"

"Dane"—he slaps a hand on my shoulder—"you were going to think about her. You're going to keep thinking about her because you're her burst. That type of connection doesn't just break."

Steve vibrates on a different frequency than most people—or as Aria puts it, his worldview is unique. Sometimes, it's just best to roll with it and see where you land.

"Her burst," I repeat. "And what the fuck does that mean?"

"The color to help balance the gray." When I continue to stare at him, he hooks his head toward the stairs. "Let's go." He says it like my inability to decipher the Steve of it is a burden.

I follow him up the stairs and across the grated steel catwalk to Bennett's old room. It only took one visit to learn to pop an antihistamine as I leave the airport, but I appreciate that they've kept the door closed. Little Stevie was obsessed with Bennett's bed, rooting around in the comforter any chance he got.

When we walk in, I take a deep breath. The sweet scent of her lingers and soothes me as much as the blue-purple walls we used to stare at while lying naked in the bed. Ever since the first time I stepped into her room that day at her and Keaton's apartment, I've loved being in her space. Maybe it's because she rarely lets people in.

Steve is by the dresser, staring at the painting on the wall. "See?"

I trace my gaze over the curved brushstrokes creating the delicate features of Bennett's face, buried beneath heavier strokes of exaggerated clown makeup. She said it looked nothing like her, but I think it resembles her too much at times. When the sadness creeps in after a mention of her mother or the panic she shows in a moment of raw vulnerability.

"What am I looking for?" I ask.

"The color burst," he says.

Steve holds up his palm, rubbing circles in the air near the bottom of the painting where the blaze of bright pinks, purples, and yellows encroach on the muted shades covering the rest of the canvas.

"Bennett calls it her bright spot," I tell him. Her favorite part, even though she claims to have no idea what it represents.

He chuckles. "It's you—well, your influence. When I started painting her, I couldn't envision any of these colors. She was dim, like a sheet of clouds covered her." His thumb and forefinger pinch his chin while he studies his work. "Then she looked down to check her phone, and, hello, color burst. She said it was a friend from Phoenix texting her." He looks over. "*Not* the friend getting married."

Out of love for the guy, I try to keep the skepticism to a minimum, but I am no Aria when it comes to dealing with the way he reads vibes and energies. "So, because it wasn't Keaton, you assume it was me?"

"No," he says, focused on the painting again. "I know it was you because she lit up the same way every time you were here or whenever she talked to you or about you."

I picture Bennett sitting there with her phone in her lap, smiling at whatever nonsense I'd texted. Even if it's all bullshit, I like the idea of being a source of light in her world because she was a fucking supernova in mine.

I sigh, dropping my head back. A chance to see her sounds like the exact sword I want to throw myself on.

"She'll bolt out the door the second she realizes I'm here," I say.

He tips his head for a new angle. "Or she won't."

A lovely thought, but I know Bennett. I've chased her down the street before when she saw me unexpectedly. And I won't bother pretending I wouldn't again.

"Hey," Aria says from the doorway. "The container marked with an *S* is sugar, right?"

Steve's mouth curves upward as he twists to see her. "No, babe. That's the salt. The sugar is above the stove."

She hesitates, her eyes darting back and forth before she gives a sweet smile. "I'm sure it will be fine."

Once she disappears, Steve shakes his head. "We'd better start drinking. There's a sports bar down the street. We'll get drunk enough to choke down your cake, and you can tell me how to convince Aria to be more aggressive with her 401(k)."

My fucking soul mate.

IT'S LATE WHEN LITTLE STEVIE starts pawing at the door. Having properly rung in my birthday eve, I walk a zigzag on my way to let him in. The behemoth of a tabby shows his appreciation by jumping onto the dresser rather than the bed. If Bennett were here, she'd roll her eyes and kick him out, but I like cats. Their dander just hates me.

I crash back onto the mattress and resume staring at my phone. Her name is on the screen. It has been the last several minutes while I lie here, thinking about how shitty I am for letting her walk into an ambush.

I'm drunk enough, I decide to warn her. Now. At three a.m. And fuck texting. I'm ruining my chances at seeing her. I should at least get to hear her voice while I do it.

"Dane?" She answers with a sexy rasp, and fuck, I've missed my name out of her mouth.

"Hey." I sound drunk, so I sit up to clear my head.

"What happened?" she asks, slightly alarmed. "Keaton?"

Shit. I should have realized she'd think something was wrong if I called in the middle of the night.

"No, everyone's fine. I just…" I rest my head on the headboard and close my eyes. "Fuck, baby. You have no idea how much I needed to hear your voice."

She's quiet, each second pulsing between us. I think I've lost her when the phone rustles and she takes an audible breath.

"It's almost your birthday."

I smile like she just admitted to missing me too. Because the fact she hasn't hung up yet is all the proof I need to know she does. "You remember our plan?"

"Anywhere but nowhere we've been," she says, repeating the words I told her.

We were on the back patio at Maggie's. Bennett was on my lap in one of the rickety rocking chairs, fireflies blinking in the field of flowers between us and the riverbank. After bickering over who would buy the tickets, she nuzzled into my neck and said we weren't moving from that spot until then. I was perfectly happy to oblige until she grazed her teeth over my earlobe.

I checked tickets earlier. We would have gone to New Orleans. Then, to torture myself further, I searched hotels and restaurants.

Bennett falls silent again, a familiar one I've experienced over and over. She'll be on her side, facing the empty side of the mattress where I should be, her mind busy. I keep my eyes closed, pretending she's here.

"Stop fidgeting."

She laughs, and I swear, my fucking heart squeezes in my chest. "What makes you think I am?"

"You always fidget when you're trying to avoid thinking about something."

When she doesn't answer right away, I know I called it.

"What am I trying to not think about?" she whispers the question like she does when she's afraid of the answer.

If I wanted to spare us both, I would throw out a wild response and hear her laugh again. But I'm drunk, and that void in my life she filled when I hadn't known it even existed feels vast, the absence of her louder than ever.

"You miss me, too, and how much scares the hell out of you."

I wait for her to tell me I'm wrong, to find an excuse to go, but she does neither. Maybe I shouldn't tell her I'm in her room right now. If she's anywhere near as miserable without me as I am without her, maybe she won't run when she sees me.

"I'm in San Francisco, Bennett."

Pulling the phone away from my ear, I wince and mouth, *Fuck!* This woman has ruined the chill I once had. Until her, I'd never blurted a goddamn thing in my life. I tap the phone on my forehead a few times before I bring it back for damage control.

"I only found out you were coming after I got here. Steve has it in his head he's a jacked Lindsay Lohan, playing parent trap."

Every beat without a response kills me. Death after death and then, "Oh."

Oh? I can't read *oh* over the phone. I need her eyes, her lips, a second syllable at least.

When it comes to Bennett, there are two ways past the force field. The first, you have to feel out. Give her time to panic, breathe, overthink, and come to terms before you slowly back your way in. The other, bulldoze the fuck through. Number two carries the potential to detonate in your face, but given the time frame and lack of visual cues, I'll clip the wire.

"Get on the flight," I tell her. "I don't care what reasons you come up with not to, just get on the fucking plane, baby. Two days. Two days you already promised me."

"Dane…"

I hear the doubt she'll use against me if I let her.

"No, Bennett. Two days. You can give me that. Now, lay your sweet head on the pillow and drive your sexy ass to the airport in the morning to be with me." I hesitate to push any further, but she'll either come or not at this point, so why the hell not? "I'll be here, waiting. I love you."

Before she can say anything, I hang up. Then I resume staring at my phone, expecting to see her name appear. A call or text to say she's not coming. She's sorry, but it's not a good idea. But the screen stays black for a minute and then an hour.

I fall asleep, thinking maybe she'll listen. I fall asleep, thinking in a few hours I'll be holding her again. I fall asleep, thinking I'll be waiting when she walks in the door and we'll have a second chance to figure this out—to be together here, there, wherever. I fall asleep, thinking a lot of things.

-29-
The Call

THE CALL FROM LIAM WAKES me around nine. They found the old man at his desk, like he'd claimed we would. The EMTs worked to get his heart beating again, air to his lungs, but he was gone. The doctor said it'd happened fast, a massive heart attack that would have killed him, no matter where it happened. If it's true and not only meant to ease the family's minds, then I'm glad it was there, the way he'd wanted it.

I'm out of the apartment within a few minutes, boarding a plane to Phoenix at the same time Bennett's flight should be landing. Later, a text from Steve tells me she wasn't on it. My grandfather died a few hours ago, but I'm grieving my relationship again instead of him.

I go straight to the office. Not the mortuary where my uncle and cousin are, not anywhere I will see anyone. I've shut off my phone too. Liam and Shane know I'll surface when I'm ready. We all process death in different ways. Mine involves being left the fuck alone.

The building should be locked, shut down for the next few days at least. Isn't that what happens when the leader of the pack falls—the others bow their heads? But the door gives without my key, and the alarm has been disarmed.

I know why. And it pisses me the fuck off.

"Couldn't bother to wait until his body cools?" I ask from the doorway of my grandfather's office.

Greg continues shuffling through the papers on the desk, sitting in a dead man's chair. "Ah, I see you've arrived in time to act superior."

I looked up to him once. He was a king in my mind. Then my mind aged and noted the difference between royalty and royal bullshit.

A wry smile forms as I step farther into the room, arms folded over my chest. "If you're looking for the will, it's in the wall safe."

This, my father deems worthy of his attention. His head snaps up, a look of panic in his eyes despite the calm demeanor he tries to maintain. He slouches back in the chair, his fingers steepled beneath his chin. "What do you know?"

Miles showed me the papers before I left. True to his word, my father's name appears nowhere, mine in its place. As he left me at my desk, he clapped me on the back the way he would. *Proud of you, son.*

Words he'd never spoken to his real son, who'd never spoken them to me.

The back of my throat tightens. The memory, the gesture, the rest of the past twenty-four hours hovering over me. Yesterday, I had years to decide if I would take over my half of the company. Time to sort out the life slipping through my fingers lately. Today, I have neither. A trust has kicked in, my familial duties engaged.

I readjust a golf trophy on the bookshelf and return to the door with one last look at my father. "I know enough to tell you to get the fuck out of this office."

THE STREETLIGHTS HAVE TURNED ON by the time I lock the door to leave. Crossing the parking lot, I finally switch on my phone. I only plan to check in with my uncle, see what needs to be done and when over the next few days.

This

I stop halfway to my truck, reading a text from earlier in the afternoon.

Liam: *Bennett's here.*

Another followed shortly after.

She's at the apartment with Keaton.

Then, only an hour ago, he sent, *Joyce and Patrick's. She's staying there tonight.*

It doesn't make sense for me to be angry, but I am. Instead of going to San Francisco to be with me, Bennett came here to avoid me.

The last time she showed up without telling me, she'd shut me out for days. Left me questioning every move I'd made with her until I couldn't stand thinking about her anymore. Then I saw the picture of a rainbow drink and the hand that didn't belong to me. My first taste of jealousy was bitter and unwelcome. We weren't serious—neither of us wanted to be. The lies we tell ourselves. When I looked up and saw her standing on the sidewalk outside the bar, I accepted the truth. I couldn't deny it anymore. She'd already consumed my thoughts, controlled my emotions. She could have every part of me, so long as I could have her.

I drive to Keaton's parents' house because I have nowhere else I want to go. Like I did on her birthday, I park a few mailboxes down. Tonight seems to be an eerie echo of that night. Only now, we're hours away from *my* birthday, my grandfather's heart attack killed him, and my face won't be between her legs later. She won't even know I'm here. The same way she doesn't want me to know she is.

Hey, I text her.

I rest my head back on the seat, focusing on the dots dancing on the screen. They start, stop, start again. I imagine she's torn between excuses and condolences. The question digging at me is why I'm only now receiving either. Keaton would have told her about Miles hours ago, and we both know she never got off the plane in San Francisco.

The dots disappear altogether after a few minutes.

Coward, I type, just to delete it without sending.

From where I am, all I can see is the house's shadowed porch. The light turns on, and the red door opens as Bennett steps out. Just seeing her profile again is the equivalent of taking a taser to the chest. I straighten in my seat and consider flashing my lights or rolling down my window and shouting—something to gain her attention. The entire situation feels pathetic. I can't defend sitting in the dark, so I watch her stand at the curb until a car stops in front of her. She climbs in, they drive off, and I'm irritated with her again. She should have noticed me.

I ONLY CALL MY HIGH school friend, Toby, when I want someone to drink with me to the point I won't remember my name. He knows and doesn't seem to care. We meet at a bar he chooses, and when he hears about my grandfather, he tips his beer bottle to "pour one out" for the old man.

A few rounds in, he starts ordering shots for the ladies beside us. Before he throws a drunken arm around my shoulders and slurs, "Which you want?" in my ear, I leave him and my drink at the bar. One has blonde hair, one blue eyes, and one looks like she wants to bolt. I came here so I wouldn't follow Bennett, not to screw a knockoff version.

Even though I could probably drive, I decide not to deal with my truck. Why risk the temptation of going somewhere other than my house? I fold into the back of a Honda and rest my head on the cool glass as the driver pulls away. The ride helps me decompress, gain some distance between me and one long-ass day. Almost to the house, I remember I ignored a text from Liam earlier.

Where the fuck are you?

Not drunk enough in an Uber, I send.

For as long as I took to answer, he replies right away.

On your way home? ALONE?

We pull into my driveway before I can ask why the question elicited all caps. But once I get about halfway up the sidewalk, I know why.

Bennett.

She's sitting in front of my door, her knees up to her chest and her arms wrapped around her legs. When her head stays down, I think she might be crying.

Fuck me. I can't handle Bennett crying. Her lower lip quivers, and her eyes shine while they spill tears. Devastating and beautiful.

She still hasn't moved when I lower down in front of her. I push the hair back that covers her face, her cheek on her knee. So fucking gorgeous. And asleep.

Luckily, I live in the kind of neighborhood where everyone's in bed by eleven, so no one notices a random woman sleeping outside. I unlock the door before I gather her into my arms, and she snuggles into my shoulder, her eyes staying shut as I carry her inside.

Once her head hits the pillow, she rolls over. I slide off her shoes and unclasp the hook on her bracelet. She rarely leaves it on when she sleeps. The *Seek* etched into the medallion catches my eye. I asked her about it while she was sprawled across me in her bed in SF. Why it was so important to her.

"You'll laugh at me," she said.

I nodded, my chin bumping the top of her head. *"Probably, but you're going to tell me anyway."*

She pushed onto her forearms, resting them on my chest. Her eyes stayed down, her fingers twisting in the chain of my necklace. *"Not long after my mom left, Keaton and I went to a carnival set up in the mall parking lot. While she stopped for cotton candy, I noticed a sign for a fortune teller."*

She cast her eyes up for my reaction, which I wouldn't give her. Getting Bennett to open up on command was the equivalent of catching lightning in a bottle.

"When I sat across from her, she glanced up from her book and said, 'What you desire isn't here. Seek it elsewhere.' She went right back to reading as if I weren't there, but the words felt important. Like she knew what I was missing and that it was out there for me to find. A few days later, I saw this bracelet in the window of a thrift store, so I bought it as a reminder to keep searching or whatever." She shrugged, returning her gaze to my chain. *"Crazy, I know. She probably just wanted me to leave, and the bracelet was way overpriced, considering the other side's word had worn off."*

"So, what are you looking for, Bennett?" I'd asked this once before—before I knew how much I wanted the answer.

"I'm starting to think I won't know until I find it." Peeking up at me again, she added, *"But I'll let you know when I do."*

As I lay her bracelet on the nightstand, I reach for my chain out of habit, but nothing's there. I lost it a few months ago—somewhere in Colorado. It was a graduation gift from my mother. I'd found it in a drawer before I left for college, wrapped with a note reminding me, no matter where I went or how long I was gone, to come home. Seems fitting I lost it the last time I visited Bennett.

Maybe I should go to the couch, let her sleep, but I strip off my shirt and jeans and crawl in beside her. I pull her to me, needing to remember how she feels. When I press a kiss to her forehead, her eyes flutter open. She stays against me, holding my gaze, and I know she won't go anywhere. Not tonight at least. Which means I need to memorize everything about having her here with me before she leaves again.

"I'm so sorry," she whispers.

I slowly breathe out, hesitant to lose the calm settled between us, but I've gotten the condolences. Now I want the explanation. "Why didn't you go to San Francisco?"

"Because your grandpa died." She readjusts, moving her head onto the pillow so we're nose-to-nose. "Keaton called this morning, so I flew here instead."

"And you didn't think to text? Or call?" I shake my head, confused why she wouldn't tell me. "I thought you stood me up."

"Liam said to leave you alone and that you'd reach out when you were ready. Then you did, and everything I tried to say sounded terrible, so…" She presses her lips together and looks down. "I came here."

And I went anywhere else.

She pulls away. I almost fight her until I realize she's checking her phone. She rolls back to me, her face only inches from mine.

"It's your birthday."

"Ask me what I want," I tell her.

A hint of tension creeps into her forehead, and her voice drops low. "What do you—"

I cover her mouth with mine and remember what it's like to breathe. She gasps, but then her hands move to the sides of my face. Her lips part, and our tongues collide as I jerk her body closer.

"Dane…" She puts little weight behind what I assume she means as a warning that nothing has changed. I'm not allowed to ask her to stay, and she doesn't want me to go.

"Bennett"—I push my forehead against hers, my hands already nudging down her shorts—"I don't fucking care."

Her eyes dart back and forth between mine before she nods and teases her fingers inside the elastic of my briefs. I kiss her, convinced if I stop, she'll stop, and I need her to keep touching me. I need more than memories and dreams. I need Bennett for however long she'll give me.

I'll deal with the consequences of losing her again. The pain when she walks away will be real, brutal, and I'll only have myself to blame. But who the hell am I kidding? I'll destroy myself over and over for her.

-30-

Goodbye

I CAN'T FALL ASLEEP WITH Bennett in my bed. If I drift off with her weight on me, I risk waking up alone. So, I creep out of my own fucking house at five in the morning.

To avoid being a complete asshole, I leave a note on the kitchen counter. A white scrap paper telling her I need to take care of a few things. At first, I wanted to write out a sticky note. Place a kiss on her forehead before pressing it on her pillow. But it felt sacrilegious, a tainting of something beautiful.

Liam's truck is at the gym when I get there—twelve hours ahead of our usual workout time. Even before seeing him hanging out in the locker room, I assume his purpose is to find me. Understandable, since I returned to ignoring the world after I found Bennett outside my door. I should stop by his parents' house later. Apologize for checking out on Shane and everyone else.

I toss my bag on the bench. "Am I that predictable?"

He shrugs. "If it makes you feel any better, Keaton went to her parents' in case Bennett was the one to bail."

"Nope. I can't say that helps in the least."

He hovers, waiting for me to change. "Are we pretending it's not your birthday?"

"Yep."

"And that you didn't fuck your ex last night?"

I'm tying my shoe and jerk my head up. "You want to try that again?"

When I straighten, he holds his hands out and takes a cautious step backward. "Down, boy. I'm just getting a feel for how today is going to go."

"Not well if you say shit like that again."

My cousin has a habit of pushing the line, but he typically watches himself when it comes to Bennett. He dismisses the glare I set on him and shakes his head. "I'll risk the ass-kicking and guess you two haven't talked much then?"

I clench my jaw, and after a long sigh, he heads for the door.

"You two are fucking exhausting."

And I couldn't agree more.

BY THE TIME LIAM AND I finish our workout, he's filled me in on the details. A wake tomorrow with a private service the day after. The old man might have acted like he would outlive us all, but it sounds like he was rather set in what he wanted.

I shower at the gym and pick up my truck before returning to the house. No part of me expects Bennett to have hung around, so when I walk in and see a blonde on my couch, I freeze in the doorway. Then I recognize the dye job.

"Get out," I say to Aubrey, dropping my bag by the door.

And just to make my fucking day all the better, I step farther in and spot my father. He's scanning the frames on the mantel over the fireplace, scowling at pictures of the wife he deemed unworthy and son he sees as competition.

"You too," I add. "And if you're looking for any proof of you in those photos, we burned them all. Bought a fire pit just for the occasion."

Greg tugs at his collar, uncomfortable in the house that has brought him nothing but annoyance. How much money did he bleed into it just to keep her from raising hell in his personal life?

She gutted him on alimony, as one should when they're left because of a terminal illness. Then, with every fuckup after, she found a way to make him pay.

Without any other greeting, he holds out his hand, a slip of paper between two of the fingers. "Happy birthday, son."

He stops a decent distance away, and I reach for the check. Reading the amount, I let out a disgusted laugh. "We both know you don't have half a million lying around. Not with that one's surgery schedule."

Aubrey narrows her eyes at me and mouths, *Asshole*.

I shrug and return to the other glare set on me. "So, what are you bribing me for?"

Greg glances around and gestures at the walls surrounding us.

"Fuck you," I spit. "You think I'd let you anywhere near her house?"

He tried the same bullshit before I left for college. Twice since then. This place is a splinter festering in his palm, and by tearing it down, he'd finally one-up a dead woman.

"You aren't happy here, Dane." His tone carries an irritation only a father could have for his son. "You've been rather blunt about that over the past year. So, why hold on to something you don't even want?"

I cross my arms over my chest and slowly shake my head. I'll die in this house before I give him the pleasure of destroying what was hers.

"Fine," he says, waving it off. But a flash of disappointment in his eyes gives him away as he sits on the couch beside Aubrey. "Even without the house, the money's yours if you sign over my half of the business. I shouldn't need to pay anything, considering it rightfully belongs to me, but you are my son."

I'm shaking my head again, a disbelieving smirk on my face. "You just can't fucking quit, can you?"

"We both know you have no interest in being there. The only reason you came back was for Miles, and ... well"—he slides his arm behind Aubrey—"he's gone, so now, you can be too. Take the money and go wherever you want. Maybe Colorado to be with that lovely little blonde." His mouth twitches, mentioning Bennett, and I'm one *lovely* past fucking losing it.

"Out," I warn. "Before I fucking throw you out."

Aubrey prickles at his side, her reaction to his comment as subtle as mine. "Greg," she says, giving me a rare look of understanding, "I want to leave."

My father holds my gaze as he rises, and I wonder when I became such a threat to him. Even without the shit with my mother and grandfather between us, I can't imagine anything more than a mildly apathetic relationship with him. The same father-son dynamic he'd shared with his father until he started acting like an entitled fuck.

Aubrey drags him through the living room, giving me one last look before they disappear out the door. And as much as I hate to admit it, all I can think about after they leave is the check. Still in my hand.

DESPITE AGREEING TO PRETEND IT'S not my birthday, Liam's incessant messages demanding I meet them for dinner wear me down. I park at the restaurant, thinking about something Aria said during my short time in San Francisco.

While we ate my shitty birthday cake, Steve went to feed Little Stevie. The way she watched him from the living room made me ask her, *"When did you fall in love?"*

I'd had enough to drink at that point, the current slice was tolerable, so my filter wasn't on.

From Steve's ramblings, I already knew his side. He'd fallen in love the moment he saw her—across the bar when her hair was cut in a pageboy and she wore her eyeliner thick. The black words on her pale skin showed him her soul, and he recognized it. But seeing the soft, memory-driven smile on her face, I needed her side.

"I've been in love with him since he was born." She glanced over, her smile growing when I tipped back my beer to keep from mocking her Steve-ism. *"I'm serious."*

"Okay," I said. *"And here I thought, you were the sensible one."*

Aria laughed and shifted to face me. *"The first time I realized I loved him was a few months after we met. He dragged me into a dollar store, bought sidewalk chalk, and then drew my portrait in the parking lot."*

"A reasonable answer. So, how do we get from five years ago to over twenty?"

"When I saw pictures of him from high school and learned what he was like, I fell in love with who he had been then. And again, after watching his family movies from his childhood, and in the picture they had taken of him right after he was born. I loved him at every age throughout his entire life. I just didn't know it until I was standing in the center of his chalk art."

It reminded me of the first time I had gone to dinner with Bennett. Here. At this restaurant. I was supposed to meet up with a chick I'd met at the gym on the other side of town that night. I'd spent the day telling myself I wouldn't cancel, but deep down, I knew I would. Just like I knew the hook-ups after her wouldn't be enough to get her out of my head. I couldn't figure out why back then, but now I know I've been falling in love with Bennett since the first time I saw her. It just took a long time to understand that's what it was.

THE OTHER THREE ARE ALREADY at the table when I walk in. Bennett gives me a sweet smile when I slide into the chair next to hers.

The check is on my dresser.

Waiting for the server to take our order, Liam and Keaton seem determined to steer us through an obstacle course of conversation in which Bennett and I have no reason we need to speak to each other directly. It would be amusing if it wasn't so unnecessary. We order, and before the server has walked away, I have my phone out under the table.

Hi, I text her.

If I wasn't next to her, I wouldn't notice her sliding her phone out from under her leg on the chair. Her eyes dart to where my hands disappear under the tablecloth, and her lips tug up on one side.

Hey, she sends.

Maybe I could leave, help Shane run the office remotely. *Fuck,* I can't seriously be considering this because of a one-word text message. I need to get my shit together, remember what I was like before she sank her claws all the way into me.

You look hideous.

Sparing my first glance since sitting down, I see her eyebrow arch at my message. She looks at me fast before nodding at something Keaton said, but I know the smile is for me. Her hands move under the table

Her: *Tell me how you really feel.*

I weigh my options, decide how much room I want to give her to wiggle. Then I bulldoze on through.

I've missed you in my bed and being inside you. I've missed your laugh and smile—every part of you really. Come home with me and put me out of my misery.

As soon as I hit send, I put my phone facedown on the table between us and slip my hand back under and to her thigh. She doesn't try to move it. Her leg or my hand. In fact, her fingers lace with mine.

LEAVING THE RESTAURANT, NO ONE questions Bennett following me when I cock my head toward my truck. Everyone knew she'd leave with me. Regardless of what I'd thought up until yesterday, Bennett and I aren't over. We're fucked up and tormenting each other until one of us bends. She wants me to return to being a weekend boyfriend, and I want her every fucking day.

Back at the house, I toss my keys on the counter. Bennett's still hovering by the door to the garage when I turn around.

"Come here," I say.

She listens, but her steps are too slow, so I reach for her waist and haul her against me. One side of her mouth turns up at my impatience, and her hands run up my arms. In my dreams, she never touches me.

"When do you leave?"

"Liam's taking me to the airport tomorrow after the visitation. Unless you want to take me?" She blinks up at me, as out there as Bennett will put herself.

I nod. "I want. We'll make an appearance and then bail early to screw in my truck."

She laughs, and I brush my lips over hers.

"But first…" I lower my hands over her ass and keep going. "I've gotten the smile and laugh. Now for the rest of the things I've missed."

She squeals my name when I pick her up by the backs of her thighs, her legs locked around me as I carry her to the bedroom. We have a lot of shit we need to say between now and when I drop her off at the airport, but I'll worry about it tomorrow. Tonight, I'll love her and sleep.

The check is still on my dresser.

I SQUEEZE IN AS MUCH time with Bennett as I can over the next twelve hours. Then, in the afternoon, I force myself to go to the mortuary for the first time since my mother's funeral. It's the smell that hits first—distinct and unlike anything else I've experienced. An overload of flowers along with the combined scents of the waves of people who've passed through the building over the course of a hundred years. Second is the lighting in the viewing area—a rosy tint cast over the room.

Liam and I dutifully shake every hand extended for the next few hours, repeating, "Thank you. That means a lot," and, "He sure was," depending on the sentiment offered.

Most of our clients make an appearance along with a great aunt we've only met a few times who lives in Sarasota. When Willis comes in, he makes his rounds before slipping me an envelope and a wink. I open the flap enough to see inside and tuck it in my pocket, not sure how to feel about a bereavement bonus.

Greg might be the only person I've seen openly drinking at a visitation before. The more scotch he downs, the more laser-focused his glare is on me. Eventually, I ignore him, refusing to bother with the stare-downs he keeps trying to lock me into.

The crowd thins, and my eyes are Bennett-hunting. She snuck in with Keaton earlier and gave me a reserved smile. I might have been joking about screwing her in my truck, but the bailing early part? All I want to do right now.

I head toward the back where I last saw her. The door to the small room for the family to take a breather is cracked open. I start to push the handle but stop at the sound of Greg's voice on the other side.

"…and so beautiful," he says.

I pull my hand away, unwilling to walk in on anything between him and Aubrey. I saw enough at the company Christmas party. But I only get a few steps before I notice my stepmother picking at her manicure in a corner next to a flower wreath.

And then I hear it.

"I really should find Keaton."

My blood runs cold at Bennett's voice on the other side of the door, holding every note of uncomfortable with the slimy tone Greg uses on waitresses and secretaries coming through right behind it.

"It's a shame you and my son couldn't work something out. But … maybe it's for the best."

"Mr. Masters," she says fast. Then, "Mr. Masters, stop!"

When I throw the door open, Bennett is backed against a table with him in front of her, his fucking hand on her waist.

Her panicked gaze shoots to me. "Dane!"

Greg glances over his shoulder, and she takes the opportunity to shove him away. She rushes toward me, but I pass straight by her. Greg barely gets turned around before I have him against a wall with my forearm to his throat.

After my mother's funeral, I found Greg at the house, stuffing anything of value into a duffel bag. Miles had to drag me off him, my father's face bloody and my hand broken. I'd never experienced blinding rage until then. And it feels the same after all these years.

"You're going to regret ever fucking touching her," I growl at him.

His hands calmly rise to pull at my arm, so I push harder on his windpipe until he squirms. It feels better than it should, seeing the smugness drain from his face as it reddens.

"Son," he chokes out.

"Don't fucking call me that."

"Dane!" Bennett tugs at my other arm, trying to pull me away, but I stay with my eyes locked on Greg's, which are blinking faster, the longer I hold him to the wall. "Please, don't. Nothing happened. I'm okay."

"The fuck it didn't," I say through clenched teeth. "You couldn't get your hands on the house or company, so you thought you'd put them on her?"

My father's frantic attention darts behind me, then back, and I safely assume we have company.

"Fucking Christ." Liam sounds more irritated than anything else. "Down, boy."

When he appears beside me, I step back.

Greg drops to his knee, hunching over and gasping for air. He glares up at me, yanking at the knot of his tie. "We're done," he spits.

"We've been done for years." I pull the bullshit check out of my pocket and throw it at him. It lands on the floor between us, acting as the official battle line on the ugly shag carpet. "Start looking for a new firm because you won't work at mine."

I shoulder past my cousin, his eyes mid-roll, not slowing down when Bennett calls my name. She chases after me, trying to stop me until she catches up in the parking lot.

"Please don't walk away from me."

Her plea brings me to a stop. Not because I promised I wouldn't walk away from her again, but because all the exasperation toward her emerges after being buried. She steps back when I stalk toward her.

"Why the fuck not? I've watched you do it enough."

Her eyes widen at first, and then she folds her arms over her chest. "That's not fair."

I laugh, scrubbing my hands over my face. "You know what's not fair? Being in love with someone who is too wrapped up in their shit to care about yours."

"I care," she says, but it's flimsy.

"Do you? We can only be together, so long as I abide by what you want and don't want. Never once have you considered what I want. What I need."

Maybe—just *maybe*—I'm displacing some of my anger onto her, but right now, I have too much to get off my chest to stop.

I move closer, my eyebrows drawing in. "I was abandoned, too, Bennett. Your mother might have chosen to bail, but mine left too. And now, you keep doing the same, and I let you because I have this fucked idea that, one time, you won't. That, one time, you'll stay with me." I shake my head, forcing myself to dry-swallow something I should have realized long before now. "But you never will. There will always be an excuse why you won't let me all the way in. And as much as I thought I could, I can't do this with you anymore."

She swipes at the tears on her cheeks, lips trembling. Devastating and beautiful. Fuck, it hurts, and I have to look at the ground, biting back a sting in my own eyes.

"Liam can take you to the airport." I bend down and kiss her temple. "Goodbye, Bennett."

The words strangle me on their way out, my chest on fire at the thought of them being real.

With every step toward my truck, I will her to say something. To give me a reason to stop, to believe, one day, we'll be enough for her to quit running from all the shit she refuses to sort out inside her head.

But she doesn't, and I drive away.

Neither of us would bend, so all that's left to do is break.

-31-
Broken-Heart Chic

THE NEXT FEW WEEKS, I exist in what feels like a montage. A funeral, sorting through documents, lawyer meetings. The days are split between fast-laning everything I need to know to keep the business running smoothly and dealing with Greg's constant attempts to sink us. The battle line drawn wasn't only between us personally; it was all aspects.

As expected, he contests the will for his inheritance, as well as the trust that passes ownership of Masters Financial. His claims range from the old man was senile to Shane and I coerced him into changing it at the last minute. He doesn't have shit, but it will keep the company's lawyers busy with litigation for the foreseeable future.

The best part is, I can't fire him until everything settles down or else I chance giving him ammo. So, I saddle him with a babysitter to make sure he doesn't fuck over any investments out of spite or funnel clients into a side business or another dramatic-as-fuck scheme.

I also schedule a company photo to forever capture the awkwardness of the entire situation. I blow it up large enough to see his scowl and hang it in the lobby behind reception. The first time I walk through and see it, I can't help but smile. My bright spot breaking through the cloud of shit.

About a month after the funeral, I step into a bar I normally wouldn't in search of a face I wouldn't have given two shits about last month. How I ended up having regular meet-ups with Keaton's cousins, I have no idea. That's a lie. I know exactly how it happened. One night, Liam's frat brothers surpassed the hour-long tolerance window I reserved for them. I told him I was going the fuck back to the house unless we went somewhere else. Enter Chevy Reynolds and a questionable bar downtown.

Lincoln gives a nod as he and I pass, his sights appearing set on a redhead. I sit across from Chevy, who's leaning back in his chair with a hand and beer bottle propped against his chest.

He eyes me and cocks his head to the side. "You look like shit."

"Thanks." I reach for a beer from the bucket in the center of the table.

We went from polite acquaintances to brutally honest bros in a single night of drinking. He might not be Steve Spires—really, no one could ever live up to that legend of a man—but Chevy's a nice balance to the other aspects of my life. Straightforward and I never have to question his intentions.

"No, seriously." He waves his hand at my general form. "What are we going for with this exactly? Broken heart with a splash of broken razor?"

I scratch at my stubble with my middle finger and take a swig while he chuckles. More like a lack of sleep and a conscious decision not to shave. Broken-heart chic only lasted the first week. Now, I shower daily and change my clothes as often.

I haven't talked to Bennett at all since the visitation. I don't text her or reach for my phone, hoping she did. As far as I'm concerned, I said everything I'd needed to over the past year and a half. My subconscious doesn't agree though. The dreams have become regular enough that dream me rolls my eyes every time she waltzes into my dream office. She'll ramble on about cats, or I follow her out the door and into the SF apartment.

A few weeks ago, she moved to LA with Marco. It's the closest she's been. Every time she relocates, she creeps closer back to Phoenix. I used to think it meant something, but any pattern will emerge if we twist the details enough to fit.

"Where you been anyway?" he asks. "Lincoln's been shot down by two women already."

"Stalking my ex," I say coolly.

Since she once again lives with the king of social media, her image floods my feeds. It irritated me at first, but now I scroll through, specifically looking for Marco's posts. It's what I was doing before I came inside. I consider it stockpiling potential material. If she's going to insert herself into my dreams against my will, she can at least show up in the fucking sundress she wore a few days ago. Legs, hips, tits—none of which my dream self will touch.

"Moving on at its finest." Chevy raises his bottle to be an asshole, but I drink to it anyway. Then, getting all the touchy subjects out of the way early tonight, he asks, "How's the dad shit been going?"

I shrug, watching the redhead wrinkle her nose at his twin in either disgust or amusement. "On a scale of hugging and making up to murdering each other, I'd say we're just shy of cutting the other's brake lines."

"I don't know how you put up with it every day. Fuck, I don't know *why* you put up with it. If I had to tolerate Bentley and his bullshit as often as you deal with your family's, it would drive me mad."

"What else am I supposed to do? I promised the old man I'd take over when he was gone."

"Yeah, well…" He thinks it over a second and lifts a shoulder. "I don't know if that would be enough for me."

Lincoln strides over then, a smug grin on his face when he drops into the seat between us. "Well, I'm done for the night." He tips his head, eyes squinting. "What about you?"

"What about me?" I glance at a chick walking past. Short black hair, long legs in skinny jeans.

She looks down long enough to smile and keeps going. When my attention returns to the twins, Lincoln's arms are crossed over his chest.

"You come out with us at least twice a week," he says, checking with his brother for backup. "You dodge women all night and leave alone. I think it's about time you take your balls back from Lex and end the abstinence streak you have going."

Chevy kicks his chair. "Maybe you should quit worrying about his dick and focus on your own." He nods toward the woman Lincoln planned on leaving with, strolling out the door with another guy.

"Shit. It really feels like a redhead kind of night." Lincoln strains his neck to see around people and jumps to his feet. "There's another in the back. Wish me luck."

"He has a point, you know," Chevy says once he's gone. "At some point, you need to let go. Lex is great, and I'll rip the skin from anyone who tries to hurt her, but she needs to fix herself in a lot of ways. Waiting for it to happen is a dangerous game to play."

I don't respond, instead staring at my beer bottle. Then I decide fuck it and stand up. I head to the bar, to the chick with the legs. We talk; she laughs. I've always been good at saying the right thing and choosing the right moment to move closer. She has a steady job and a yearlong lease, and her life plan includes buying a house in the Phoenix area. She has a friend, so Chevy joins us soon. Lincoln comes over with his fourth redhead.

We stay until last call, all of us making plans to go somewhere else after.

"I'll be right back," I say into her ear.

She nods, and I hear her squeal, grabbing on to her friend's arm as I walk away. I don't know if she notices when I keep going, but Lincoln and Chevy do, both of them giving me a quick wave as I reach the door.

Next time, Chevy texts.

I reply, *Yeah, for sure.*

Then I check Instagram.

-32-
Keep Dreaming

THE FRIDAY BEFORE LABOR DAY, everyone is getting ready to leave for a long weekend. I've been in meetings all day, my mind on the verge of numb. Greg caught Willis at dinner the other night and filled his head with ideas. I've been scurrying around to minimize the damage from that. Then, this morning, my father announced in the middle of an all-staff meeting that he was planning to start a competing business and would be hiring anyone who left Masters Financial with him.

I'm almost to the point that I'm ready to say screw what the lawyers advise and fire him. Publicly, if possible. Maybe I'll have his company car towed from the employee lot just to hit it home.

My tolerance for him has been in steady decline, but today, I have less than usual. Probably because I slept at the office last night. I've slept here all week, showering at the gym and only stopping by the house long enough to grab a change of clothes.

Hell of a life you've got here, Masters.

I'm poring over audit reports, my elbows braced on the desk and the heels of my hands pressed into my forehead, with thoughts of what Chevy said—about whether it's worth it—on the fringe of my consciousness when my door creaks open. I glance up long enough to see Aubrey strutting in. She has a popped bottle of champagne hugged to her chest and two flutes clutched in her other hand.

"What the hell is this?" I ask as she closes the door behind her.

Since the encounter at the house on my birthday, she's been quiet. Respectful even. But, today, she's wearing what I can only describe as her daddy issues. The electric-blue dress suffocates every curve, and if the hem slips any higher up her thighs, the entire office will know her waxing preference.

"We're celebrating," she says.

I've already gone back to the papers in front of me, but I lift my head when the lock clicks.

Aubrey spins around with a dangerous grin. "You officially own half of Masters Financial, Dane. That's huge, and since no one's bothered to throw you a party or anything, I'm setting it right."

I lean back in my chair as she steps around the corner of my desk. Official is pushing it. The trust still isn't settled, thanks to Greg. Not to mention, the reason I'm half-owner is hardly grounds to assemble a planning committee and hang a banner.

After filling both the glasses, she holds up one and wiggles the other at me. "Come on," she whines when I don't take it. "Let's make a toast."

Curious of her angle, I humor her and clink my flute to hers. "Here's to firing your husband at will."

She cackles, bumping her knee against mine. It stays there, and her eyes never leave me as we drink. A much less subtle play for my attention than the nudes. Or it is until the knee glides up my thigh, and she crawls onto my lap, straddling me in my office chair.

I force my eyes up from the anniversary-gift tits now in my face. "Aubrey."

But she dismisses my warning.

"Greg wants to destroy you." She runs her hands up to my chest. "You have his house and his business. So, why not finish the job? Take *everything* that's his and ruin him first."

Her fingers tug at a button, then greedily go for another when I don't stop her. I should be stopping her, but for the first time,

I'm entertaining her sick little game. People passing by will hear her moaning and tell Greg. Or maybe he'll charge in with a new accusation and see his wife bent over my desk.

The last one reminds me of the *click* when she came in.

"The door's locked?"

"Uh-huh." She slides my hands up her bare thighs. "No one's getting in."

Aubrey bucks her hips against me, and despite my dick's obvious interest, I can't look away from the damn door.

All my dreams about Bennett happen in my office. I'm sitting in this chair when she walks back into my life. When she smiles and laughs her wild laugh.

The subconscious is easily influenced. If I screw Aubrey in here, then in the next dream, she might be the one on the other side of the door. Or Bennett will pound for me to let her in, but I won't be able to work the lock.

Shit. Not even my neglected dick is willing to risk losing a dream version of her I can't even touch.

Loving this woman is a sickness, missing her a disease.

When Aubrey tugs my lip between her teeth, I pull back.

"You need to get off me."

Her hips stop moving as she sits back. "What?"

"We're not having sex, so you can get back at Greg. We're not having sex at all, so you need to get the fuck off."

"Wait, think about it," she starts, planting her hands on my chest.

Except I've already thought about it, and rather than let her finish, I do what I should have done in the first place. I stand up, and her ass bounces off the carpet. When I moved back to Phoenix, I swore, I wouldn't play into the soap-opera level of drama waiting for me. Now, I'm one bad line away from a starring role. Revenge houses, disinheritance schemes, illicit affairs.

Aubrey scrambles to her feet, her cheeks red with embarrassment. I won't add to it. I simply grab my keys and phone off the desk. "Shut off the light when you leave."

I walk straight from my office to Liam's. Most everyone is gone. Shane passes me on his way out, his eyes warm, and he gives a firm pat to my shoulder. I've always admired his ability to stay above the bullshit within these walls, envied how he taught Liam to do the same.

I collapse into a chair across from my cousin's desk. "Go for a drink with me before Keaton gets off work."

He squints from behind his glasses. We haven't been to a bar, just the two of us, in almost a year. Since before I chased Bennett into a dressing room where we exchanged promises disguised as something else.

"Am I playing therapist?"

"I don't need therapy," I say.

After a long pause, he sits back in his seat. "So, I'm back to being your wingman?"

Loyalties die when we let them. Some we cling to, not knowing how to let go even though they drain us, turning our lives into something unrecognizable. Other times, we hold on to a promise long after it's not required anymore, just in case.

"I don't pick up chicks at bars," I tell him, standing up. "Come on. I have a proposition for you, and I'm thinking you'll want to stop at the hardware store after you hear it."

His eyebrows rise. "For...?"

I smirk as I turn to leave.

"WHAT ABOUT THIS GREEN?" LIAM asks, pointing at a can.

We've been in the middle of aisle nine for the past thirty minutes. The last time I helped him pick out spray paint, we spent our entire lunch break here, debating color choices. I don't know why I thought the process would go any faster on our second go-around.

I lean down and swipe the can from the shelf. "Is there a real difference between this and that?"

He wheezes out a laugh, shaking his head. "Seriously? One's hunter green, and the other is forest."

"Oh," I say dryly. "My mistake."

"You're sure about this?" Liam moves toward the oranges. "Because once I tell Keaton we have a house to move into, she's going to do her squeal." He looks back, dead serious when he says, "And we don't fuck around when it comes to the squeal."

"So you've said."

He continues staring me down, waiting for confirmation. I don't blame him for being skeptical. The idea to let him and Keaton live in my mother's house went from concept to offer in the same amount of time we've spent in the hardware store.

But while my father's wife was trying to dry-hump me in my office chair, I had an epiphany. A moment of clarity I should have had weeks ago. Or months even.

I'd been ready to leave everything in Phoenix behind for Bennett. No hesitation, I would have gone with her that weekend, never questioning the decision. I told myself it was *because* of her, of how much I loved her, but I was using her as an excuse to do what I really wanted. She was my chance to escape all the parts of my life I couldn't walk away from on my own—promises made to dead people. Love gave me permission to break them. Except I never needed her to be the reason.

My sanity is enough. My happiness.

"I'm sure," I say. "We'll figure out rent, and whenever you two are ready to buy, we'll subtract what you've paid."

Leaving the business won't be as easy. Even after the lawyers settle everything, Miles laid out a succession plan in his trust to be sure it stays in the family. I might be ready to move on, but I won't abandon Shane and Liam to deal with Greg swooping in because of some loophole. He'd dismantle everything if given an opportunity.

Liam's fingers trail along the cans, closer and closer to the glow-in-the-dark paint he chose last time. He picks it up and turns to me with a shrug. "No point in remixing a classic."

I shake my head, walking away, and call back, "Until your name is on the deed, spray-painting shit on walls is over the second I give you the keys."

While Liam pays, I play with a display of key chains. The mass amount of cliché sayings hanging from the hooks makes me want to roll my eyes. Cheesy or not, I slide one off and toss it onto the counter with the can. My cousin shoots me a look as the clerk swipes it, but he stays quiet until we reach the parking lot.

He tosses over my purchase. "Are we pretending I didn't just buy you a key chain that says *Keep Dreaming* in giant, pink-sparkle letters?"

"Yep," I say. "Unless you want to be evicted from a house you haven't moved into yet."

Holding his hands up, he backs around the front of his truck. "Nope. Collect all the eleven-year-old girl shit you want."

I tuck the key chain in my pocket, where it stays until that night when I lay it on my nightstand. Then, in the morning, it goes back in my pocket. We keep reminders of what matters most close to us. Especially when the real thing will always be out of reach.

Part 3

-33-
Picture Frame

Bennett

LA.

Marco might have threatened my life if I didn't move here with him, but he hasn't needed a single one of his Krav Maga classes to convince me to stay. The merging of styles and people and the sounds coming from around every corner is intoxicating.

My time spent snapping pictures of houses in Colorado morphed into a gig of photographing food at restaurants around the city. The pay is decent, and they send the food with me afterward. Marco and I taste our way around the globe out of carryout boxes in our one-bedroom loft and return to exploring on our days off. We're in our Portland groove.

Within the first week, he brings up *Darkest Desires*. "So, if you really finished the book, are you a Denton or a Daphne?"

"Denton," I answer fast.

Given the eye roll, I should have said Daphne. I search for the book later but still can't remember where I stashed it. Some things are meant to remain a mystery.

I've been here short of two months when I pick up Keaton from the airport. Liam is going camping with her cousins for the weekend. Having experienced our whining on previous trips, he bought her a plane ticket to spare them both. Her visit works out perfectly, though, because Marco's leaving me for a family reunion back in Oregon.

When we get to the apartment, she dives at him for a hug. The alarm in his eyes quickly gives way to annoyance, but he manages to pat her on the back. Only once.

After he takes off, she and I spend the afternoon walking down Rodeo Drive, well aware that we can't afford anything but drooling on the windows nonetheless. On our way to a more rational shopping locale, we pass one of those buildings with a random collection of offices. A dermatologist, interior designer, accountant, a psychiatrist.

And that's when I see it.

A single, wayward glance shifts my entire universe before it collapses.

Keaton continues walking, rambling about the benefits of power naps, but I've stopped dead center of the sidewalk. Someone bumps into me, but I hardly notice. The blood seems to have drained from every other part of my body to gather in my chest, pooling and throbbing while my mind races to make sense of what's carved into the side of the stone building.

"Bennett?"

My head snaps to Keaton, who's standing next to me. I force a swallow, blinking as I look around, my breath coming faster.

Then I dash through the door, driven by disbelief or shock or some other emotion I can't even name because I've never felt anything like it. I only realize Keaton's following when she grabs my hand, stepping onto the elevator. She squeezes tight, like she's reminding me I'm here. I'm real. This is real.

The receptionist jumps when I throw the door open, banging it against the wall.

"Miss, do you have an appointment?" she says. Then, with more panic when I don't slow down, "Miss, you can't go in without an appointment."

But I do, closing the door behind me.

The walls of the office are cream, displaying degrees and paper clippings. Calm, tranquil colors make up everything from the art to the baby-blue couch I drop onto. No invitation needed, I figure. Movies always show people lying back, but I never have—until now. I sink into the cushions and stare up at the exposed wood beams on the vaulted ceiling. After a few steady tick-ticks from a clock on the wall, I take a deep breath and start at the only place I can.

"I asked my mother if she loved me once. Flat-out, no bullshit." My feet are propped up on the arm of the couch, and I pull an extra throw pillow onto my chest. It's a soft yellow, relaxing to look at and easy to crush to me.

"I was terrified of her answer, but when she barely glanced up from the papers on her desk, I asked again. She was emotionless when she told me no. That it's impossible to truly love anything if you don't love all the parts of yourself. You can pretend, but deep down, you know it's not real. You know it's not your truth, and the longer you lie, the more of a disservice you're doing to them and yourself."

It was the most honest she'd been with me, and nothing in my life has ever wounded more. That was when I lost faith in love. I stopped believing this all-consuming emotion could transcend people's faults and fill the empty places inside us. It might work for a little while, but it won't last. The pieces will fall apart again worse than before. Our hearts more twisted.

My mind jumps to Dane, and I sniff to dismiss the stinging in my eyes. The pillow's not so soft anymore, the walls not as tranquil. I swing my legs around, sitting up.

"A few weeks later, I was dumped at a friend's house. Like fucking laundry or an old toaster she had no use for. An inconsequential thing she needed to purge from her life."

I overhand the pillow across the room and send a picture frame on the desk crashing to the floor. But she doesn't even flinch in her brown leather chair, the same impassive expression I grew up with staring back at me. I strive for equally indifferent and smooth my shirt.

"So, tell me, Dr. Ross, if the person who brought me into this world could throw me away and never look back, how do I trust everyone else won't do the same eventually?"

The clock ticks again, deafening through the silence, and before I lose the cool-bitch edge I have going, I'm walking back across the room. I snatch a different picture frame off a shelf on my way by and pause at the door. I wait for some moment of reflection to turn me around, a latent emotion to send me running into her arms. Or for her to say something. Anything. But then I notice the headline of the article hanging on the wall in front of me. From her practice's grand opening.

Six years ago.

She's been in LA this entire time and never once tried to find me. Then again, why would she? I am not and will never be who she's searching for.

"Goodbye, Mom," I say, turning the knob.

Keaton is waiting by the receptionist's desk, ready to fight if the woman so much as thinks about moving. I pass them both, and she follows me into the hall. I hand her the frame once we're on the elevator and slump against the wall, trying not to collapse. To breathe.

"She's still using these?" Keaton asks, glaring at the frame clenched in her hand.

I blow out air and nod. "That was the only one I saw. The others were just regular silver frames."

The doors close, my mother's name plaque disappearing behind them. Should I be crying? It feels like I should be. My body is exhausted, my mind reeling, but the emotions aren't there. I broke into sobs when I lost my favorite therapist, fought back tears while thinking about Dane a few minutes ago, but now ... nothing. No overwhelming sense of relief. No earth-shattering revelations.

Nine years of buildup and fucking nothing.

I pinch my arm until my eyes water.

"Screw her." Keaton rips the back off the frame, taking the stock photo of a little girl out. "She doesn't even look like you."

The picture falls to the floor as she returns the cardboard back to the homemade picture frame. There were three at one time, each with a different message I painted on top. *Mommy and Me*, *Happy Mother's Day*, and the one in Keaton's hand, *I love you*. Even though I added my name in blue on the bottom of each and drew the stars and hearts, my picture has never been in any of them.

As soon as we step out of the building, Keaton jerks me to a stop on the sidewalk and shoves the frame at me. "Hold this." Her emotions are all over enough for the both of us as she fishes her phone out of her purse. She swipes under my eyes and does the same to herself, and then she holds her phone out to take a selfie of us.

"What are you doing?" I ask.

"What she should have done when you were seven. I'm taking a picture of you, and we're going to a drugstore or wherever you go to print a picture and putting it in this frame, where it belongs." She turns to me, all the tears she wiped reappearing. "You deserve better than that woman, Bennett. She brought you into this world for selfish reasons and then left you to fight through it on your own. Just because you weren't the answer for her, she made you think you weren't enough, but you are. You're my answer for a million things, and I love you forever and all that shit, so on three, say, 'I love you, Keats,' and smile for the damn picture."

None of the tears flooding out of me are self-induced, and when she lifts her arm again, she counts down.

I tell her, "I love you, Keats," at the same time she says, "I love you more, Bennie," and taps the screen.

Our faces are blotchy. Eyeliner is smeared, and mascara-blackened streaks stain our cheeks.

But within an hour, the picture is in the frame, and inside of two hours, the frame is on my nightstand.

KEATON'S ASLEEP WHEN I SNEAK up to the loft to Marco's bed. The comforter tents over my head, blocking the light from my phone as I sit in the middle of the mattress. I stare at the screen. My background is mostly covered with apps, but even if it wasn't, no one would know what they were looking at.

Except for Dane.

Our clothes in a pile on my bedroom floor in San Francisco, zoomed so far in all you see is the pocket of his jeans and a splash of white lace from my bra. He set it as my background, so I would think of him naked anytime I saw it. I kept it because it reminds me of him, and I want to remember how we were before I ruined it. Ruined us.

I cried for two days after he left me in the parking lot of the mortuary. Maggie would pull my head onto her lap and stroke my hair, humming an old lullaby she said her grandmother had rocked her to. She'd done the same thing after the wedding, but after my last visit, it felt different. Final.

The only other time I tried to call him since then, his phone went to a voice mail he hadn't set up. I was packing to move to LA and found his necklace. My heart hurt for him. The way it does now.

The silence between rings is louder with each one. I scrape my nails over the silver bar hanging around my neck. I'm expecting the voice of the woman to tell me his mailbox isn't set up when—

"Hello?"

A low, hushed voice confuses me, and I check if I hit the wrong contact, but the screen says *Snake*.

"Lex," Chevy says after a beat, and I bring the phone back. "You all right?"

"Why are you answering Dane's phone?"

He snorts. "He's passed out on a log after playing one of Lincoln's drinking games. The better question is, why are you calling it?"

Keaton didn't tell me Dane was going camping. She hasn't mentioned him much at all lately, even though she's been sharing a house with him the past month.

I was awarded another middle-of-the-night phone call when Liam tagged their apartment wall to tell her they were moving. Through the squeals and flood of decorating ideas, she mentioned Dane was going to let them live there rent-free until they could get approved for a mortgage. I wanted to ask what happened then. If Dane left, never to be heard from again.

I drag both of Marco's pillows under the comforter with me and stack them, bending in the middle to lay my head on top. "Because I'm not all right, Chevy," I say, answering both his questions.

Then I tell him about my mom. How she would barely look at me and how she had already been living here when Keaton and I were in the car accident that earned me a week in the hospital and during both my graduations. I admit how the apartment has felt wrong since we got back. The entire city too small and suffocating now that I know she's out there.

Chevy lets out a sigh. "Where to then?"

"I have no idea," I say.

I press my nose into the pillow. Marco smells amazing, and I frown at the thought of leaving him. He has a cousin itching to take over my half of the lease. The same cousin who knew a guy who had a friend who was Aria's sister.

"Well, you know my vote, and I can safely cast another three in favor of Phoenix."

I offer an, "Ugh," in response. "You really want to bring Bentley into this conversation?"

"Fuck no." The sound of a beer opening cracks through the speaker. "I'm counting the dumbass sleeping on a chunk of wood right now."

"How is he?" My voice is barely audible. "Dane, I mean."

The clarification is unnecessary. I just wanted another excuse to say his name.

"Better than he's been for a while."

I'd ask what he means, except Chevy's not finished.

"I'll delete the call if you want me to. Dane can wake up in the morning, hungover as shit, and never know how close he came to restarting the process of getting over you."

I can't breathe under the comforter anymore, and I drag it off my head.

"It's up to you, but if you want me to leave it, you need to do something. Talk to him or get your ass back to Phoenix. Otherwise, let me delete it so he can move on."

His voice echoes through my head, and I close my eyes, waiting for the ache in my chest to stop.

The day after the bachelorette party, Dane and I went to breakfast with Keaton and Liam. We both wore our sunglasses inside. A pair of lurkers. After, he dropped me at the airport later. I looked back at him before I walked through security, and he was watching me, unmoved from where I'd left him. I imagined running to him, twisting one or two more days out of my trip. Dane magnetized, but something inside me repelled, nudging me the opposite direction, and I boarded the plane.

I'm starting to think I'll always board the plane. He needs the chance to move on without me popping back up in his life, only to leave again.

"Thanks, Chevy."

"Take care of yourself, Lex," he says. "You'd better show your face at Christmas."

BEFORE I LEAVE LA, I download a copy of *Darkest Desires* to my phone. I reread the first half throughout my trip at rest stops and gas stations. I don't need to get to the end to answer Marco's question.

Dentons are strong, steady, and always there, waiting and ready to prove he's not going anywhere. I'm a fucking Daphne—always pushing people away before they leave on their own. Dane's the Denton, wasting his soul-crushing, sticky love on one of us Daphs, who doesn't have the faintest idea what to do with it.

By the time I walk up the steps to the porch, it's dark. I open the door, and the smell of cinnamon hits me.

"I told you not to make a big deal," I say on my way into the kitchen.

Maggie's smile relieves all the tension that's been warring inside me the past few weeks. I've missed her. I've missed Colorado.

"Welcome home," she says.

And it feels like I might be close.

—34—
Flowers

THE SHOCK OF FINDING OUT my mother's been up the I-10 for so many years calls for a reset, time to regain my footing. Not that I had much to begin with, but I stand by the saying. I sit by the river and walk in the woods until I carry battle wounds from branches scratching me, and I frequently return with a slight limp from stepping in a hole and turning my ankle. But I'm a badass woman of nature now.

Weeks in, and I'm still reminding Maggie my "pit stop" is only temporary.

She always responds the same way. "Everything is temporary, my dear. You living here, me living at all. The whole damn planet will disappear one day." Then she usually pats me on the leg and offers me a snack.

She gets tired easily now, sleeping in the afternoons when she used to be out, cutting bull thistle or organizing in George's office. When I ask if she wants to get a checkup, she tsks and lectures on a woman's right to nap after nearly ninety years. The next day, the stubborn woman cleans my room top to bottom while I'm at work to prove she's not lacking energy.

After finding out I was staying with Maggie again, Katie Sayer, The Home Slayer, asked me to come back as her assistant. I have no idea why. The woman went and got *me* coffee more often than I did her.

The week before Thanksgiving, she calls me into her office. I figure she's finally come to her senses, but then she offers to pay for me to get my realtor's license. I clutch at my chest like she popped the question, asking me to swear my undying fidelity to her. The proposition is the kick in the ass I need to make a decision. Calls are made, and courtesy of a vague threat from Keats to spill something that happened at sleepaway camp when they were eight, her cousin offers me a job. She's starting her own interior design business in Virginia Beach. I have no idea what the hell a merchandising specialist does, but I'm sure one of my skills will transfer. Knowledge of mid-priced homes or my ability to point at shit on walls.

Time seems stuck on fast-forward, the days getting shorter—literally, since the sun sets at a ridiculous hour now.

Before I know it, I'm in my countdown phase, under the two-week threshold. It never ceases to amaze me how keyed up I feel, knowing I'll have new places to explore, unknown streets and faces and now an entire coastline.

My almost-daily stop at the grocery store is the last thing I need to do in town. I have it down to a science, the aisles memorized. Today, though, I get distracted with flowers displayed at the front of the store. Most are white petals, a few standard bouquets of red roses, but smack dab in the middle is an eruption of color.

Flowers fall in the same category as produce for Maggie—something that might outlive her—but the pinks and yellows and oranges remind me of San Francisco. Of Steve's tower and my painting. It wouldn't be right to leave them for someone else. Someone who doesn't know about bright spots. So, on my way to the register to pay, I set them in my basket.

I drop my keys twice, trying to balance the brown paper grocery bags while I unlock the door. As I kick the door shut behind me, I sigh and toss the mail on the table. Once I set the bags on the counter and hang my coat, I unload, pulling out the very yellow bananas first.

"Maggie," I say, "I got your bananas and peaches, but I broke the flower rule again."

I lift the bouquet of daisies out of the other bag and smile at the pop of color.

After I find a vase buried in the cupboard and fill it with water, I put the flowers on the table. It brightens the entire space. I finish putting groceries away before I head to Maggie's room.

"I know what you'll say," I tell her, opening the door, "but I really think—"

I freeze, my hand still on the knob, even though I can't feel the metal anymore. I can't feel the floor beneath me either, the ground, the earth below me. Nothing but my heart thrashing inside.

"Maggie." The name sounds wrong, not like the other hundreds of times I've said it.

"Maggie," I try again.

She stays unmoved on the bed, her hands folded on her chest and ankles crossed. I can't tell if I'm moving or watching myself move when I step toward the bed. Blue and green yarn is wrapped around the knitting needles on the bed at her side. Her eyes are closed, face peaceful.

My body acts of its own accord, reaching out a hand to touch the cool skin of her wrist. My fingers slide around to the underside, slightly lifting her hand to feel for the pulse my brain already knows won't be there.

"Maggie." This time, it comes out as a strained sob, and the silence after is never-ending.

Backing up, I swipe at the hot tears streaming down my cheeks. I shut the door. I don't know if I should leave her alone, but I close it and rush to the kitchen for my phone. My hands shake, tapping the numbers on the screen. When I turn to look at the door, I knock the vase off the table, and it shatters, hitting the floor. The operator's voice comes through the speaker as I stand in the middle of the broken glass. The flowers trampled beneath my feet.

-35-

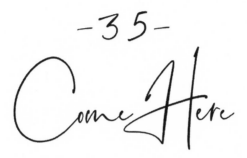

Come Here

THE NEXT SEVENTY-TWO HOURS are a complete blur.

According to the local funeral director, who doubles as the county coroner, Maggie's been prepared for this for well over a decade. Shortly after George died, she chose her casket. She dropped off the outfit she wanted to be buried in along with a picture to model her hair and makeup after. She picked her program and music. Even the flower arrangements have been decided.

"We're all waiting for something," she told me.

For her, that thing was to be with George again.

In my time living with her, I only remember maybe half a dozen people visiting the house, but there's a steady stream. They give sad smiles and reorganize the refrigerator to fit whatever food they brought to mourn over. I take most of it to the church delivering meals to the homebound and anyone in need of assistance.

The same people come to the wake. I stick to the side of the chapel, lying low in my dark navy dress. I only have one in black that's funeral appropriate. Anytime someone rubs their hand over my arm and gives condolences, I don't know what to do. I wasn't Maggie's family; she didn't have any other than a cousin. He lives in an assisted living center in Detroit and couldn't remember her when they told him she'd passed. I'm just the girl who spent spring and half a summer with her, eating her cooking and marveling at how simple life seemed to her.

I decide to sneak out the back, claiming to a lady from Maggie's church group I need air. Almost to the bottom of the broad church steps, I look up and suck in a breath. Dane is standing on the sidewalk, his beanie on his head and hands at his sides. I'm still processing him when Keaton throws her arms around me.

"What are you doing here?" I ask, high-pitched as shit, my face buried in her curls.

"Like I'd not be here," she says. "Maine or Spain."

Not ready for her to pull away, I squeeze her tighter in case she tries. I texted her about Maggie but never expected her to come. I had no idea how much I needed her here until now. How much I needed to see him.

My eyes lift to Dane over her shoulder. He moves aside to let a grocery clerk pass, heading inside to pay respects, but his gaze comes right back to mine. The three of us might stay in the odd embrace/stare-down limbo indefinitely if not for Liam. He yanks me from Keaton and down the last two steps into a hug. I haven't seen him since his grandpa's wake, and he holds me longer than he ever has.

"You look like shit, Bennett," he whispers in my ear.

I smile for the first time in days.

He rustles up my hair, and I nudge him off. Liam glances over his shoulder at his cousin before grabbing Keaton's hand and leading her up the steps. Dane hasn't moved when the ornate wooden door bangs shut behind me, his mouth in the same downturn as the last time. My fingers itch to feel the chain of my necklace—his necklace—hidden by the neckline of my dress. Of all the distances, the current ten feet is by far the worst to overcome.

"Maggie died," I finally say.

He nods. "She did. I'm sorry."

"No one I know has died before. No one close—" My voice breaks, and I tug at my bracelet, pretending not to notice. "I don't know what to do."

His head tilts to the side, his brow lowering. "Come here."

The words are a string, drawing me toward him. I walk until his body stops me. His arms fold around me as I fist his shirt in my hands, my face crushed to his chest. He stays there, letting me be the one to pull back. I tilt my chin up to him, and he brushes his thumb over my cheek. A Denton through and through. My Denton.

"I don't want to go back inside," I admit. "I know it makes me a terrible person, but..." I shake my head, unable to give a reason other than I can't function with sad eyes on me. Which isn't fair. They need to target someone with their sympathies.

Dane's eyes flash behind me but quickly return. "Okay. Wait here."

He steps past me, and I turn, wanting to grab him, pull him back to me.

"Where are you going?"

"To say goodbye to Maggie," he says over his shoulder. "Then I'm taking you home."

INSTEAD OF THE COTTAGE, DANE drives me to the motel I've been staying at the past few days. I can't sleep in Maggie's house without Maggie there. His eyes scale the walls when he flips the light on. Seventies wallpaper and several burned-out bulbs, but the couple who owns the place is sweet and they do what they can for updates.

He flicks a light fixture only holding on by a screw. "Swanky."

I shrug. "Not everywhere can afford an ice machine on each floor."

"Or more than one floor," he counters.

A smile tugs at my lips as I find clean sweats and a tank top in my bag. He doesn't have any clothes with him, no bag he wanted to get before we left Liam and Keaton at the church. All indicators he doesn't plan on staying, so it surprises me when I come out of the bathroom, and he's reclining on the bed, shoes off. I crawl in beside him, both of us on top of the bedspread.

Sweet owners or not, the bedding is not to be trusted.

He covers us with the blanket I brought from my room and rolls onto his side to face me. We watch each other like we used to, caught up in a moment where only we exist. I've missed being still with him, having his eyes on me. He reaches over to trace my face with his fingertips. My skin tingles where his skims across.

"Virginia Beach," he says without a question mark.

"You're selling your house."

He nods, his gaze following his fingers as they trail over my jaw. "You found your mom."

At the mention of her, I automatically reach for my necklace before remembering I hid it in the bathroom. I haven't taken it off since I found it, but if he sees it, he might ask for it back. Add jewelry thief to the résumé.

His touch drifts down my arm to my bracelet, rubbing over the medallion. "Was she what you were looking for?"

"No, she wasn't even worth finding."

I shift, and he looks up, bringing his hand back to my face to stop me from moving away from him. The more settles between us, a soothing blanket over top the blanket we're under.

"Stay," he says after a minute.

My belly flips, and I think he's asking me not to leave, but then he sits up to drag his shirt over his head. His jeans land on the floor a second later, and he lies back down beside me. His hand glides up my arm and neck as it returns to my cheek. I memorize the feel of his skin covering mine, not asking about the house again or if he's leaving Phoenix or if he misses me even though he shouldn't. Whatever this is, where we can be here with each other without all the noise, feels too delicate to disrupt.

I start to drift off, exhausted from staying afloat the past three days.

"Don't close your eyes," he whispers.

"Why?" My eyelids flutter open, and one side of his mouth perks up.

"Because I'm not done staring into them yet."

I laugh, sad and pathetic, and he smiles.

"Okay."

"Okay."

Neither of us says anything else. We fall asleep that way, the warmth of his hand on my cheek, and in the morning, we go to Maggie's funeral together. Then he goes home, where he belongs, and I prepare to do what I always do.

Leave.

-36-

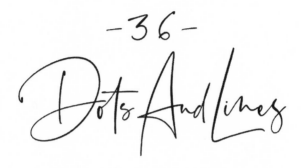

Dots And Lines

THE SLEIGH BELLS TIED TO the door of the real estate office wake me from one hell of a nap. I lift my head to the town's one and only lawyer walking in. Mr. Butteman works with Katie Sayer, The Home Slayer, often enough that I barely bat an eye until he stops at my desk.

"Can you stop by this afternoon?" he asks.

I sit back, figuring it has to do with Maggie since he's in charge of her estate. "Is this because I'm still at the cabin? Because I leave for Virginia Beach the day after tomorrow."

Maggie arranged for her land to pass to a group interested in starting a nature preserve. They've been out a few times already, scouting the area. The cottage will serve as the visitors' center, and they'll drag paths to the river and the wooded area along the back of the property. She talked about it a lot when she forced me to experience nature on our first go-around. Before I was a master woodswoman with a designated walking stick I fished out of the river on my own.

"No, no," he says. "You're fine to stay as long as you'd like. No one's in a hurry to kick you out. Maggie left you a little something, so I need you to sign a few papers."

"Oh." I scratch the tip of my pen on my desk, creating a mark I'll have to wash off.

"Just whenever you get a second, pop in. It shouldn't take long at all once I get the DVD player hooked up."

And any thought I had of conveniently forgetting he asked goes right out the fucking window.

"DVD?"

"Yes, ma'am. I finally convinced her to quit recording updates to her will on VHS tapes last year." Mr. Butteman raps his knuckles on my desk a few times. "I'll tell my secretary to expect you."

After he walks out, I glance around the empty office. Unless someone shows up with a house-buying emergency, no one will know if I duck out for a bit. Even if they did, tomorrow's my last day.

I quickly lock up and sprint after him.

Within fifteen minutes, we're across from each other at a large conference table in a room surrounded by glass walls. Behind Mr. Butteman hangs a flat screen with wires strung down to a media cart. He turns his chair to face the TV and points the remote at the DVD player, bringing the screen to life.

A pressure releases from my chest when I see Maggie in high def. She is in the exact chair I'm in, wearing the shawl she knitted before I left for LA. Her salt-and-pepper hair is pulled into a bun.

She sits without moving or talking for so long that I can't decide whether to laugh or cry.

Finally, she scrunches her nose. "Is it on?"

I throw my head back, cackling hard enough Mr. Butteman pauses the video until I've wiped my eyes. I hold up a hand in a promise to stay quiet, and he presses the button again.

"Bennett," Maggie says.

Fuck. And now I'm legit crying.

"You were a light late in my life. I only wish I could have had more time with you."

My freaking heart.

"Now, with that out of the way, I'll cut to the point." She readjusts, leaning forward toward the camera. "You can't be centered unless you know where center is, so it's time you pick one. I'm leaving you enough money to get started. Open a business or put a down payment on a house. I don't care what you do with the damn money, so long as you stay put and really make a life for yourself. Then you can go, explore, find new experiences. And when you're tired and you need a place to rest, go back to your center."

She stops talking, back in her motionless state. I shake my head, not sure I understand, but Mr. Butteman's attention remains glued to the TV.

"Oh," Maggie starts again, causing me to jump, "and for God's sake, do *not* let Betty from the church go through my George's things. She won't know what anything is, and she'll pitch it, all willy-nilly. Most of that stuff is in good condition. Box it up and take it to Wilber, the guy who repairs watches. He'll know what to do with it. Be happy, whatever you do, my dear."

Mr. Butteman pauses the video then. Maggie has her hands folded in her lap, an easy smile on her face. The way I'll remember her with all her kindness on display.

"So, if you can just fill out these papers saying how you'd like the money transferred, we'll be able to get this moving and have a check or deposit ready within the week."

He pushes over the forms, and I glance down, my eyes bulging when they land on digits.

"Eighty fucking thousand dollars?" I shriek it, then cover my mouth because holy overreaction.

"Shit, sorry." I cringe, then slip in another, "Shit."

Oh my God, Bennett. Stop swearing at this man!

"Sorry," I say again. "But she can't leave me that much money. It's insane. She wasn't right in the head."

"Maggie Elizabeth was sound of mind when she was here, I can assure you."

I narrow my eyes in response.

The woman only knew me a few months. Granted, she probably knew me better than I know myself. Hell, she sang me to sleep on more than one occasion. Not even my own mother bothered to do that when I was a child, but eighty-fucking-grand?

What if there's mold at the cabin? I should buy a test kit.

Mr. Butteman slides a pen across to me, and I panic and push it back across the conference room table.

Rather than roll it back and risk entering into a never-ending cycle, which I'm prepared for, he gives a head shake. "You said you're not leaving until Thursday. Take the day and drop by in the morning. If you're still struggling, we can discuss your options."

As much as I want to tell him to give it away right now, my reaction has caused enough of a disruption, so I agree. I've almost reached the door when I pivot. "Mr. Butteman?"

He stops gathering the papers and looks up.

I reach for my necklace, my new go-to fidget. "Even if I don't take the money, could I have the DVD?"

With a gentle smile, he nods. "We'll make a copy."

AFTER I FAKE A HEADACHE, Katie lets me leave early. I should stay, put in a real effort until my official last minute as her assistant, but I would hate to ruin my mediocre employee streak. Maybe I'll spring for lunch tomorrow to make up for it.

I stop by the grocery store, for what I imagine is the last time. They keep the empty boxes from shipments, letting anyone from town take them as needed. I find a sturdy one in the pile, large enough for my project.

For the last year and a half, my life has revolved around boxes. Packing and unpacking the same ones to a point I probably only have one move left before I'll need to trade them out for new ones. But the items inside the boxes have been mine—sometimes an extra item added in, like *Darkest Desires*, or one left out, like when I gave up a T-shirt Little Stevie would drag around like a puppy. Until now anyway.

George's workroom is full of boxes. Stacks along three out of the four walls a few feet deep, nearing the ceiling in places. Some are marked as being from George's parents, others from Maggie's. The rest seem to be their own keepsakes from throughout the years. Three families and multiple lifetimes sorted into categories that only make sense to whoever wrote with permanent marker on the cardboard sides. Crystal birds in one and glass figures that include birds that aren't crystal in another.

No matter how ready Maggie was to die, she never brought herself to part with the boxes. I've looked through several over the past week. Hidden away are a few reminders of her to take with me, including a photo album set on top of one. The last picture is of the two of us, glued in with the dates I lived with her the first time written underneath.

A lady from the church will be here later to pick up the rest. Not Betty—I checked. Martha will decide what can be donated and what needs to be thrown away. Except for the items on the desk set against the wall, of course.

I lug in the box I marked *George's Workstation* and drop into the squeaky roller chair that gives off a puff of dust. Pliers, cutters, beads, and curved spoon handles with holes drilled in each end are waiting like George went to grab a snack and will be right back. One bracelet looks finished, lying next to a tool with a sharp tip that I decide is for engraving. I turn the worn metal over in my hands, running my fingers along the design bordering the edge. I leave it out and pack away the rest.

Most papers appear to be notes and measurements. Something catches my eye on one of them. Three black lines with a dot, followed by more lines and dots with the word *Love* scribbled above them. I lift the page and uncover another beneath it. The entire alphabet is represented the same way. Morse code.

I pull Dane's necklace from under my sweater and hold the silver bar between my fingers, examining the markings I've rubbed at hundreds of times, noticing the spaces between certain ones.

Oh, holy shit.

Reaching for a pen, I drag the chain over my head. I have to scratch at the paper a few times before the ink flows, and I start drawing the symbols and matching them to what George sketched. They're not random etchings but purposeful.

Dane must not know, or he would have said something when I asked why it was so important to him. All he told me was it was the last thing he'd received from his mom. More than enough reason to always keep it close. Until I stole it.

Found it, I remind myself.

But I did steal it, didn't I? I stole his necklace, and I stole his love, knowing full well I had no rights to either. Although he took mine, too, as hard as that is to admit.

When I decipher the last letter, I slump back in the chair, blinking rapidly at the two words in front of me. What has been around my neck for months. Over my heart.

Come

Home

Dane has nothing to do with the message, but I feel him in it. The way he would tell me, *"Come here,"* sounds the same in my head, and I let out my breath on a sob that surprises me. Tears fall on the paper to bleed the fresh ink and give life to the old.

Come home. Come home. Come home. I hear the words in his voice and cry until I hurt.

All of me hurts. My head, my heart, my soul.

I spend the night with every blanket Maggie ever knitted piled on top of me. In the morning, I load my boxes into my car along with George's, and then, even though it's freezing, I take one last walk to the river. I stop at my favorite rock, feeling along the cable of my bracelet to the medallion. The *Seek* has started to wear off like the other side. I'm surprised it's lasted this long, considering the shape it was in when I bought it. I rub my finger over the word one more time before I unhook the latch holding it on and throw it into the water.

I watch it float down the river, knowing I'm done looking. No blues or grays or crazy clown hair pulling me in every direction. I know where I want to go. Where I'm supposed to be.

"Come here," he says, and it's time I listen.

Time I go home.

And most importantly, it's time I stay there.

-37-
Wrong Address

Dane

"AND YOU'RE SURE?"

Liam has asked the same question a dozen times in the last few minutes. Every time he turns the page or signs his name, he pauses and peers at me over his glasses.

"If I were going to change my mind, it would have happened at some point in the past few months. Not while you're signing the papers."

He nods. Again. Then he swipes the pen across the last signature line and tosses it down. "Done. You can't take it back now. I own the house."

As relieved as he looks, it doesn't compare to what's washing over me right now. Step one of unburying myself from the mess of a life other people have left me in is finished. The Revenge House is now Liam and Keaton's home, warm and filled with all the things it should have been from the start.

The only thing to do now is wait for the lawyer to draw up the paperwork to relinquish my claim to Masters Financial. I haven't mentioned it to Liam yet, but an out was easier to find than expected. Based on the old man's succession plan, my shares will pass to my eldest child involved in the company when I retire. Since I'm fresh out of offspring with a finance degree, it will go to the next eligible person within the family. At two years younger, that's my cousin. I'll turn over my half, and once Shane retires, Liam will inherit the rest to become sole owner.

What I'll do after I officially have nowhere to live *and* no job, I have no fucking clue. Who knows? With no one else to consider and no obligations to fulfill, maybe I'll return to my meandering ways. Put on some music and drive until I forget everything from the past year and a half.

Until then, I'll crash at the house with Liam and Keaton. I mean, after I let them live there rent-free, the least they can do is take in my vagrant ass for a couple of months.

Leaving the lawyer's office, Liam checks his phone. I realize he's not following me down the sidewalk and turn to see him stopped in front of the building. He stares at his screen, his expression irritated and bordering on pissed off. "What the fuck, woman?"

"Everything good?"

He glances up at me, shaking his head. "Just when you think there's a break in the crazy…"

The way he trails off, I assume it has to do with Bennett. It always has to do with Bennett.

Before I figure out a nonchalant way to pry for details, he glances across the street at a boutique.

"Hey, I told Keaton I'd grab her one of those fizzy bath-explosion things that smell like chocolate or something. I'll meet you back at the house."

I almost offer to go with him. Then I remember I'm not the whipped one and head for my truck.

The two of them have been going through something lately—settling into marriage maybe, but it feels bigger. Keaton's been staying at work late and bailing on their dinner plans. Even before the holidays, she was acting off. And Liam. Fucking Liam is a patient man, but I swear he's one more, *Hey, babe, I'm going out,* away from losing his shit.

She's avoiding me, too. We've stopped spending time together and going to lunch so she can vent about Liam. I dismissed it as nothing at first. Busy schedules and distracted minds. But last week, when she realized we were at the house alone, she got up from the couch and walked straight out the door without a word. I didn't see her again until hours after Liam came back from the gym.

I've known the woman long enough to know she would never screw around on him, but I'll admit, I've been tempted to follow her. Do everyone a solid and solve the mystery surrounding her disappearances and odd behavior.

When I get back to the house, she's in the kitchen. She's flipping through a magazine at the counter, propped on her elbows. Our new normal involves a nonverbal exchange, so I give her a tight-lipped smile on my way through, but Keaton surprises the hell out of me with a full grin in response.

"Hey," she says, her tone light. "I left your mail over there."

"Thanks." I grab the envelopes and lean back beside her to sort through them. "You're a homeowner, by the way."

She beams even brighter. "Does that mean I can kick you out whenever I want?"

Glad she seems back to herself, I smile and bump her with my shoulder. "Sure, but you'll have to deal with Liam screaming when he finds a spider in the shower."

She cackles at the memory. "I've never seen someone climb a vanity so fast."

He'd probably still be up there if I hadn't shown him photographic evidence that I'd released it outside.

I pause on the second to last letter in the stack from a gutter company I've never heard of before. Unlike the junk mail, it's addressed to me directly instead of Current Resident. I open it, curious if Liam requested a quote. Of all the updates, I can't remember the gutters ever being replaced.

"What is it?" Keaton asks, glancing at the invoice in my hand.

"A bill for having new gutters installed last week. They must have mixed up accounts."

She quirks a brow as I pull my phone out to dial the number at the top. After closing her magazine, she wanders toward the hallway. "Good luck."

I spin around at the counter, braced on my elbows when a lady answers, "Desert Bloom Gutters."

"Yes, I received an invoice, but I haven't had any work done."

"All right, honey. That's going to be Lenny in billing. I'll transfer you over." The line cuts off with about ten seconds of cheesy hold music filling the time before a gruff voice breaks in.

"This is Lenny."

I straighten up and try again.

"What's the name on the invoice?" he asks.

"Dane Masters." A few beats of silence tick by. "I'm not sure if my mother had work done from you guys before and there was an address mix-up or—"

"At 1030 Le Clare?"

"Yes."

"Right. I remember this one. The place of install was different from the billing address. Max, our service coordinator, made a note on the order. It's not that uncommon for people fixing up homes before they move in to have the bills sent to their current address."

I nod despite the fact he can't see me. "Makes sense, except I'm not moving anywhere."

Lenny lets out a grunt, and papers shuffle on the other end. "I've got it right in front of me. Supplies and guys went to 615 Wicker Lane last Tuesday. And Max marked he was told to send the invoice to Dane Masters at 1030 Le Clare."

"By who?" I can't hide the irritation in my tone, but someone trying to hook me for two grand is a decent reason to be mildly pissed off.

He blows out a breath. "I have no idea. That's all Max wrote down. I can ask him next week when he gets back from vacation and let you know."

I give Lenny my number. He assures me he'll let me know once he sorts it out, but I'm already on my way out the door. Since I fired Greg last month, he and Aubrey have dropped off the grid, but it looks like he might be finished licking his wounds and ready to revamp his bullshit. And if it's not my father, then whoever's using my name won't be after today.

"Where are you going?" Keaton calls after me.

"To deliver this asshole's bill myself."

As I pull out of the driveway, I program the address into my phone. It isn't far, less than five minutes of cruising through neighborhoods similar to mine. I park across the street from a small Tudor-style stucco with brand-new fucking gutters and grab the invoice off my passenger seat.

In front of the house are two large trucks and a van, all with different logos on the sides. A contractor, plumber, and electrician. Given the squeal of saws and pounding that floods out the open front door, the place is under a full renovation. Lenny was probably right about no one living here yet. Someone's around though. The brick driveway goes up the side of the house with a gate blocking my view of the garage in back, but the roof of a car is just visible on the other side. Aubrey drives a god-awful pink Hummer, and it's the wrong color for the Mercedes I let Greg keep.

A guy with a shoulder full of two-by-fours steps out, and I move aside to let him by.

"The owner inside?"

He glances over his shoulder and nods. "Kitchen. But hang a right through the living room to get there."

I walk straight in without knocking. It would be pointless with all the power tools.

The wood floors of the entryway have been sanded, ready to refinish, and it looks like more walls have been torn down than built. Following the only path without plastic sheeting or sawhorses, I head through the living room. I spend a minute checking out the space. Large and open with what will be a skylight when they finish the ceiling. Splashes of exposed brick and a sunken seating area.

"I wasn't sure about the skylight at first."

I still at the sound of her voice behind me, unconvinced it's her and not the universe playing a cruel fucking joke. The dreams are moving into full-blown auditory hallucinations. But when I spin toward the unfinished kitchen, Bennett's leaning against a wall stud. She's wearing the same camouflage pants she wore the day I found her, a paint-splattered T-shirt, and her hair is in a messy bun.

So fucking beautiful.

She straightens. "Then I realized I could stargaze from my living room."

My breath quickens as I absorb the last part. *Her* living room. If I could, I'd scan the place again. Search for any sign of her inside these walls. Only, right now, I'm barely capable of lifting the paper clutched in my fist.

"Why am I getting bills meant for you, Bennett?"

She looks at the sawdust-covered floor while playing with her necklace. No. *My* necklace. The chain wraps around her fingers, the silver bar dangling under her palm.

After seeing her in Colorado, I gave up the idea of getting over her anytime soon. Part of me always figured if I did leave Arizona, I'd end up in Virginia, searching for the girl who still haunted my dreams on a semi-regular basis. But now, she's here. In Phoenix. In a house she's remodeling.

I slowly close the distance between us. I need her to say it. To tell me what she's doing here.

"Bennett," I repeat. "Why am I paying for new gutters?"

"Because I was mad you never asked me to stay." Her gaze comes back to mine. "You should have asked me, Dane. When I came back or when you were in Colorado. You never asked, not once."

"You told me not to."

"Well," she says fast, "then I'm mad at you for listening when I obviously had no idea what I was talking about. Either way, you're making it up to me with gutters. Unless you'd rather it be with floors. Although you did yell at me and make me cry last time I was here, so I should get both. And don't think I've forgotten about the shit you pulled the first time I drove in snow."

Now I look around. All the renovations. "You bought a revenge house?"

I can't help the amused smile forming because this woman is fucking certifiable, and I love every neurotic inch of her.

"No." She pauses and reaches for the necklace again. "It's just a regular house, but the down payment wiped me out, so the least you can do is cover the repairs if we're going to live here together."

I rewind and replay the last part as she continues to ramble, "We'll need to figure out utilities and the mortgage, and your name isn't on the deed yet—"

"Live here together?"

She looks away, hitching up a shoulder. "Only if you want—"

"I want." The invoice falls to the floor. I grab her face in my hands before she can step back, and her eyes come back to mine. "Fuck, baby, do I want. I'm just trying to catch up. You never moved to Virginia?"

Bennett shakes her head.

"You've been in Phoenix the entire time."

"At Joyce and Patrick's."

The avoiding and sneaking around—Keaton's been cheating with Bennett the last several weeks. So close the entire time I've been missing her.

"And after dumping me, claiming you didn't want any of this and forcing me to exist without you for months, you just bought a house for us to live in without even asking me?"

Her throat bobs when she swallows, and her chest rises faster.

I huff out a laugh, staring down at her. "You're fucking crazy."

She nods. "If you haven't figured that out by now, you're hopeless."

My face dips down, lips hovering over hers. Torture, considering how long I've been dying to taste them, but a delicious kind I can end whenever the hell I want to. "Always have been when it comes to you."

I press my lips to hers and drop my hands to the small of her back, holding her tight against me. "Stay," I say into her mouth. "Stay, stay, stay." I could say it all day, but she laughs, and I groan. That sound will ruin me.

When I pull back, my eyes fall to her wrist, no black braided cable or medallion. "You're not wearing your bracelet."

"I don't need it anymore. I've found what I was looking for."

"Oh?" I say, wrapping my arms around her waist. "So then, what were you looking for, Bennett?"

"This." Then she shrugs, her lips curving into a smile when she looks up at me. "Whatever this is."

"Love, baby. This is out-of-nowhere, *what the fuck have you done to me* love." I kiss her and grab her ass to lift her, tying her legs around me.

"Dane!"

Fuck, I'll never hear my name enough out of her mouth. And I plan on making her say it a lot for the shit she's put me through to get here.

She locks her arms around my neck as I carry her through the living room toward the torn-apart kitchen. "What are you doing?"

"Checking out our home."

But, really, I'm looking for a basement. You know, just in case.

Epilogue
Almost 2 Years Later...

Bennett

HEY.

I smile at the pink sticky waiting for me on the back door when I get home. Dane ran out of his original supply a long time ago, but he steals more from Keaton and Liam's house whenever we are there. He isn't subtle, purposely dropping them in front of her, but she has yet to notice her stash depleting.

When I get inside, I drop my gym bag and still-unused yoga mat. By the time I locked up the photo studio, I'd blown any chance of making it to class. Not that anyone was expecting me, since I've successfully missed every one since I signed up last month. At least today, I had an excuse that doesn't involve stopping for an iced coffee. My last client was bossy, and her husband was an absolute nightmare. I swear, if pregnant Keaton wasn't so fucking adorable, I'd have kicked her and Liam out of their own maternity shoot hours ago. Liam almost lost an arm when he reached for my camera, claiming he had a better angle.

I drop my keys on the kitchen counter and notice another mini-mem.

> *I know how you like to look for things, so … find my notes and then come find me.*

A laugh bursts out of me, and I glance around, spotting another on the archway leading toward the living room. I peel off my message, my belly doing a familiar flip when I read what he wrote.

> *Marco followed me weeks after I already started to creep his Instagram for pictures of you. I couldn't stop. A man obsessed.*

Another is stuck on the frame hanging over the fireplace. The sun beams at the perfect angle through the skylight at this time of day, highlighting what has somehow become the focal point of the entire room. Offering to photograph Steve was a mistake, but I thought it would be sweet since he'd painted me. If only I'd known the portrait would wind up hanging over my mantel. Not only is he in a full tuxedo with his chin jutted up, but he's also proudly holding Little Stevie.

Reaching up, I pull down the sticky.

> *And the reason I was late to the engagement party was, I'd tried to convince myself you weren't special. Just a woman I needed to screw out of my system.*

The next is on the coffee table.

> *Rendered pointless the moment I saw you again. You were the embodiment of what I never knew I wanted—even in flats.*

Each note is a confession from him to me, and I follow the trail of pink through the house.

> *Real talk, it was always a date.*

You inspired three more playlists, each cheesier than the last.

My first trip to SF turned into three allergy shots. It was worth every second with you.

I stop at the bedroom door and sigh at the one on the knob.

Even when I tried like hell for it not to be you, it was you. ALL I see is you, Bennett. I loved you then, now, tomorrow, always.

Adding it to my pile, I open the door and roll my eyes on my way inside. Dane's standing in front of a wall covered entirely in pink sticky notes with a giant question mark drawn in the center.

"You're ridiculous," I say.

He shrugs one shoulder. "You're beautiful. And now, you're going to answer my question." After a few blinks, he smirks and shakes his head. "Did the playlist teach you nothing?"

The playlist...

I look down at the stack in my hand, then squint at him. "Really?"

"Really, Bennett." He stares at me, serious. "Check them again."

I flip through them, starting with the first confession—only this time, I notice the first letter of each is darker than the others.

M

A

R

R

Y

M

E

My eyes shoot back to Dane, who's holding a ring.

"Well?" he asks. "What do you say, Angel?"

I laugh, tugging at my necklace—his necklace—and nod with tears in my eyes.

He breaks into a smile and mouths, *Come here.*

And I do. I jump into his arms and kiss him without letting him put the ring on my finger. But when he does, I see the inscription inside. Dots and lines I know by heart, spelling out the four-letter word that best describes Dane.

Home.

Acknowledgements

I have to start with Gina Baker. For *not* inspiring any therapist in this book and being there when I wasn't sure I needed anyone. A genuine smile and willing ear attached to an open-heart. You have no idea how grateful I am for you and the hours you spent listening to a dramatic teen sorting out her shit.

Joseph Laurence, how are you still here? Seriously, you deal with me better than I deal with myself. You're my silver-medal, yo. (Because we both know Franco is gold.)

Have ya'll *seen* the cover? Murphy Rae—all I can say is daaaayum. I hope the inside is worthy of the outside. Thank you for magic.

So much thanks to my editors. Truly, madly, deeply. Jovana, you have no idea how much your notes made me smile. And Madison, you put up with so many *this* jokes. I'm sorry.

Emmily, I can't write a book without you. I claim you for the rest of time. Thank you for always being there at all hours and carrying me away from the ledge.

My Tuesday Writers—you all inspire me in so many ways, and I appreciate all the thoughts and love toward my writing. And me. Also, a shout out to the PRW gals for taking me in. I mean, I'm still not a part of the FB group but still.

Love to my family for blindly supporting me without reading any of my books. Any of you who have, please pretend you didn't. I'll be watching for awkward looks at Thanksgiving.

And of course, infinite thank yous to my early readers, bloggers, and you, if you've read all the way here. Like, whoa, you are possibly one of my favorite people. Even if you're only still reading out of spite, I still thank you, just with less enthusiasm. Either way, a review would be appreciated.

Thank you all for being bright spots,

CG
xx